Last Night

A Novel

JJ Lane

Cover design and illustration by Jenna Rees Borstelmann

Printed in the United States of America

ISBN-10:0-991-29270-7
ISBN-13:978-0-9912927-0-7

Table of Contents

PROLOGUE

The Turn Over

The jumbo postcard arrived in Baltimore on Wednesday, exactly half-way into JJ's vacation with the guys. The huge card poked out past the rest of the mail in the stack, and a slim smile warmly edged across her face as she plucked the piece of mail from the middle of the pack. The picture on the front was of "Mount Mitchell, The Highest Point East of the Mississippi." She knew JJ had chosen the large card just so he'd have plenty of room to write. Her smile grew as she turned it over and read the message.

Honey, can you believe I talked the guys into camping up here in the mountains? I figured we were on our way to Myrtle Beach again, but I talked them into it on our way out of town. They weren't real happy about the idea, but I'm sure they'll come around. It's a good thing I packed my boots! We had to stop at Bigmart to buy a tent and provisions on the way. We just checked in here at the campground. There aren't many other campers. I guess it's early in the season. Tomorrow we're going hiking in the morning and tubing in the afternoon. The ranger said there have been a lot of bears around lately. Maybe we'll see one. My phone isn't working up here. You'll need to call the park office if there's an emergency. We're camping at Cabin Mountain Park. It's on the river, at the western base of Mt. Mitchell.

Don't worry about me. This isn't Myrtle Beach. Not even Frank and Izzy and I could find any trouble out here in the wilderness, even if we went looking for it!

Love JJ

She turned the card back over and studied the photograph. Her smile began to wane and a strange look spread across her face. "It's odd," she thought, "that the top of the mountain is bright with sunshine, yet the base is dark and shrouded by the clouds. It makes me feel like the mountain is covering up something mysterious, like it's guarding some big secret."

Her smile was gone now. She was starting to worry.

1

A Turn to the End...Or an End to the Turn?

"You *are* going to tell me *exactly* what you've been up to these last seven days. I need to hear *everything*. I want names. I want places. I want times. *And I want reasons!*"

JJ squirmed in his chair and wondered, "How could a simple vacation have come to this?"

The interrogation continued. "Do you understand what trouble you're in? I'm not buying your story and neither would anyone else in his right mind. I'm giving you one last chance to explain yourself. The night is getting late. I'd like to close this book and move forward."

By this time JJ was growing weary. He looked off into the distance for a minute and thought, "I just hope Frank and Izzy remember it the same way I do."

He turned back and answered. "Once again, you've misread my character. I'll explain it one last time. I don't think I have any other details left in me. It was a *very long* week."

JJ let out an anguished sigh, but then a devilish smile slowly crept across his face as he went on. "I know it may sound hard to believe, but strange ideas don't seem so crazy when you see them through your own eyes. I'd like to close the book on this whole ordeal myself. But this is my story and I'm sticking to it..."

2

The First Turn

"Get up JJ. You need to get up now. The police want to talk to you." Izzy gently shook JJ, as Frank nervously glanced back and forth, hovering over Izzy's shoulder.

JJ sat up, yawned, and stretched his arms. He took his time shaking the cobwebs out of his head, and finally said, "I had the craziest dream last night. The whole world was taken over by Alien Robo-Zombies from Mars. It was in stark black and white, like a 1930's movie. When the dream started, I thought the invaders had secretly infiltrated our society just to eat our brains. You know, just a regular dream. But then the dream became much darker. The Aliens were after more. Much more. They took the humans' brains, all right. But they started with the brains of the politicians. Next the politicians sucked in the brains of the people and made them believe things they never should have believed."

Frank reached past Izzy and shook JJ also. He interrupted JJ's story, "We want to hear more about your dream, but get up and save it for later. The police officer out there wants to talk to you."

JJ ignored Frank and continued recounting his dream, "Next, the blood-thirsty mongrels enacted all kinds of laws against nature. They made laws to make sure *they* were in control of all the money. They made laws that enslaved the people. They took control of the airwaves, so that all that remained was corporate TV and radio. They made laws in Congress to help the NY Yankees. They let the pinstripes pay absurd salaries to steal all the best players so they could win all the trophies. And worst of all, the Aliens coerced the people to pay heavy taxes to finance their whole, evil operation."

Frank broke into the story again to urge JJ along, "Tell us the rest later. The cop is waiting. You need to get up and go talk to him."

"No, I'm almost done," replied JJ. "Next the Aliens made us believe this was all for the good of humanity. Meanwhile they deforested the entire earth just to make the paper to print all the money they could print. They strip-mined all the metal just to make all the Yankees' trophies. Then they loaded all their money and trophies into their ships and sailed back off into space. They left behind them a devastated planet. No trees. No food. No farm systems. The only beings that survived were the ones lucky enough to find shelter in caves."

"That doesn't sound that far-fetched to me," said Izzy. "Now the Area 51 cover-up makes sense. But seriously, JJ, we need to go talk to the cop now. The park ranger has your name on the reservation. The officer wants to talk to *you*."

JJ didn't have any idea what was going on, but he stood up and walked out of the tent and across the campsite to speak with the officer. Frank and Izzy led the way, yet were also completely behind him. They reached the policeman, who was steadfastly standing still and peering over the whole campsite in a very studious manner. JJ asked, "What can we do for you, officer?"

"Well, you can start off by telling me exactly what was going on around here last night," replied the police officer, very matter-of-factly.

Before JJ could answer, Frank barked, "Nothing! Nothing at all. Nothing has been going on around here." He looked at Izzy and JJ and said emphatically, "I vote we head straight to Myrtle Beach. This camping trip was a bad idea to begin with."

The officer was stoic and unswayed. He looked over at the picnic table in the campsite, and it was piled high with trash and empty beverage cans. So was the ground surrounding the table. Then he scowled back at the three campers, and said, "It certainly *looks* like something occurred here last night. I've already questioned the other three campers registered at the office. They all reported that something most definitely *did* happen last night. Right here, *in this* campsite. One guy said there was a ruckus going on that sounded like Bigfoot and the Boogie Man at a drunken frat party. Another said he *saw* Bigfoot running around your campsite, and when he woke up this morning, everything was missing out of his cooler."

Izzy and JJ both winced and glanced at Frank, who, of the three, was the closest in stature to Bigfoot. Then Izzy sheepishly asked, "What did the other camper say?"

"It doesn't matter. He's not a credible witness," the officer responded.

"Less credible than the two that saw and heard Bigfoot?" asked Frank.

"He smarted off to me, so I had to issue a citation," explained the officer. "Now that he's a criminal, I can't take his testimony seriously."

"But weren't you just going to his campsite to get his testimony to begin with?" asked JJ. "I mean, it is *very* early, and we're all on vacations."

"Are you smarting off too?" asked the officer.

"No, not at all," replied Izzy, as he stepped in front of Frank and JJ. "We'll get Bigfoot's mess cleaned up right now, officer. Thanks for stopping by and being concerned at such an early hour. It always makes me proud to see my tax dollars being judiciously spent."

"So it *was* Bigfoot! I knew it!" exclaimed the officer, with a wry smile. "Why didn't you just say so? I was beginning to think you guys were troublemakers too. But I wonder how Bigfoot just keeps disappearing into thin air?"

JJ stepped over to the cop, looked up to the sky, and said, "The air just keeps getting thinner and thinner every day, doesn't it, officer?"

The policeman looked up to the sky with a puzzled look on his face and nodded in agreement. Frank said, "Officer, we'll keep an eye out for Bigfoot tonight and we'll report anything suspicious."

"You do that," replied the policeman. "While you're at it, watch out for yourselves, too." The police turned back towards his patrol car and took several steps before stopping. He abruptly spun back around to face Izzy and said, "Don't clean up Bigfoot's mess. I'm coming back in an hour to analyze this crime scene. I need to swing by the station to pick up my lab equipment. Maybe Bigfoot left some clues this time."

With that, the officer hurried back to the squad car and drove away. As the officer sped off, the three friends from Baltimore looked at each other in disbelief. They were still trying to wake up as the sun rose over the gap and sliced through the foggy mountain air. The sun's rays were cracking through the break in the mountains, and directly into their bleary eyes.

"*That* was unusual," said JJ, stating the obvious. "What a wakeup call. Was that guy for real?"

"It sounded like it to me," responded Izzy. "I guess we shouldn't clean up the mess. But I'm starved. I'm going to start cooking breakfast." He walked over to the cooler to fetch the bacon and eggs.

"I'll grab the charcoal and pans," said JJ.

"I think the cop *was* serious," Frank declared. He began walking towards the picnic table, talking loudly along the way. "What kind of clues could he possibly be looking for? This is all *your* fault, guys. If you hadn't stayed up late last night partying, this would be a non-issue. Now we'll have the police hanging out at our campsite the rest of the morning."

"Give me a break!" cried out Izzy. "Frank, not only did you leave all that mess just laying around, but look at *this*! You ate and drank everything in the cooler." Izzy held the empty cooler up in the air and shook it. "Now we need to go back to the general store for food. How late did you stay up carrying on, anyway?"

"And you raided the neighbors' cooler too, I suppose?" asked JJ.

"Frank," added Izzy. "What were you thinking? We don't have anything for breakfast now. Maybe you should make the drive alone, and let JJ and I go back to sleep."

"I don't think we should drive off," said JJ. "The cop might think we had fled his 'crime scene' if he actually comes back. It's a short walk to the general store. Frank could be back in twenty or thirty minutes."

"Absolutely not!" Frank declared. "I didn't stay up any later than you two, and I certainly didn't take anything from anyone else's coolers. Our cooler was still plenty full when I went to bed. It had to have been one of you two!" Frank thought for a split second and added, "Or *both* of you! And if I have to walk, we're all walking. You talked us into camping, JJ, so we're all in this together, like it or not."

JJ and Izzy both shook their heads in disgust, resigned to the fact that they were going on an early morning hike before breakfast. So all three began their walk, more of a dispirited trudge really, to the campground's general store. Although no one was paying too much attention yet, it really *was* a perfect backdrop. The forest was beautiful, with many stately hardwoods mixed in with the pine trees. It was early summer, so the air was still a little crisp in the morning. It was shaping up to be a perfect sunny day in North Carolina's mountains. Their campsite was near a large stream, and they could hear the rushing water as it splashed over the river rocks while they walked. There weren't many other campers around to spoil the spectacular ambiance either. But Frank, Izzy, and JJ could take care of *that* by themselves.

They walked in silence for several minutes until Frank declared, "This vacation had worked out great for four years. Why did we need to change? We could have gone back to Myrtle Beach and I could already be eating. Instead we're walking. I mean, JJ, I just want an omelet right now. This is my vacation. I'm *this* close to voting that we break camp and head straight to Myrtle Beach for the rest of the trip."

"Yeah, me too," grumbled Izzy. "At least in Myrtle Beach we can watch the games on a big screen somewhere. I don't want to miss the Orioles games this weekend. Don't forget, we're starting the rookie on Sunday. This hike is kind of our own fault, though. We shouldn't have downed everything in the coolers, which ever ones of us actually did it." He looked suspiciously at Frank and JJ as he continued, "We need to pace ourselves. We're supposed to be here for a week."

"Can't you two quit complaining?" asked JJ. "It's a breathtaking mountain morning and we're on vacation. We have our whole day ahead of us. What else could possibly go wrong?" Frank and Izzy contemplated things that could possibly go wrong for a few moments, while JJ continued, "Have you guys noticed how many people are constantly in grouchy moods lately? There's no need for us to be like that too. Why can't anybody just look on the bright side anymore?"

"You're right about the breathtaking part. I hope we get there soon," Frank wheezed. "But to answer your question, when that sun blasted into my eyes this morning, I was looking right *into* the bright side. I can't decide what mood I'm in under those conditions. The light was blinding, and I'm still squinting. It's going to take me a while to get back to normal."

"That may actually *never* happen," Izzy observed.

"That's kind of the point of this whole vacation, isn't it Frank?" JJ asked. "I, for one, am trying to snap out of *my* post-recessionary hangover. I'm done plodding along straight through life with tunnel vision. I'm hereby snapping out of my prolonged funk. I'm ready to embrace a whole new air of adventure."

The three friends kept walking and bickering about which one of them was to blame for the missing food and for everything else that happened last night. After twenty minutes or so, Izzy started wondering where they actually *were*. "By the way, do either of you even know where the general store is? We've been walking forever, and this trail doesn't seem familiar at all. Or recently traveled either."

"I haven't really been paying attention," replied Frank. "I thought you guys knew where we're going, plus I haven't eaten since last night."

"And your senses are a little dulled from last night," reminded JJ.

"Speak for yourself. I actually *know* we're going in the right direction. I was just testing you," replied Frank. "*You're* the one that needs to come back to your senses!"

"I think we need to *turn* in the right direction, which is left," Izzy suggested. "I think we're just going south right now. This shouldn't be that hard. We were just at the store yesterday."

"I'm not sure, but I don't remember being this far down a hill," conceded JJ.

"The problem with both of you is you're going downhill quick, and it looks like today is going to be an uphill battle." Izzy shook his head disgustedly at his discombobulated friends, and one thing was for sure: He wasn't going another step further in the wrong direction. "Look, I'm taking this fork to the left. You two stay straight. At least one of us needs to be there when the cop comes back. Whichever of us gets to the store first can get the food and we'll all meet back at the campsite soon. Make that *eventually* in your cases."

"Good idea, but we'll be eating first," boasted Frank.

"*Think* what you want to *think*," Izzy yelled back, as he was heading off on the new trail. "I'll go ahead and cook omelets for both of you. Just in case you actually make it back at all."

So JJ and Frank kept going straight, and further and further downhill. And Izzy's voice faded off into the distance. As Frank and JJ hiked down the hill into thicker and thicker vegetation, it was becoming clear, to JJ at least, that Frank's senses were not right. Or even left. Who knew, after last night? The friends were no longer bantering anymore, either. The downhill slope wasn't going to get any less slippery.

Just as JJ was inclined to tell Frank, "We're lost, let's turn around," the path came to an abrupt end. Right in front of them was a cave and the entrance was just wide enough to walk through.

Frank walked in a few feet and saw daylight at the other end. "This must be a shortcut to the general store. I think we're finally out of the woods. Let's go."

JJ thought, "This is probably not the best idea Frank has ever had, but if we go a little further, we can still turn around, and by that time Izzy will be back with our breakfast."

So JJ followed Frank into the cave. They walked in about twenty feet towards the light at the other end, but the light was further away than it first appeared. Nonetheless, they were hungry and curious, (which are two similar states of mind that aren't always reconciled), so they walked all the way into the cave until it got pretty dark. The cave was just tall enough that they weren't going to hit their heads, but not very wide. They could see a faint light up ahead, so the further they went, the easier it was to navigate the rest of the way. They had to walk single file, with Frank leading the way, until they got close to the far end.

The cave widened a little as they approached the exiting point, and daylight was streaming in. Now they could see that graffiti was painted on the cave walls. One message read, "Bigfoot was here." Underneath that another said, "So walked I, Loginnoggin. No I didn't. Yes I did. No I didn't."

Frank feigned a chuckle, "Ha ha. These mountaineers have a real sense of humor."

Frank walked another twenty feet forward and reached the cave mouth, with JJ right behind him. He realized there was a heavy iron gate sealing off the exit, except that it was slightly ajar, making it easy to open and walk through.

JJ took one look at the gate and became immediately alarmed. He cautioned Frank, "I don't think we should go in. This is obviously some kind of restricted zone. Lets just go back to the campsite and wait for Izzy to get back with the food."

Frank wasn't really paying attention to JJ. He was studying the old rusty iron plaque on the front of the gate. It only had a few words, but they were hard to read through the crust. As he realized what it said, he became excited, and exclaimed, "Look! It says 'FED – ATE LAND'. That's perfect!" And he impetuously pushed open the gate and walked out. Or was it in? JJ followed, pleading with Frank to turn around.

But it was too late.

3

An Unlikely Turn of Events

As JJ and Frank walked out of the cave, the gate slammed shut behind them. Two sentries had stepped out of a guard booth, and they were wearing black police uniforms the likes of which neither of the campers had seen before. The guards' badges read "Border Patrol." One of the officers was holding a strange looking contraption in his hand. It looked like a Geiger counter from a 1950's science fiction movie. It was silver, with flashing red and blue lights.

The other officer stepped between the gate and Frank and ordered, "Stand your ground! Both of you! Our meters picked up your thought frequencies as soon as you entered."

"I thought we had exited, not entered," responded JJ. "And Frank doesn't think with any frequency. He's just hungry and thinks this is a shortcut to the general store."

"Well it must be *your* thoughts we detected. You're under arrest."

"For what?" JJ cried incredulously. "What kind of police are you? What authority do you have? And what county are we in now?"

"We're the Border Patrol. You're under arrest for thinking unknown thoughts. Don't act like you didn't think it was a serious crime. And don't add to your problems by making county jokes. You have the right to remain silent or speak, either way your thoughts can and will be used against you."

"Thinking for one's self is what everybody does, right? I mean, what do you sentries do?" JJ retorted.

"We follow orders. Specifically, the orders are to arrest thinkers and other trespassers and transgressors like you."

Frank started thinking, along with JJ, that they should run.

The thought meter started beeping loudly, and one of the sentries shouted, "That one just thought a crime too!"

So Frank and JJ started running as fast as they could away from the sentries, the gate, the cave, their campsite, and Izzy, who probably had their breakfast by now.

The senior border officer responded in swift order. "The ringleader tricked us, and the other one thought too. This is serious. We need backup. Lets notify the station."

JJ and Frank kept running down the path until they came to a two-lane road. There weren't any signs to indicate which direction they should go along the road, but they hoped it would take them to the general store. Izzy turned left, and he was apparently right to begin with, so they decided to do the same, although they were so disoriented there was no telling if their bearings were correct. They walked at a fast pace for five minutes or so.

"This feels like we're going in the right direction now, don't you think?" Frank obviously wasn't too sure about it. "I guess we should have listened to Izzy and turned with him to begin with, though. Turning in a new direction just didn't feel right at the time."

"Or maybe you could have turned around at the gate, like I said you should do. You know, sometimes you can go astray just by going straight and not changing your direction," mused JJ. "We don't have time to reflect, though. We need to figure out how to get back on the other side of the mountain. And we need to move quickly. I don't know what the story is with those police, and I don't want to find out either. I would think this was some kind of prank, except those gates were real."

"The cops seemed real to me," Frank said. "But didn't it strike you as strange that they weren't carrying guns? They almost *invited* us to run away."

"I thought the same thing," agreed JJ. "Maybe that's when their thought meters started beeping so loudly. Those meters almost looked ancient or alien, didn't they? I've never seen anything like them."

As they rounded the next curve in the road, they came upon a small town. It had no more than twenty businesses flanking either side of Main Street. It was a typical, quaint mountain village. The buildings were old and in need of paint and repairs, but it was a busy scene nonetheless. Quite a few villagers were walking up and down the street, obviously locals, not tourists. It looked like a scene from a forty-year old movie. Except that in an old movie everything would have been freshly painted, and everyone's clothes would have been in style. As JJ and Frank approached the first building, they saw an old worn-out sign that read "Welcome to Hillsville."

"This isn't *your* first worn-out welcome, is it Frank?"

Frank wasn't paying attention to JJ. He was focused squarely on one of the buildings up ahead on the left side of the road. "I can't believe it. There's a diner!"

"I haven't eaten either, but I don't think we should stop. Those police were really mad. I think we need to get out of here and find our campsite and Izzy. I'm sure he's back at the campground with all the breakfast we can eat by now. He probably has it cooked already."

Frank pleaded, "Look, if you're hungry too, then you'll get that I'm too hungry. While we're eating we can come up with a new plan, then we can try to find our way back. Maybe they know the way back to the campground at the diner and can give us directions. Once we've eaten we'll have our full wits and energy about us, so it will be a lot easier trip."

JJ hesitantly agreed, so they walked into the diner and sat down in the window booth facing Main Street. There were only a few other people in the diner, all sitting at the counter. They appeared to be regulars and were having a discussion with the cook, who was the only employee on duty. JJ and Frank couldn't hear what they were talking about, but sensed there was something going on out of the ordinary. Something about a town meeting they had all attended last night. The chalkboard inside the window listed the daily special: Western omelet with grits and toast.

"An omelet! Perfect!" Frank couldn't have been happier.

"I think I'd like to see a menu," suggested JJ. "I don't want to hike around all day after such a heavy meal. Maybe instead of a western omelet I could get a fruit salad or something light."

The cook had watched from behind the counter as the new guests seated themselves. He was in no particular hurry to get to their table, which was making JJ nervous. The cook seemed more interested in his discussion with his patrons at the counter than anything else. Eventually he ambled over to take the order.

Frank immediately offered, "I'll take the omelet and grits, please. With coffee, no cream."

"May I see a menu, please? I still need to think about it a minute," JJ asked thoughtfully.

The cook quickly barked back, "Think? What do you mean a menu? Can't you read? The special is the western omelet with grits and toast."

"Yeah, what's there to think about?" echoed Frank.

"Hey, wait a minute. You aren't those two dangerous escapees are you?" growled the cook anxiously. "I heard those felons had a thought frequency that could be picked up a mile away. The most dangerous fugitives to come through Hillsville in years."

The other patrons had all turned around and were listening intently. One said, "I heard it was a mile and a half."

JJ and Frank were getting very nervous. They could see through the window there was a gathering of four police officers walking down the street heading towards them, and one of them was the guard from the gate. He was carrying his thought meter and studying its gauges.

The cook was getting nervous too. "Look, I don't want to arouse any suspicions here. I have my own agenda to worry about. I could be in big trouble if you don't get lost right now."

"Good thinking," responded Frank. "We excel at getting lost, don't we JJ?" Frank quickly turned back and asked the cook, "Where's your back door?"

"It's in the back. Where else would it be? Those old meters must finally be broken if they picked up any thought frequency from *you* two boneheads!"

JJ and Frank went running out of the back door, but it only led to an alley, which curled straight out to the main street. It led them back to within ten feet of the police! As they anxiously peeked out from the alley, the thought meter started beeping very fast and loudly.

The officer carrying the thought meter became very excited. "They're right here somewhere, men. They're probably in the diner. One of them said they were hungry. And look! The cook just posted a new menu sign in the window!"

The new sign read: Last Minute Special! Hot pastries. Fresh out of the oven. Discounts for senior citizens and police. The officers stormed into the diner and JJ and Frank went running for the hills!

Meanwhile, back in the diner, the thought meter's beeping tapered off quickly, so the police decided it must be broken. Besides, this was a good chance for them to help build community spirit by sitting with the locals and talking about last night's town meeting for a while. So the police abandoned their search and sat down at the counter to discuss politics over pastries.

As JJ and Frank cleared their second hill running from Hillside, just off in the near distance, they could see another cave entrance. This one didn't have a gate and only had one sentry, and he didn't have a thought meter. The cave entrance was smaller and didn't seem as important as the one they had originally entered (or exited) through. But it was large enough for them to walk into, and it must lead back out of wherever they were, or else a sentry wouldn't be guarding the exit!

"*I'm sure* that cave leads to our campsite," Frank reasoned. "We need to get by that sentry, quickly, before the thought squad catches up to us."

"Brilliant thinking, Frank," whispered JJ. "I guess the thought meters only measure how hard someone is thinking, not the quality of their thoughts. Maybe you should take it down a notch. I sure hope you're right about this one, though. But remember, there are fine lines between belief, hope, and delusion." JJ paused briefly, and added, "I have an idea, just follow me and play along."

So JJ stepped out of the foliage he was hiding behind, and walked right over to the sentry. Pretending to be out of breath, which wasn't far from the truth, he excitedly told the sentry, "Sir, we just saw those two thought crime fugitives. They're right over that hill!" JJ pointed back towards Hillsville.

The sentry stepped forward. "How do you know it was them?"

"I heard one of them say, 'I think, therefore I am.'"

"He said 'I am, *what*?'" barked the sentry.

JJ stepped a little closer, and lowered the tone of his voice. "He didn't say anything else."

"That doesn't make any sense. He's not even talking in complete sentences anymore. He must be even more dangerous than previously suspected. I should call in for backup."

"We'll watch the cave for you if you want to go nab them yourself," JJ prodded.

"Great, thanks. This might get me that promotion! I'll go nab these nuts myself and be right back." The sentry went scurrying off and Frank and JJ slipped into the cave. The cave went both to the left and the right. They instinctively bore to the right and had walked just a little way into the cave when they could already see light coming from another exit to the left.

"Do you think the police will chase us through the cave?" Frank wondered aloud.

"No, it's probably out of their jurisdiction," guessed JJ. "Lets just hope this exit up here takes us back near our campsite and away from wherever we just were."

They were far enough along by then that Frank was breathing a little easier. "JJ, that 'I think' thing was great! I can't believe the cop fell for it. This reminds me of college, for some reason. 'He's not even talking in complete sentences anymore,' the guy said! That was great."

"Complete sentences could also mean years for whatever it is that we may have just done wrong," pointed out JJ as they moved along.

"You said that with too much conviction. Let's *keep* moving," Frank quickly said.

Within another minute they had reached the cave exit, and it was narrow. It was not much more than a crack, just big enough to slip through. As they were exiting the cave, they heard the police officer holler, "Hey get back here. You're under arrest, you're under arrest!" He was chasing after them, running through the dark cave with a flashlight, and gaining quickly. "I see where you're going! You're not getting away from me now!"

Frank and JJ looked at each other nervously and fled quickly down the path that led from the cave exit. They were still in the woods, but they had entered a totally different environment. The land was more of a low-country topography. The air was foggy and damp. Spanish moss hung from the trees. Pines and large southern oaks abounded. To their left they could see a marsh filled with cypress trees. The air was filled with the sounds of bullfrogs and crickets. They slowed to more of a jog until they soon came upon a creek. In front of the creek was a small clearing with an old shack in the center. Then their jaws dropped in disbelief. Sitting right in front of the shack, sat two large crawdads, a turtle, and a beaver. They were *playing checkers*.

Just then the police officer ran up behind them and announced, "Now I've got you wise guys."

At some point in most people's lives, they come under duress for one unordinary reason or another. That is precisely when they reach a realization that the status quo is different than they had ever known it to be. Between the crawdads, the police, and being hungry, Frank had just reached that point.

"How are you going to arrest both of us at the same time without any backup?" Frank asked the officer.

Then one of the crawdads looked over at the humans, and cried, "Can you guys keep it down? We're trying to concentrate here."

Frank, JJ, and the officer were dumbstruck, especially the cop, who wasn't used to getting talked back to. But before they could snap out of it, two large black bears walked out of the woods from their right. The bears both stood up on two legs and let out a bone-chilling growl. The three humans were scared out of their minds and quickly turned around to their left to run. But when they turned, they were staring face to face with two huge gators that had just walked out of the marsh from the opposite direction! The gators were also standing up on their back legs and were menacingly gnashing their teeth. They looked hungrier than Frank! With the bears already growling and closing in from the other direction, all three humans went tearing off as quickly as they could run back to the cave exit.

As the humans were disappearing into the distance, the bears, gators, crawdads, turtle, and beaver all burst out laughing. One of the bears slapped both gators on the back and said, "You timed that perfectly! Did you see the look on their faces? I *love* scaring the humans. That gag never gets old! What do you guys want to play today, checkers or poker?"

"I think we'll have time for both," answered one of the gators. "We have a lot of politics to discuss today."

Frank, JJ, and the police officer ran straight through the cave exit and kept running down the cave, away from the bears, gators, and Hillsville for that matter. They never looked back, apparently too scared to see if they were being gained upon. They quickly ran up on another cave exit to the left, which they dashed right into, and then stopped. All three looked at each other with a sigh of relief, and tried to catch their breaths.

The police officer finally became able to speak and said, "So, back to the arrest. You have the right to remain silent or speak, either way your thoughts can…"

His advisement was cut short by loud rounds of gunfire. Guns started blasting from every imaginable direction. At least ten of them, firing round after round. This reverberating wall of rat-a-tats was coming at them in full stereo sound. They couldn't tell where the shots were coming from, but they quickly realized the guns were aimed *towards them*! They immediately jumped back into the cave, with bullets flying all around them.

They ran a little further up into the cave, and stopped. At that point the police officer looked at Frank and JJ and exclaimed, "You guys *are* dangerous! I hope you don't mind, but let's put the arrest off until later. I'm going back to my post. If it's not too much of an inconvenience, would you mind waiting until the next shift is on duty to turn yourselves in? Good luck and goodbye."

As the police officer disappeared down the cave, JJ and Frank finally had the time to relax and to survey their surroundings for the first time since they had run into the cave. The cave was ten feet wide and the rock ceiling was about eight feet high in the center, and arched over to either side. Looking down the length in both directions, it appeared the cave kept fairly uniform dimensions. The floor was layered in small gravel and sand, and the ceiling had very small stalactites hanging down just a few inches. It wasn't particularly damp, like most caverns, but it was a lot cooler than it was outside. The most striking feature of the cave walls was the graffiti painted all over it. Looking back towards Hillsville, the painting covered the walls floor to ceiling, as far as the eye could see down the cave. It was mostly crudely drawn words and caricatures of animals and people, but there were also tic-tac-toe grids and other kids' games. The cave writing was mostly modern or recent, but there were some drawings that looked much, much older, hiding behind some of the recent wall art. They could make out some old words written in an ancient language they didn't recognize. On the opposite side of the entrance from which the gunshots came, the wall didn't have any painting, just a bunch of bullet divots and a pile of the resulting gravel piled up on the cave floor. Looking away from Hillsville, the graffiti thinned out as the cave wound off into the distance.

"I think we got up on the wrong side of the sleeping bags today," JJ mused. "I don't know what to do now, or what to make of all this. I guess we should keep going forward in the hopes that we'll find a cave exit that takes us back to the real world."

So they pressed on. It wasn't too much further up that the cave forked in two directions. It was pitch black to the left, but there was a faint light coming from the right. The cave also narrowed considerably heading towards the light. There was very little writing on the cave walls at this point, but there was a recent sign painted that read "Bigfoot's Place this way," and it had an arrow pointing down the fork to the right.

"I think we need to stay to the right anyway," reasoned JJ. "So maybe we'll see Bigfoot. I'm pretty sure that's the right direction we need to take to circle back around to our campsite."

Frank chuckled about possibly seeing Bigfoot, and agreed.

The faint light was very far up in the distance, but it shone like a welcoming beacon. They could just see well enough to feel their way through that section of the cave. Maybe it was just their imagination, but this section of the cave seemed more rugged and remote. It was obviously much less traveled than the part of the cave they had already walked through. There certainly wasn't any more graffiti, so it was definitely off the beaten track. Most foot traffic must have gone to the left at the fork. Eventually they reached the cave exit, which was on the right side, and they walked out into another wooded land.

They had entered a very thick forest of mostly large hardwoods. At first this area appeared normal, and looked like the same woods as their campground. So Frank and JJ started getting excited that they had found their way back. But not very far inside the cave entrance, they walked up on a small mountain-style gift shop, museum, and meeting room. The gift shop was open-air and was covered by a shed roof, which hung out from the front of the small facility. It was of log cabin styled construction, and the whole complex was covered with an old rusty tin roof. As they walked up to the gift shop they were shocked to see that seated behind the checkout counter was an eight-foot tall *yeti*! Frank and JJ were standing practically face to face with the yeti, and could see she was sporting an ID badge that read "Mrs. Bigfoot, Museum Curator."

At first they were petrified, but Mrs. Bigfoot was smiling and was disarmingly cordial. She welcomed her new guests, "Come on in and visit. Tour the Bigfoot Museum. Just ignore the conference going on in the Meeting Room."

Of course, that made Frank and JJ look straight over at the Meeting Room, and right through the glass into the conference. Seated at the conference table were two men in suits, with briefcases open, and sitting directly across from them was Mr. Bigfoot, all eight feet of him. He was clearly *very* agitated.

JJ turned back to Mrs. Bigfoot, and asked, "Who is he meeting with? He looks really upset."

"Internal Revenue Agents. They're questioning why he's never filed a tax return. I told him he should keep a lower profile. But look at all these gifts he sells." As she was explaining, Mrs. Bigfoot waved her hand and arm towards the huge array of souvenirs, all lined up on the gift shop's sales shelves. "One footprint plaster cast after another! And I *told* him he should stop selling the fuzzy photographs of himself. He thinks it's hysterically funny. Every day he sells one, he laughs at the dinner table over it. But before he opened the gift shop he was just a legend, completely off the grid. Now everybody knows he's real, especially the revenuers. This is what happens to legends these days. The jealous wolves of the world just want to knock them off their pedestals."

Mrs. Bigfoot glanced over towards the conference room with a worried look on her face, and said, "I sure hope he's holding up okay in there. He has an anxiety disorder, more of a phobia really, about being around people. Especially more than one of them."

Frank and JJ looked at each other incredulously, shrugged their shoulders, and began looking over the souvenirs for sale. By this time, Frank and JJ had realized that they might as well just try to fit in. It was time to acknowledge that they were in a different world or hallucinating, and may as well just make the best of it.

JJ picked up two souvenir "How to Spot Bigfoot" mini flashlights and set them on the checkout counter. He told Frank, "These will come in handy."

Frank said, "Good idea." Then he pulled a stuffed animal out of a bin that was full of odd souvenir creatures, about half of which were of Bigfoot. It was a four-headed turtle. He held the turtle up in the air and turned to Mrs. Bigfoot and asked, "*What* is this?"

"That's Loginnoggin, the four-headed terrapin," answered Mrs. Bigfoot. "He's legendary also, not to mention very elusive. He's a good friend of ours and visits from time to time. Very few people realize they've seen the *true* Loginnoggin, even if they have. He likes to keep three of his heads tucked inside at all times, so others think he's just a normal, six-hundred pound terrapin. He only comes all the way out of his shell when he's around his closest friends. That's the only time he shows all of his personality and wit." Mrs. Bigfoot smiled faintly and looked back through the glass into the conference, and nervously added, "Mr. Bigfoot and I can relate to Loginnoggin. I hope those revenuers don't get my hubby *too* distressed."

That caused Frank and JJ to look back into the conference also. Just then, Mr. Bigfoot started roaring, stood up, and flipped the whole conference table over. Frank and JJ realized it was a great time to leave. They quickly gave Mrs. Bigfoot a warm "thank you", purchased the two souvenir mini-flashlights, and then went running back out of the cave. They headed to the right, but stopped after just a few yards and hid in the shadows. They didn't want the revenuers breathing down their necks either.

When the revenuers went running in the opposite direction back towards Hillsville, JJ and Frank continued through the cave, heading in the remote direction. They only used one of the flashlights, in order to conserve resources. The cheap flashlight barely worked, but they could see well enough to walk at a normal pace without running into anything. The cave zigzagged back and forth, and kept getting more and more narrow as they went. They pressed on for at least half an hour without passing any other exits. There was no more graffiti on the cave walls, and it was clear that this area of the cave was very seldom traveled.

They were getting discouraged and began to consider turning around and going back to the fork, but eventually they came to a very small jog to the right. The main cave was hooking around to the left at that point, and the hole branching off to the right was just wide enough to slip through. JJ and Frank reasoned that right was the correct direction to get back to the campsite, so that's the path they chose. The small cave winded around to the right for forty feet or so, and then took a sharp turn to the left. As soon as they made that turn, light came streaming in from a small cave exit straight ahead. Fortunately they arrived at the turn just as the flashlight's batteries died out. "What a tourist trap Bigfoot's place was," muttered Frank in disgust, as he stuck the dead flashlight in his pocket.

This cave opening was not very big, just large enough for Frank to fit through. JJ followed him out. Or was it in?

Last Night

4

A Fateful Turn

Frank and JJ walked out of the cave into a grand painted desert. It was a totally different world than the other places they had just been. The view was astounding. They could see mountains far off in the distance, all in beautiful shades of reds, purples, greens, and grays. Cactuses were everywhere, and there were several different species. In fact, near the cave entrance there was an entire forest of them. Some mountain pine trees helped form the forest too, but cactuses dominated the landscape. They could see a narrow mountain stream meandering through the valley below, making its way to a large blue lake. The sky was a canvas of unusual, vibrant colors. The hues were so powerful that they almost radiated energy. The whole scene was surreal. JJ and Frank felt almost as if they had entered a collaborative work by Dali and Maxfield Parrish. They were awestruck at first, standing at the top of a valley overlooking a plush desert. It was topography neither one of them knew existed.

Then JJ did a double take while surveying the river, and asked, "Did you see that down there? It looked like two crawdads floating down the river on a raft, both of them wearing orange suits."

"No. And I thought *I* was losing it!"

They slowly began to realize the forest of cactuses was moving in a way they had never seen either. At first they thought it was the breeze making the forest sway, but it soon dawned on them that there was no wind blowing at all. That's when they realized the cactuses were actually moving around! In fact, two cactuses had quietly moved in behind them, blocking their path back to the cave. One was eight feet tall and had a scaly trunk, with a big bushy top. The other was short and wide, and looked kind of like a clump of prickly pears.

"I think we should get out of here," Frank said with a shaky voice.

The tall cactus began to *talk to them*, in a very polite tone, no less. "Who are you? Where are you from? Why are you visiting us?" The cactus had a wide, smiling mouth, and two eyes that emitted a radiant gleam. It towered over JJ and even Frank, but seemed gentle.

JJ and Frank were in a state of shock, which took a moment to recover from. JJ regained his faculties first, and was thinking to himself, "This cactus *seems* harmless, I guess I should be civil and talk to it."

"I'm JJ and this is my friend, Frank. We're from Baltimore, but we're wondering where we are now. Even in Baltimore, we've never seen talking cactuses! We're here accidentally. We were running from the thought police and found you."

"Welcome to our home. You're humans, aren't you? Unlike you, we don't have names here. We know whom we're talking to and who is talking to us. We share our ideas in a way you probably wouldn't understand."

"If you aren't offended," JJ offered, "I'd like to call you Yucca. You look like a giant yucca to me. We need to call you something. We humans don't know that someone is talking to us unless they call us by name. Otherwise we may just hear someone talking, but not listen to what is being said. Most humans need to know in some way they are being talked to *directly* in order to pay attention. I hope you understand."

"No, I don't understand, but it's okay with me if you call me Yucca. I've always wanted to see the human world. I discussed this with the last humans that came to visit. They were rude and left abruptly. But *you* seem friendly enough. Humans are very curious beings, always worried and moving quickly. I'd like to see what world produces these behaviors."

"No you wouldn't," insisted JJ. If you came to my world you would just get arrested for being different. And I mean *a lot* different. You're a talking cactus. Look at me, for example. I'm only a little different than other humans. I guess that is why I was being chased."

The other cactus had been cautiously inching closer to JJ and Frank as they talked to Yucca. It had eyes and a mouth too! Once it got up the nerve, it began speaking to JJ and Frank very energetically, "I want a name. I want a name. I want a name too!" It quickly looked back at Yucca and said, "I like your name, Yucca." Just as quickly, it asked JJ and Frank, "Can I get a name as good as Yucca's?" Then he went back to Yucca, "Ask them some more questions. Ask them more about humans." Next it turned back to JJ and Frank again, "Yucca's really good at asking questions. He'll ask one after the other. One after the other." Yucca stared down at him as if to say it was time to stop talking.

JJ answered, "I think we should call you Peppy. What do you think, Frank?"

Frank nodded his head in approval and added, "Peppy's a great name. But JJ, can we get out of here now? I'm really hungry and pretty freaked out about this place. We need to go find Izzy."

Yucca had been listening to JJ, deep in thought. He stared down at the two humans and asked, "What are the thought police? And why were you running from them? And why should I be afraid of your police? I thought crimes were only committed by the evil. Are you evil? You don't seem to be, and I can sense these things. I'm not evil, either, so why wouldn't I go to see your world? Surely I couldn't be considered to have committed a crime if I don't even know what the laws are, and I'm not hurting anyone? Right?"

"That's not the way it works in my world," JJ replied. "Sometimes if the police don't like the way you look or act, they simply *suspect* you did something wrong. They can even put you in jail just because they think you might hurt *yourself*, much less anybody else. And no, I'm not evil. But, I don't know anything about the thought police other than that they were chasing us. Apparently Frank and I were thinking for ourselves too hardly."

Yucca wanted to make sure he clearly understood the crime issue, so he pressed on, "But if I don't knowingly do something wrong, doesn't that mean that I'm innocent to begin with? I can't understand why, in a society as advanced as yours, that if someone is truly naïve to breaking a rule, that they could be held accountable. The other humans I've talked to were quick to let me know that your society is much more advanced than ours, but I'm not so sure now."

"That's kind of what the laws say." Trying to explain more clearly, JJ continued his thought, "They say that we are innocent until proven guilty. But it's not really true in practice. In my world we have the right to go to court and spend all of our money to try to prove that we are innocent, or even to get out of jail while we're awaiting trial to begin with. We don't get those resources back if and when we are found innocent. The police and the judges and the lawyers and the bail bondsmen get to keep all the money. A lot of the people in jail are those who didn't have any money with which to defend themselves to begin with. Some of these people's parents were born without money, and some of them don't even have any parents at all."

"And what, exactly, is money? I've heard of it, but I'm not sure I understand how it works."

"Money, or dollars, is what the wealthy people have. It buys things like houses, cars, clothes, and food." JJ was getting tired of all the questions, but didn't want to be rude.

"So the wealthy are the police, judges, and lawyers?" Yucca reasoned.

At that point Frank broke in and insisted, "JJ, stop talking this nonsense and let's figure out how to get out of here."

Peppy stepped in too, looked up at Yucca, and said, "Yeah, Yucca, stop asking all the questions. You're aggravating the humans. They don't want to play this game." Then Peppy turned to face JJ and Frank and warned, "I told you guys he'll keep asking questions. Yep, one question after another. One after another. He's playing the game. You can either play the game, or walk off, but good luck getting around Yucca if you walk off. You'd have to be *very* agile and artful to dodge Yucca and *his* questions."

JJ briefly considered Peppy's advise, looked at Frank, and said, "Be patient just a second. I want to finish my explanation to Yucca." Then he turned back to Yucca and continued with his original train of thought. "See, the way our system works, it really helps to have money if you expect to be found innocent in court. If you're found guilty, like a disproportionate preponderance of poor people are, then you go to jail."

"But how would someone locked up in jail find nourishment? It sounds like that is a death sentence."

"That's not the way it works, Yucca. When someone is in jail, the jail keepers give them food and water. They may not get any intellectual nourishment, but the criminals are there for punishment, to be sequestered from society. They are allowed to physically subsist with enough to eat and drink, though."

"And *why* is this punishment? What kind of punishment is it if criminals are given food and water without having to forage for it themselves? It seems like they are getting rewarded for committing crimes."

"Well first of all," JJ tried to explain. "I don't think a lot of them committed much of a crime to begin with. Many of them only committed minor drug possession crimes. Nine out of ten of them committed nonviolent crimes. I'd like to remind you that I am here because I was escaping the thought police. I think that officially makes me a criminal. So I'm not the expert to ask much about the jail system. But the real, hardened, criminals in jail are there to be taught a lesson."

"What is the lesson? To learn in captivity what no one bothered to teach them in freedom? Why is this punishment just? In my world we would educate these beings while they are young and free to make a decision on their own, instead of keeping them in captivity and forcing it on them."

JJ was beginning to agree with Frank about winding down the question and answer session, but continued. "It's the parents' job to communicate these lessons to their kids, not the government's job. And a lot of kids have crappy parents that don't convey these messages. I mean, look, we have a broken system, no doubt about it."

"I'm not sure what a system is exactly, but if something is broken, shouldn't somebody fix it?" Yucca questioned.

"Yes, but that's not *my* job." JJ stressed.

" What is your job?"

"I'm a cabinet maker," JJ answered with a twinge of pride.

"So, if a cabinet was broken, you could fix it?"

"I could try, yes, I would think so," responded JJ, who was wondering where in the world Yucca was going with this line of questions.

"Then you need a system maker. *That* is who could fix your broken system," Yucca concluded, a broad smile across his face.

Frank was really getting agitated. "JJ, Can we *please* just get out of here? I want to go eat and I can't take any more questions or answers."

"Yeah, Yucca, stop it with the questions," chimed in Peppy. "Now you're really antagonizing the humans. They don't want to play the game. This is no way to treat our guests. The elders said we should be respectful of other species. Leave them alone so they can leave."

Ignoring Frank and Peppy, JJ jumped right back in. "Look, we don't have system makers or fixers. We have a congress that we elect to do that sort of thing, but they never change anything for the better. They are lazy. They only argue back and forth with each other, just so they don't have to ever actually do anything. Our options are limited: We just try to choose the least lazy ones to be in congress. In my world, we rely on movements to fix the system, not congress, and movements don't happen very often."

"Why do you need a congress that doesn't do anything, if you have movements that actually do something? If your system is truly broken, then maybe you should find something else for your congress to do, like gardening for example, and let your movements fix your problems."

"That's actually not a bad idea," JJ thought, even though he knew it wouldn't work in practice. He continued on with the answers, "The problem with a movement is that a lot of people have to work together and believe in the same idea, and they have to do it on their time off from their jobs. Theoretically, the reason we elect a congress is so we don't have to do that kind of work on our own."

"Have you talked to your congress about these thoughts? It seems to me that if people aren't doing the job they are supposed to do, they should find some other work to do. Since you elect them, then maybe *you should* find some other work for them to do."

"Unfortunately, regular guys like me can't talk to congress. Only the very wealthy people get to talk to them directly. Even if a guy like me *could* talk to congress, they wouldn't answer me back."

Yucca wasn't satisfied with JJ's answers to the congressional questions, so he continued to grill JJ, "I don't know anything about the wealthy, but why do they get to talk to your congress and you don't? Maybe congress isn't as lazy as you think they are. Maybe they are *working very hard* for the wealthy who get to talk to them. You need to figure out a way to go talk to your congress. And what is so different about a wealthy person that congress would listen to them and not to you? Do they look a lot different? I think you are funny looking creatures. You behave very oddly and unpredictably. Maybe that's the problem. Congress may just be scared of you."

Frank's patience was spent and he angrily raised his voice a notch. "Hey JJ, stop talking to this cactus guy. I can't take it any longer. We need to find some food and water. I haven't eaten since last night! We were *this close* to eating omelets. But Mr. Fruit Salad himself had to *think* about it. *That* thought *was* a criminal action, by the way. There must be some food around here somewhere. Let's get looking for it."

"Yucca, stop it!" Peppy urged. "This is ridiculous. You need to stop badgering the humans. I told you they don't want to play the game."

Yucca, looked at JJ, and noted, "Frank is very forceful. Maybe he should be the one to talk to your congress. Is he wealthy?"

"No, but he's hungry. Surely there must be a place to eat around here somewhere. Otherwise we really need to get going."

"We don't have the kind of food you eat, I don't think," said Yucca. "We just plant our roots into the ground and garner the nourishment we need. Then when we want to roam around, we pull up our roots and go where we want to go. What exactly do you eat, anyway?"

"Preferably meat, vegetables, fruit, those kinds of things."

"You mean you eat living things?"

"Yes," answered JJ.

Peppy jumped in and quickly urged Yucca, "*Now* I hope you realize you've been out of line. We need to see these humans off on their travels. Stop hassling them. Stop it right now. And they're hungry too. There's no telling what they'll do next. Stop playing the game now, please!"

Ignoring Peppy, Yucca scolded JJ, "That is so barbaric. I'm beginning to understand why congress avoids you. Have you ever considered…"

Frank cut him off mid-question. "I'm not listening to another one of Yucca's questions or *your* explanations, JJ. I'm leaving. Come on, let's get out of here."

As he turned to walk out, Frank realized Yucca was standing directly in the path to the cave entrance, defiantly blocking him from leaving.

JJ sized up the situation, and asked Peppy, "What, exactly, *is* the game Yucca's playing?"

Peppy exclaimed, "That's the end of Round one! Yucca won the first round 30 -16 1/2. The game is called 'Do Ask, Do Tell.' See, according to the rules of the game, round one is over after 30 questions, but not until the last team asks their first question. Each team gets one point for every good, probing question they ask, and half a point for each good answer they give. Round two is the final round. Each member of the losing team gets to ask one question. Quality counts in this round. The scores are weighted. Your questions will have to be very thought provoking. You don't have much of a chance to catch up to Yucca's score. But don't feel bad. Yucca always wins. Only the elders can beat him."

"Okay then, I'll go first." Frank volunteered, impatiently and half-heartedly. Here's my question: "Why are you asking us so many stupid questions?"

"You humans are very unimaginative," replied Yucca. "That's the same question every human has asked me, all ten of you that I've met. You apparently don't care to question the world around you, or you'd be more enthusiastic about doing it. To learn interesting answers, you need to ask interesting questions. Anyway, to answer *your* question, in my world the way we learn is by asking questions of our own authority figures, the elders, and of the visitors we meet from foreign lands. We understand this is the way to accumulate new wisdom. *That* is why I ask so many questions, because I learn by asking questions. Humans apparently never even learn to ask questions."

JJ was listening intently to Yucca's answer, and had to agree with him on his perspective. "We go to school to learn, but our lessons are already prepared for us by the teachers. At school we are generally dis-couraged from asking questions because it disrupts the flow of the class for everybody else. Maybe that's how we develop the tendency to only learn, or believe, what we're told. I think learning by asking interesting questions is a great idea. And in that spirit, now it's my turn: Who are the elders? Are they talking cactuses too?"

A big smile spread across Yucca's face as he explained, "They are the older members of our family. If you want to call us cactuses, that's fine with me. The Elders all tend to stay together in one grove over on the other side of the mountain. They know all of our collected wisdom. I go visit them whenever I learn something new I'd like to discuss, or if I am wondering about the answer to a difficult question. They share their knowledge with us whenever we ask."

"Yeah, and sometimes they share it with us even when we don't ask," added Peppy.

"They *do* wander around from time to time to check on all of us," agreed Yucca. His big smile grew larger when he heard Peppy's observation. "They let us know if we're not conducting ourselves in a civilized and befitting manner, that much is sure."

"The Game's over," announced Peppy. "Yucca won as usual. Frank gets a zero for his unenthusiastic question. JJ gets a 6 for a good question he seemed genuinely interested in learning about, but Yucca earns a 3 on the same question. Final score: Yucca 33, JJ and Frank 22 1/2."

"Great! We can leave now," exclaimed Frank.

But Yucca stood firm in the path to the cave. His large smile continued to beam across his face and he leaned down towards JJ in a friendly manner. He said very softly, "This game is *not* over. I'm changing the rules. There's a round three this time. And JJ, in round three I *am* going to travel with you and Frank back to your human world. Let me explain. I've played 'Do Ask, Do Tell' many times before. And I've always been able to make some sense out of my opponent's responses. I have generally understood the way their answers to my questions fit within the contexts of their ways of life. But I'm not satisfied with your answers. I know you're telling the truth, but the truth just doesn't make any sense to me. I need to see your world with my own eyes to understand it."

JJ looked over at Frank and said, "It looks like we have a new companion on our vacation." Then he turned back to Yucca and asked, "Is the best way out of here through the same cave we came in through?"

"That's the only way I know. I've never left before. We'd better get going quickly, before the elders hear about this. I'm going to be in trouble when I get back."

Then Yucca looked back down at Peppy and asked, "Can you keep this quiet? And please only tell the elders where I went if I disappear for too long."

Peppy was *very* concerned. "Yucca, you know you can't do that. Have you lost all your senses? Please don't go. I'm worried. This is a really bad idea, the worst one you've had yet."

And Frank was very perturbed. He pulled JJ aside, out of earshot of Yucca and Peppy, and said, "I don't know about this, JJ. Do you really think we should bring Yucca with us? We're lost as it is. We don't even know how to get back to the campsite yet. He could slow us down. It's not fair to him *or* us. Plus, he's always asking stupid questions, like about money. What does he care? He doesn't even have pockets."

"It'll be fine, Frank. Just settle down and stop worrying about pockets. We're not *that* lost. And he seems pretty quick on his toes, so to speak. I don't think he's stupid at all. He has that twinkle in his eyes that makes me think he gets it. You know that look, don't you? Not many you meet have it. He might even provide an interesting new perspective and be fun to have around on the vacation. Wait until Izzy meets him! He's going to freak out!"

"Who's going to freak out, Izzy or Yucca?" asked Frank, who then hesitated for a second before adding, "And he *was* asking stupid questions, whether he's stupid or not."

"He was asking simple questions. Not stupid questions. The answers that some people give to simple questions are stupid. He was just asking simple questions about our way of life, and I was trying to explain things. I think that sometimes the answers to simple questions should be very complex. Maybe the answers to very complex questions are simple, who knows?"

Frank let out a sigh, resigned to the fact that they now had a new companion. "Ok ask me a complex question, then. Never mind. The answer is D, all of the above, and I'm still hungry."

JJ and Frank walked back to Yucca and Peppy. JJ promised Peppy they wouldn't do anything dangerous, and that they'd have Yucca back within a week. Peppy said a nervous goodbye, and the three set off for the cave.

5

A Quick Turn on a Dime

So JJ, Frank, and Yucca, set off into the cave in search of their campsite, Izzy, and food. Their second "How to Spot Bigfoot" flashlight guided the way. They walked through the desolate cave for over an hour without seeing anything of note. The cave made some zig-zags and jogs and went up and down, but always left just enough room to get through, although Yucca scraped his top leaves on the cave ceiling a few times. This stretch of the cave was very remote, as if almost no one had ever passed through. Eventually the flashlight batteries started to run down, until soon the cave became almost pitch-black. They realized they really needed another flashlight or a new set of batteries to navigate forward in this direction. Their only other option was to double back towards Hillsville and the thought police quickly, before the batteries ran completely down. But surely, Frank and JJ thought, they could find their campground by going forward without needing to go back and elude the Hillsville police again.

Soon the flashlight died altogether and they were stranded in almost complete darkness. JJ and Frank had no choice but to stop to discuss their options. They could definitely retrace their steps without panicking, even without much light. Luckily, Yucca's eyes radiated a glow that shone just enough light that they could see the cave walls around them. They had only paused for a minute when they were stunned to see lights flickering in the distance, and bobbing towards them. As the lights drew nearer, they could make out the silhouettes of two people approaching, carrying old-fashioned lanterns. JJ and Frank quickly became very nervous. They weren't used to having nowhere to hide. When the oncoming party finally reached JJ, Frank, and Yucca, the two approaching travelers stopped to greet them.

The man in front politely asked, in an even tone that belied his own unease, "Who do I have the honor of meeting, and where are you going?"

JJ stepped forward and responded, "I'm JJ, and these are my friends Frank and Yucca. We're headed back to our campsite, hopefully. We're looking for food too, although our friend Izzy has food back at the campsite. Have you passed a place to eat in the direction you're coming from? We're hoping there's an exit up ahead that will take us in the right direction. Oh, and who are you?"

"I can see you're nervous," responded the mystery traveler. "But there's no reason for *you* to be on edge. *I'm* the one that should be uneasy. You have two quite imposing companions with you. Forgive me for not introducing myself sooner. I'm the Economist and this is my friend Statistic. We're here looking for clues to the answers. This search is my mission. I seek high and low and near and far for every bit of evidence I can find. No stone is left unturned in my hunt for clues."

"But have you turned up anything to eat in your search?" asked Frank.

"I don't know of any place to eat anywhere near here, but I haven't explored all the surrounding areas. And I haven't seen your friend or any campgrounds either."

"What kind of clues are you looking for?" asked JJ curiously.

"Hints of inflation or deflation, mostly. But other things too, like demand changes, shortages, surpluses, and such. Even the most minute evidence of fluctuation or the slightest change in economic barometers must be examined closely."

Yucca had never heard of an economist before, and was also getting curious. "What does an economist do, exactly?" he asked.

"I'm an expert on the economy," replied the Economist, who acted quite surprised to see Yucca talk, but was nonetheless happy to see that he had an interested audience. "You see, the economy is the sum of all the collective money, wealth, and productivity in any nation. My friend Statistic is an average guy who helps me predict the productivity part of the wealth. He's kind of a jumpy fellow. It's important for me to carefully measure how far he jumps and when he jumps, so I like to invite him to travel with me. That way I can keep an eye on him at all times."

Now Yucca was getting even more curious. "Does it matter to you what direction he jumps in? And why? I guess it doesn't, or else you'd be following him, and clearly he is following you. I'd be excited to hear more from an expert on money, because I've just recently learned about the wealthy. As I understand it, they are the leaders, so maybe you can lead us to the food and Izzy. Since you're an expert on the wealthy, then you must be one of the *wealthiest,* and therefore one of the most influential leaders, right? Maybe you can even help JJ talk to congress!"

Frank butted in. "Lets stop the small talk. I still haven't eaten since last night and it doesn't look like Statistic has either. Lets go find some food."

Then Statistic weighed in. "Economist, I agree with Frank. I'm leaving your search for clues for the answers, and joining Frank's team to look for food. Good luck on finding clues, but I'm hungry."

"Good luck to you too, Statistic. It's been a pleasure working with you. I'll be in touch when we both return from our journeys. I'll still dig up some clues to report without you. Somehow. Somewhere."

The Economist had taken Statistic's change of direction in stride. He had at least seemed cheery as he immediately headed off in the direction JJ had just come from. He was on his own now, and was being quick about it.

Last Night

6

The Head Turner

JJ, Frank, Yucca, and Statistic continued walking through the dark cave. Yucca looked back, wondering if he had made the right decision to keep going, as he saw the Economist's light flicker into the distance. Statistic's lantern was lighting the way now. Forward.

After almost two hours of walking, the group came to a fork in the cave. They paused to decide which direction to go in. Luckily, Statistic was able to shed some light on the decision.

He said, "The Economist and I just came from the left cave and didn't pass any place to eat, or anything that looked like an exit to a campground either. Yesterday we were exploring further up into the right side of the fork. There *is* a place to eat in that direction, but it's at least two hours away, maybe more. There are also some other exits between here and there, but we didn't go into any of them. Maybe your campground could be in one of those areas."

"Let's go to the right, then," Frank said. "I'm sure that's where the campground must be. If not, at least we know we'll find food eventually."

JJ hesitantly agreed, but was beginning to think they should turn around. The farther they went forward, the longer it would take to retrace their path. And that was quickly becoming a likely scenario. They had traveled another fifteen minutes when they spied another cave exit coming up in the distance. As they drew nearer, the whole cave became very noisy. They inched closer. The ruckus coming from the entrance was so great, they didn't know what to expect. Or maybe it was the exit, it just depended on one's perspective. It sounded *to them* more like an entrance into *something*.

They carefully walked out of the cave and into a frantic scene. Hundreds of large critters were running all over the place, chattering, squabbling, and in general acting very confused. JJ and Frank had never seen critters like these. They looked a lot like prairie dogs, but they were three feet tall and were standing upright and scurrying around on their hind feet.

That was what they heard and noticed first. Then they saw what was flustering all the critters. It was a massive rig of some kind. It was brand-new and state of the art. Steam appeared to be belching from its giant smokestack, not black pollutants. It was methodically pumping up and down in powerful thrusts. The rig had five massive, ten-foot tall gears that were all working in tandem. It sported a big banner that read "brought to you by EcoCo: The New Eco-Friendly Fricking & Fracking Machine." There was a huge pipe going from the rig straight up towards the sky that never seemed to end. There was another pipe extending across the flatland for as far as the eye could see.

The machine looked starkly out of place. It was sitting in the middle of a seemingly endless prairie. Despite the complicated mass of equipment and flustered critters running amok immediately before them, JJ and his friends could see that in the distance this land was otherwise a large, serene habitat. It was a sweeping, flat plains region. There was a scattering of short, gnarled trees and small bushes spread across the prairie, but mostly the vegetation was just miles and miles of plains grass.

JJ, Frank, Statistic, and Yucca had walked right into the chaos. Two critters who had been in a heated argument, eyed JJ and his friends as they walked into the fracas. Both critters stopped arguing and hurried over to the group of strangers, and welcomed them to their home.

Yucca jumped right in to question mode and asked the critters, "Can you two please tell us what is going on here?"

Critter 1 answered, "Well, the politics of what is happening here is very fractious."

"No, they're frictious, not fractious," Critter 2 responded.

"Frictious isn't even a word, so they're *not* frictious, they're fractious."

"I think they're more frictious than fractious," Critter 2 retorted. "I don't care who sanctions *your* official words, but there is a lot of friction involved here, so frictious describes it. I asked a lot of the other critters their opinions on the situation. Half of them agreed with me whole-heartedly, a quarter strongly disagreed, a third think you're a jerk, and a quarter think Bigfoot is a scam artist. Those are frictions, not fractions. See, fractions need to add up. Frictions don't add up. But somebody had better be paying attention to them, because they sure can add up into one big problem for us all!"

"How many think *you're* a jerk?" responded Critter 1.

"Just a small fraction."

Yucca intervened. "Can you two tell us something more constructive? It seems like you're just arguing for the sake of arguing."

Then another critter invited himself into the fracas. "Why don't you settle it by playing 'pen, sword, dollar'? That always decides who's right."

Critter 1, glaring at the 3rd critter, said, "I don't like that game."

"I'll play!" Critter 2 said excitedly.

"What is 'pen, sword, dollar'?" asked Frank.

"It's an age-old way to settle an argument," explained Critter 3. "On the count of three, both arguers extend their right hand into the shape of a pen, a sword, or a dollar. Whoever wins, wins the argument. It's easy to play. The dollar is a flat hand, the sword is your finger pointing out, and the pen is your fingers curled up, like you're writing."

"That sounds like a game we play back home called 'rock, paper, scissors.' But how do you know who wins?" JJ asked.

"It's *always* obvious, isn't it? It just depends on which way the wind is blowing."

"Shouldn't the dollar always win? Like in real life?" Frank asked what they were all wondering.

"More often than not, but not always. Anyway, that wouldn't be much of a game would it?" answered Critter 3.

"It would be a game for the ones playing with the dollars, *just* like in real life," JJ noted.

Critter 1 stepped back in, answering Critter 3, "Forget about the game. It's too hard to tell which way the wind is blowing right now anyway." Then he turned back to JJ and explained, "Everything was just fine here until Mr. Big from EcoCo showed up and started asking a lot of questions. We were okay with Mr. Big's visits for the first few months or so. It seemed harmless. Then they started delivering all this big equipment. More and more of it!"

Critter 3 quickly moved forward and said, "Mr. Big read us a long story about the facts concerning the safety of fricking and fracking. But I think the most important fact is that it's embedded within human nature to break all the rules when there is a profit to be made, so the rest of the facts don't really matter."

Critter 2 chimed back in too. "Yeah, then we started realizing they might be taking over, so we filed a complaint with the EcoBureau. The EcoBureau insisted EcoCo follow the eco laws and use only eco-friendly equipment. That didn't really help us. Most of us still needed to move to new homes."

"Yeah, they put a lot of us in nice, shiny new homes. But we don't really feel at home in them. As new as they are, they don't have the soul that our ancestral homes had. There's no grit; the memories are gone. So is the soul."

"There are also no leaky roofs like we had always been fixing, but I know what my friend is saying. It's more like we're in hotels or something, not our homes."

"So what are you going to do next?" asked JJ. "Everyone seems to be in a total state of disarray. Do you have a leader of some kind that can unify the constituency?"

"We're working on it," explained Critter 1. "We're not lacking volunteers for *that* job. Most of us are against the new policies being forced on us by Mr. Big. But we keep arguing amongst ourselves over the details of the issues."

"Details like whether the same idea is frictious or fractious?" Yucca wondered.

Critter 2 nodded. "Exactly, but it *is* important to properly frame the issues."

Their voices started drowning out over an increasing roar coming from the distance. A long convoy of massive tanker trucks started rolling in from the plains. They pulled up to EcoCo's rig. They were brand new, state-of-the-art tankers, with big advertising slogans on the sides proclaiming "Another Public Service from EcoCo. All the energy to make your family happy!" The first truck pulled up to the rig and attached a pipe to a hub in the center of the rig. A few minutes later, it detached the pipe, and drove off, driving back down the dirt road it had come from. Each truck in queue pulled up to the rig, one by one, performing the same maneuver.

Looking upward, Yucca asked, "Why is the pipe going up? And to where are the trucks driving off? And where does that other long pipe stretch off to across the prairie? It looks like all the energy is being carted off to make the families happy *somewhere else*."

Critter 1 shrugged his shoulders. "That's what *we're* wondering. We have heard there is a large tunnel on the other side of our land that eventually connects with the Great Sea, so I'm sure that's where the trucks are coming from and going to. No one will tell us anything else, though. We may have to wait until the EcoSummit to find out."

"What is the EcoSummit?" asked JJ.

Critter 1 was eager to talk about it. "It's a huge conference called by the Right Governor. His directive is that there will be a meeting of the representatives of all of the Federated Lands this weekend to hammer out a new set of eco laws to insure the mutual well being of all of us. The Right Governor is very in tune with our interest in the green movement. It's a big deal. Why haven't you heard of it?"

"We're just passing through, hopefully. We're humans, from Baltimore. Except Yucca is some sort of talking cactus. We met him in a cave earlier in our travels, and Statistic is human, but I don't think he's from Baltimore," explained JJ. "Yucca, is your land part of the Federated Lands?"

"I'm from Virginia," Statistic quickly inserted, but no one was listening to him. He wasn't charismatic enough to be paid attention to, apparently.

"We're not part of the Federated Lands, to my knowledge," answered Yucca. "My friends and I back home never really thought about lands and governments, or even oil and money. We just listened to the elders and contemplated their favorite subject, something they called 'metaphysics'."

Critter 1 frowned towards Yucca. "Well that doesn't mean you're *not* a member. We didn't know we were members until Mr. Big showed up and told us we were!"

The severity of the situation was beginning to soak in on JJ. "You critters need to have a meeting as soon as possible. I'll help you organize it if you want. You need to try to settle all your minor differences, and identify some common goals. Then you need to elect some officials who will go represent all of the critters at the EcoSummit. The only way you'll get a fair deal at the summit is if you stop all your inner squabbling and present a unified front. You should also commission a study to find out where those pipes go and who is profiting from Mr. Big's rig. And by how much they're profiting."

"You're right. It looks like the pipeline goes straight to the top. And I'm not feeling so fractious all of a sudden," acknowledged Critter 1.

Yucca was frowning now. "JJ, do you think I should be concerned about my own land and my friends? What if Mr. Big put a rig in my woods?"

"Maybe a little. I don't understand what is going on exactly. I think we should explore the cave system some more. It's becoming clear to me that EcoCo is spread out through more than just one land. It must be a huge conglomerate with the kind of state of the art equipment they have here in Critterland."

At that instant Critter 1 exclaimed, "Hey look! Here comes the EcoCo guy now. It's Mr. Big himself!"

"I don't like this guy," muttered Critter 2. "He's always smiling and scowling at the same time."

"Me neither," added Critter 1. "He's obviously *a liberal!*"

"Liberal?" Frank blurted out. "He looks like a big shot to me. Look at all those medals on his chest! Usually only staunch conservatives would wear that kind of hardware. *Why on* earth would you call him a liberal? Wouldn't you think he's a conservative?"

"Look, Frank, I don't know where you came from, but he *invaded* our land. He brought in all that heavy equipment and displaced most of the native inhabitants: *Us*! He didn't ask us for our opinions and we didn't get a vote in the matter. We had no say whatsoever. I hardly find this brazen behavior *conservative*," replied Critter 2. "And to make matters worse, he's clearly *humane!*"

"Yeah, in fact, the only way he could do this to us was through *very liberal* interpretations of the laws, I'm sure. Only a human would take those liberties," argued Critter 1.

Critter 3 looked at JJ and Frank and said, "Please let me explain about humane liberties. 99% of those folks that exist in our world are conservatives or liberals. It's only the 1% that are both."

Mr. Big wasted no time striding over to the group. "What are you humans doing here in Critterland? What is your business? And why do you have this cactus with you? Where did you find it, and how did all of you get here? And, pray tell, what are you saying to these fine, law abiding citizens of Critterland?"

Frank gulped and was nervously *thinking* about asking Mr. Big, "I'm just hungry and looking for a diner. Have you seen one? JJ and Yucca have been dragging me all over the place for no apparent reason, and now Statistic is lost and hungry too."

JJ stepped in between Frank and Mr. Big. "It's none of your business why we're here or how we got here. I was just discussing with the critters our mutual concern about the safety and integrity of their environment. All of this big machinery can't possibly be good for the ecosystem. The critters are not happy with being displaced into temporary homes while the drilling is going on, and they're worried about what will be left of their ancestral homes when the drilling is done. What assurances can EcoCo give to the critters?"

Mr. Big stepped right up to JJ with a large scowl on his face and answered, "Son, it is my job to make sure all the business here is eco-friendly. It is my job to make sure the critters are taken care of. And it is my job to make sure that the entire process goes smoothly, with no problems from any outside troublemakers."

Yucca was studying Mr. Big very closely. "What are all those medals for? There sure are a lot of them."

"Thanks for asking, cactus. They are lifetime achievement awards. I have earned 27 of them."

That answer didn't satisfy Yucca. "Forgive me for asking, but how can you earn that many lifetime achievement awards? It seems like you could only earn one of those."

"Well you clearly have never worked a day in your life! Otherwise you would know what it takes to earn one of these." Mr. Big looked very agitated.

"I'm sure they were hard to earn," Yucca answered. "I'm just wondering how you could have worked for 27 lifetimes? And you're right. I have never worked a day in my life. I'm just now trying to grasp what working actually is."

"Son, I *earned* my first one when I was 25 years old. When I was done with that first one I realized it was my duty to keep working. You need to realize the same thing and get working. What kind of parents did you have, not teaching you a work ethic?"

Yucca was deeply offended. "Well excuse me, but I didn't have parents. And I don't like the indignant tone of your voice, even if I did. JJ, is this the way you humans talk to one another when you get old? I'm sure this guy believes he has the right, as decorated as he is, to be mean to me, but I don't like his pompousness."

JJ looked at Yucca and responded, "No, this guy is being a jerk and I don't understand the lifetime achievement awards either." JJ turned back to Mr. Big, and said, "Mr. Big, we all respect that you've achieved a great deal in your life, but don't be rude to us. I mean, surely you can see that Yucca's not human, and somewhere in your lifetimes of achievement you must have learned that cactuses don't have parents, so why cop the mean attitude?"

Mr. Big stepped menacingly towards JJ. "Son, you're being insubordinate and I'm glad you mentioned cops. I'm reporting you to the police immediately for insubordination and felonious meddling. You and your band of criminals are going to pay for this one! Nobody treats a hero like me like that." Mr. Big motioned to a posse of police officers who had accompanied him on his junket.

Frank nudged JJ and whispered, "We'd better start running again." So they ran right back into the cave, with Statistic and Yucca following closely behind.

As the police were chasing JJ and his friends towards the cave, Mr. Big turned and addressed the growing crowd of Critters, who had been scurrying over to see what the commotion was all about. "Now that those scallywags are gone, I'd like to address you critters concerning a most *positive* development. The Eco Council has received several written complaints from you about the way EcoCo is conducting business here in Critterland. In response, EcoCo is announcing a new initiative. This will be very beneficial and will help your mutual financial stability.

I am proud to say that EcoCo is going to hire five Critters from your community to highly paid positions within the company. These will be lucrative jobs, with twenty-year contracts and retirement pensions. We will begin taking applications immediately."

One of the critters asked, "Do I get preference for the jobs if I was one of the letter writers?"

"No!" bellowed Mr. Big.

"That idea doesn't sound half bad," said another critter.

"It doesn't sound half good either," responded a scowling Critter 1.

"If it's not half bad *or* half good, then what is the idea? Half baked?" asked a frustrated Critter 2. "I'm confused. I can't tell whether this plan is frictious or fractious."

"It's both!" Critter 1 exclaimed. He suspiciously began to grill Mr. Big, "How do five jobs help us? There are over five *thousand* of us. Why wouldn't you distribute the money evenly so we can *all* improve our lives, although modestly, instead of giving five of us gobs of money? That kind of money might build a new school that all the critter kids could attend, for example."

"Because we want to show you critters that everyone has the chance to live 'The Federated Dream'. It doesn't matter what species you are, how undereducated you are, or the degree of squalor you have been living in. Everyone has the chance to live it. Each of these five individuals will work hard for twenty years and will proudly *earn* their money. And they will do so with the knowledge that the government will defend their growing wealth vigorously. We will not let any of the masses of non-producers hornswoggle these upstanding citizens. There will be no wealth redistribution in these Federated Lands. We want every one of you critters to believe in 'the Federated Dream' and know it is possible to achieve. Why, this could be your way out, son!"

"Out of what?" one of the Critters wondered aloud.

"So landing an EcoCo job is kind of like winning a lottery, isn't it?" asked Critter 3. "And the odds of winning are low, just like in any government sponsored lottery?"

Mr. Big was becoming annoyed at so many questions about his grand announcement, but he gruffly answered, "You *need* a lottery to be fair. You see, son, usually to land a job of this caliber, you would need to *know* somebody or be qualified. None of you critters have any of those assets."

"It doesn't cost anything to play, does it? Where do I apply?" Critter 2 asked Mr. Big.

"That's the spirit, son!" Mr. Big slapped Critter 2 on the back.

"But what about the rest of us?" protested Critter 1.

"Son, you obviously don't understand how big this opportunity is. As if your newfound belief in 'the Federated Dream' wasn't enough, you will also see the infinite benefits of trickle-down economics. The new hard-working class of critters will pass along some of their hard-earned money to the non-producers. For example, they'll pay tips to critters that carry their luggage, serve their dinners, or shine their shoes. *Everyone* will benefit from this generous gesture from EcoCo."

Critter 1 frowned at Mr. Big, and then at Critter 2. "You're not really applying are you?"

"It beats getting trickled-down upon."

"If we get the job, do we *have* to wear shoes?" asked another Critter.

Last Night

7

The Turn Up

Meanwhile, JJ, Frank, Yucca, and Statistic kept running through the cave in the direction they had been heading earlier. Statistic's lantern was guiding the way forward, until finally they realized they were far enough away to take a breather.

JJ asked Statistic, "You've been through these caves before. Are there any exits we could duck into coming up soon? We need to get off the beaten path for awhile."

"As I was trying to tell you earlier, there are several cave exits not *too* much further up. The next one on the right might be a comfortable place to stop and catch our breath."

They arrived at the next exit, and walked out through the mouth of the cave. They realized they were in a thick forest. This path didn't seem traveled very often.

"Statistic, do you have any idea what is in this area?" JJ wondered.

"Yeah, like hopefully a diner and a hotel, for example," stressed Frank.

"We passed by here and didn't go very far in. We didn't see any civilization, or anything else interesting, so we left."

"It looks like it will be getting dark soon," JJ observed. "I vote we go a little way down the path, then veer off a safe distance and set up camp for the night."

Frank grudgingly agreed. "Ok, I guess we don't have much choice. But we'd better get up early and start looking for food. I can't believe it's already tonight and I still haven't eaten since *last* night. Once we've eaten we need to make our way back to the campsite and find Izzy."

Statistic tried to reassure Frank, "We'll eat in the morning, I'm sure. The exit I know of with food is only another hour and a half up the cave. I'm sticking with you, and it looks like Yucca is too."

So, the friends found a safe clearing in the woods, far from the police. They took a few minutes of rest to catch their breaths, and then looked for wood so they could build a campfire. Soon they had a roaring fire, and as they got comfortable, they began reflecting on the day's events. Yucca wasn't too fond of the fire at first, but JJ and Frank explained that was part of camping in the wilderness with friends. Plus, humans don't hold up any better in a fire than does cacti. Everyone simply needs to know to keep their distance from the flames. Respect the danger, but enjoy the ambiance and intrigue, just like life in general. But remember to pay attention, or you could miss something important.

As Yucca started to get comfortable by the fire, he became contemplative. "I'm still very troubled by what Mr. Big said. I don't understand why people would be so mean to someone else. I don't understand how someone's train of thought could be so singular that they wouldn't consider other people's perspectives before forming an opinion, much less before even speaking to them. And I don't understand the concept of getting more than one lifetime achievement award. It seems to me that one would be enough."

"I don't get it either," agreed JJ. "I know that in our modern world people feel like they need to work constantly. And it seems like we all need to accomplish a lifetime quickly. Even young people now think they need to live a lifetime in a few years instead of paying their dues the way I have been doing as I have been growing up. Life is nonstop these days. If you stop working, then your competitors might pass you, because there is no reason to believe they are taking a break either. Being idle is the same thing as falling behind for most people now. They're always afraid they're missing something happening somewhere else."

"So your world is kind of like one big race?" Yucca asked with a degree of puzzlement.

"Yeah, welcome to the human race. Why do you think JJ and I are here?" Frank reflected. "We wanted to get away from the race. But somehow we got lost. I guess it's still a break from the human race, though. But I don't feel like racing anymore. I'm just hungry."

"It's not *really* a race," JJ explained to Yucca. "In our world, a lot of us are very relaxed. Many people work hard all day and then are very calm at night, spending time with their families, or reading a book or something. Some people are unemployed and wish they *could* work all day. Those people probably stress out more than the people working. But some people feel they *need* to work constantly. They are so driven to succeed that they work very long hours, never really stopping to enjoy life that much. Those people are always worried. Worried about their competitors working longer hours than they do, getting the same ideas or even better ideas than they themselves have, or just being better prepared in some way than they are. These people feel a need to work so hard that it seems more like lifetimes before they can even take a vacation. I myself am one of those people. I need to learn to relax a little more. Of course, with Frank here as my wing-man, I guess I shouldn't start relaxing now."

"Look, JJ, I haven't eaten since last night, so give me a break," Frank responded. "But I've never understood awards to begin with. It seems like some people feel an egotistical need to win an award just to be recognized by their fellow man. Ball players want the MVP awards, guys like Mr. Big want medals, managers want employee of the year awards. Who decides who gets the awards anyway? What is the measure? Why would any secure person want to show off medals just to let the rest of the world know that *someone else* thought they had done some good? Personally, I've done a lot of things in my life I thought were good. The world doesn't know it, but I do. But the only *award* I want is the *reward* of knowing that I am proud of myself for living an enjoyable life, and for being a good neighbor, husband, and father."

"JJ, do you think Mr. Big feels *rewarded* twenty seven times over?" Yucca was clearly really troubled by this whole concept.

"I'm guessing he has more than one pension," JJ answered. "He probably has pensions paid by the public directly, and others paid by the private sector, so I would say he probably feels rewarded many times over."

"I don't trust people like Mr. Big who flaunt their own accomplishments," Frank added. "Like I just said a minute ago, who decides who gets the awards anyway. So why should I care about who?"

Statistic had been sitting silently, listening to everything being said. But now he was ready to weigh in. "You know what, I like the relaxing and talking we're doing now. JJ, I get what you're saying about working too much. I do too, but I *need* to. I have a wife, two kids, a mortgage, car payments, and forget about college savings. I mean, my wife and I can't even afford vacations anymore. After the bills are paid and social security and taxes are deducted, there's not much left. My only getaways now are moonlighting my second job, assisting the Economist. He's a nice guy in most ways, but always prodding me, asking boring questions. I wish I could be spending that time at home, sharing boring questions with my wife and kids. Then the boring questions would be special questions."

Yucca looked at the humans, and they were all nodding at each other understandingly at what Statistic had said. He was warming up to the idea of the campfire chat. The flickering light from the fire made Yucca's eyes light up with a warm, yet even more quizzical, and piercing glow. His eyes looked especially beaming to Statistic, who was sitting next to Frank, directly across the fire from Yucca. "What is social security, Statistic?" Yucca asked next.

"It's a government program," explained Statistic. "Our government withholds a percentage out of each of our paychecks for our whole life. Then when we reach the age of 65 we get to retire. That's when the government starts giving us back monthly checks to live off of."

"If I understand this correctly," Yucca observed, "The government borrows your money, and then gives it back to you when you get old? Why don't they just let you keep it to begin with? Couldn't they let you save the money on your own? You might be able to retire earlier. In fact, the government keeping your money *and* telling you to work until you're 65 just to get it back, sounds like *forced slavery* to me."

"Well technically, Yucca, they take your money and pay you back with money they take away from the kids who are working. By the time I retire, for example, the government will have already spent the money they took from me. They will have probably spent it just paying interest on the loans and bonds that exist from before I was even born."

"They *take* the money from the kids? They *make* the kids take care of the parents when they get old? Isn't that what kids should *want* to do? These elderly people raised these children. Where's the gratitude? The government shouldn't be obligated to get involved. What kind of kids wouldn't take care of their own parents when they become too old to take care of themselves? You must have some very nasty, vile kids where you live. I've never heard of such callousness. Kids should realize this would be the most rewarding experience of their lifetimes, caring for the ones that gave them life to begin with!"

"Let me explain further," Statistic continued, "Some kids are actually very helpful and loving to their elderly parents, but some of them *are* just waiting for their inheritance. See, when an elderly person passes away, they generally leave their estate to their kids."

"I see now," expressed Yucca. "The government *is* doing the right thing, after all. When they take the social security out of the paychecks, they are punishing those ungrateful kids. By not letting people save and invest their own money, they are taking away part of those nasty kids' inheritance. Plus if the government is keeping the kids' social security too, the kids *are* being properly punished. It also seems to me like one big pyramid scheme by the government, but at least their hearts are in the right place."

At that point Frank *had* to break in, "Yucca, that doesn't make any sense at all."

"It doesn't make any sense to me either," agreed Yucca.

Frank was still shaking his head when he changed the subject. "You know JJ, we're always joking around about our jobs. I thought we have always been honest with each other, but I never realized how truly burdened you are with your work ethic. I've always admired that a little, but kind of made fun of it too. Are you really saddled with that much extra baggage? I realize you own your own company, but is it really worth fretting and beating yourself up over? Can't you be just as successful as you are now, but separate yourself from your work after hours? Is that why you make digs at me sometimes, because I have a normal forty-hour workweek? And that perhaps you think I don't care about my job in the least when those forty hours are over?"

"No, not at all," replied JJ. "I know you care about your job, and that you have a lot of responsibility. I wish I could set aside my concerns when the workday is done, like you're able to do. Instead I continue to plot scenarios well into the evening a lot of the time, trying to think of ways to better affect the outcomes of tomorrow's events. Sometimes it's not just my work I fret about. Even though my sphere of influence does revolve around me, I'm concerned with other things happening in our world too. Occasionally all the worrying gets the best of me and I can't sleep at night. *That's* when I start to stress out over the things that I know I can't control, and I wonder to myself 'Or could I?'"

Yucca sighed and observed, "You humans have a lot to worry about that I don't." Yucca thought through a moment of silence, then looked across the campfire at Frank and asked, "Frank, what is your job? I understand that JJ owns a cabinet making business, but what do you make?"

"I guess I don't actually make anything, just money. I'm a systems operations manager. I'm responsible for the direction and the over-sight of all operations within my division. Technically my job title is

'President of Operational Oversight.' See, I oversee my corporation's oversight office. The job title sounds impressive and the job pays well, but it's a thankless, crappy job. Unlike JJ, I try to forget about my work after hours. Personally, I have a lot of heart and a lot of soul, and a lot of other problems too. But I put up with my job because I have a very comfortable home life. My wife and I own a nice house and have two great kids. The family activities keep me busy, and I also have good friends like JJ and Izzy to hang out with on my time off. I have a lot to be thankful for. So does JJ. He has wonderful kids, wife, and home too, and I'm sure this trip brings him a lot of mental relaxation, no matter how unsettled he may seem to be at times."

"Frank, it sounds like your job affords you some peace of mind that JJ doesn't have, so it can't be *that* bad. President of Operational Oversight sounds very important to me," noted Yucca. "It must take a lot of wisdom and be a great honor to be vested with the power to overlook things in behalf of your whole company. Just imagine how much money the President of Operational Oversight for EcoCo must make! He must overlook more than just about anybody else in the Federated Lands!"

JJ, Statistic, and even Frank laughed at Yucca's view of Frank's job, and JJ said, "I never thought about it that way, but maybe our congressional oversight committees actually *are* doing their jobs, after all!"

Frank stopped chuckling and explained to Yucca, "*My* oversight office is really in charge of *overseeing* the company's operations, not *overlooking* anything. JJ is making reference to our congress' oversight committees, which are responsible for investigating improprieties within our government and it's laws and lawmakers." Then Frank, who was not known for his tact, went on to tell Yucca, "You know what Yucca? Getting back to JJ and I being worried about things, I'd be a little concerned if I were you about Mr. Big coming into your land. What if the EcoBureau doesn't recognize the same rights for cacti as for critters?"

"I don't want anything to do with those rights, if that's what you want to call them. Mr. Big acted like he didn't know where I came from. That's a good sign."

"I wonder if there's a way to keep it that way? How many ways are there to get to your land?" asked JJ.

"I only know of one way out. I'm not sure about in." Yucca contemplated for a minute, and then said, "I sure hope nothing wrong comes of all this back home. I'm getting an uneasy feeling that bad things may be inevitable, that we may have unhappy clashes in our future. But the Elders are so sure of themselves, that it is hard for me to actually believe."

"You know what Yucca?" asked JJ. "Nothing is ever cemented into eternity. I mean, technically it might be, but not really. People in *my* world *think* they set things in stone. People save for retirement. They take out life insurance policies. People get married. They may land the 'perfect job.' Congressmen may pass a law. These people think they have planned perfectly. They may think that from that point forward everything will go just as they may have planned. The problem is, once they've reached that juncture, they stop trying. And once they stop trying, things change. Even my country's founding fathers knew the government they provided us with would need to be reworked as our country evolved. Yucca, there is never an ending to *anything*. You just have to believe that you have thought the things through in your life that are worth thinking about as best you can. You need to help teach the youth as best you know how. And whenever you think you've reached an apex, you need to try your best to go a little higher. And then keep moving on from there."

The friends thought about things and were quiet for a few minutes. They were starting to get sleepy sitting by the fire, even though it was still pretty early in the evening. They were all silently self-reflecting on the long day's events.

JJ eventually broke the silence again. "Statistic, I hope I'm not offending you by asking, but why is your name 'Statistic'? I've never heard the name before."

"No, I'm not offended. I get asked all the time. My dad was a high school math teacher, and it was his idea. I was embarrassed by the name for years, but as I grew older I started to appreciate my name's unique individuality. That's kind of ironic, isn't it? I get my dad's quirky view of the world and sense of humor now that I'm older.

There was another long moment of silence, then JJ asked, "Statistic, what was the Economist *really* looking for? He doesn't need to walk all over the place looking for clues. He can stay at home at his desk to analyze numbers. He doesn't even need you following him around. And Yucca's right, it seems like if anything, *he* should be following *you* around anyway. He shouldn't feel a need to pay you if he's just analyzing your reactions, either. What kind of science is that? Some things here are not adding up. He was looking for something, just not the clues he was speaking of."

"I don't know. He always said he was just looking for clues. Come to think of it, though, just last night he did say that he was on the cusp of discovering "the whole tamale." But we were on our way to dinner, so I didn't think anything of it."

The mention of food brought Frank back to life. "Tell us how good the tamales were. Were they smothered in hot sauce? Man, I'm hungry."

"No, actually we had Chinese." Frank slumped back down. A few seconds of silence elapsed, and then Statistic said to Frank, "Come to think of it, I still have my fortune cookie from yesterday. I tossed it in my backpack. Here, do you want it?" Statistic reached into his backpack and handed the fortune cookie to Frank.

Frank perked up, and devoured the cookie. Then he asked, "Do you guys want to hear my fortune? It says 'Time keeps moving on, no matter how you decide to use it.' I wonder what that's supposed to mean?" No one volunteered any interpretations, but Frank tucked the fortune in his wallet anyway, just in case it made sense to him later.

By that point they were all getting very comfortable and sleepy from the warmth of the fire. It was still quite early in the evening, but they had just finished a very long and eventful day. Then suddenly they were all jolted back awake by a rustling in the woods. In the near distance a flashlight became visible. It was someone approaching quickly. The whole group was petrified. A human silhouette stepped out of the shadows into the campfire light.

8

Right Turn

"Izzy!" Frank exclaimed, "We've been worried about you. Where have you been? How in the heck did you find us? And what's in your backpack? Please say food!"

"*You* were worried about *me*? That's funny," answered Izzy in a sarcastic tone. "*You're* lucky I was worried about *you*, because I did bring food. I brought plenty of snacks: trail mix, jerky, chips." Izzy opened his backpack and pulled out bags full of power snacks. He said, "Here, dive in. You guys sure have had a long day, judging from everything I heard about you on my way tracking you down here. You seem to have made people mad all the way here."

"I take it you made it to the general store?" JJ ascertained.

"Yeah, it wasn't too much further to the left than I thought it was."

"Did the police come back to the campsite?" asked JJ.

"Oh yeah," Izzy replied with a sarcastic tinge back in his voice. "He had the Park Ranger with him this time. He spent two hours analyzing the evidence. His results were inconclusive, so he decided we had been smarting off earlier and issued citations to all three of us. We'll need to deal with that when we get back. The larger problem is the Park Ranger doesn't believe in Bigfoot and he's really peeved at what we did to his campsite. He wants to question us when we get back. We'll get citations from him too."

"Great," replied Frank, also in a sarcastic tone. "Did you clean up the mess?"

"The Campsite? Yes," replied Izzy. "Was I able to smooth over the mess with the Park Ranger and police officer? No. After another hour went by, I realized you two knuckleheads were totally lost. I was worried because I knew how fast you were both going downhill, so I followed the path you had taken looking for you."

"And you didn't get arrested by the thought police in Hillsville?" asked Frank.

"No, but they warned me to watch my back while I was visiting. They were busy on a manhunt looking for two dangerous criminals that were on the loose. At first it didn't occur to me it was you two, because the police told me you were wanted for thinking. I never would have drawn *that* conclusion!"

At that point Izzy had started sizing up the new members of the expedition. He looked at JJ and asked, "Are you going to introduce me to your new friend? And where did you find the giant cactus?"

Yucca's eyes flared back up as he looked at Izzy and responded, "I'm Yucca. JJ and Frank came to my homeland after they escaped the police. They cordially invited me to come along on their trip back to your world."

Izzy was stunned to hear Yucca talking, but was already warmed up to the idea that he was in a different world, having talked to the critters already. "Wow, you walk and talk! That's unbelievable."

"Did you not go through Yucca's land of talking cactuses?" JJ was surprised. "Oh, and our other new friend here is Statistic, from Virginia, by the way."

"No, I never saw the talking cactus land. But I sure would like to. Let's plan on stopping there on our way back to the campsite. I'm assuming you guys are still lost, right? I know my way back to the campground from here, so don't worry. We'll need to pass back through Hillsville, though. The worst-case scenario is the police take you into custody. But once they start questioning you, it won't take them long to drop the thought charges. Anyway, from Hillsville I followed the caves straight to Critterland. I poked my head into several of the other exits, but didn't see anything of note. Critterland was very chaotic. The critters told me the whole story about how you stood up to Mr. Big, JJ. They were very appreciative of your attempt to help. They pointed me in this direction, but told me about a shortcut. I came in from the south, down by the villages."

"You mean there are villages here?" Now Statistic was surprised too. "The Economist thought this land was uninhabited."

"Yes, there are villages down south of here. They're kind of abuzz right now about the EcoSummit, just like the Critters are. In fact, one of the towns is having an EcoSummit Caucus this evening, and there's just enough time for us to make it. Do any of you want to go with me? I'm curious."

"Why don't you and JJ go," volunteered Frank. "I'll stay here with Statistic and Yucca and keep an eye on the fire and the food. I'll save some food for you, JJ."

"Sounds good to me. I'm curious too." JJ jumped up off the log he was sitting on, ready to go.

It was a short walk to the village. On their way in, they passed a small sign that read "Entering Wrightsboro." It was a small hamlet, but a lot larger than Hillsville. The buildings were much better maintained too. Many were newly painted and the town commons was freshly mowed. It was clear the residents of this town took a lot of pride in their community. They reached the Town Meeting Hall, and the sign outside read, "Tonight 9:00 PM Community EcoSummit Caucus of Southrightmost County, District 1. All welcome members of our community are invited to attend." JJ and Izzy slipped in the side door and sat down in the back row, not sure if they were invited *or* welcome.

The Chairman commenced the meeting. "Community, we are gathered here to conduct a forum to discuss our positions at the Eco-Summit. I am Edwin Jones, chairman. After this discussion we will hold a caucus to name our representatives for the EcoSummit. And most importantly, during this caucus we will agree on our platform concerning the issues brought forward by The EcoCouncil."

"As you may know, the EcoCouncil has specifically identified the following issues for which we should be prepared to debate: Water Purity, Air Pollution, Erosion, Drilling and Mining, Invasive Species, Toxic Spills, and Deforestation." I'd like to start by discussing the topic that seems to be of the most interest to all of us, the Invasive Species issue. Does anyone have any opinions they would like to share on the matter?"

A man immediately stood up and spoke. "My name is Elroy Jones and I have lived here my whole life in the homestead my daddy grew up in. My grandparents settled this land alongside most of *your* grandparents. They worked hard to build a homeland they could call their own. They built it from scratch out of a lawless wilderness that was previously inhabited by who knows what. I can no longer sit still and watch the invasion of our great land by the *Intellectuals*! This land used to be completely free of them. They're not native to it. It's not natural for them to be here! At first there was just a few of them. Now they've taken root and are over-running the place. I talked to one of them once, and he couldn't understand a word I was telling him. Plus, they're stealing our jobs! They're choking us out, and they're using all their fancy new words to change the way we live! Who ever told them they could come here anyway? I didn't. Did any of you?"

He looked around the room. The whole caucus shook their heads no. "See! They're here *without permission*!" There was a murmur of agreement in the crowd that lingered for a minute.

But the crowd was quieted when the Chairman stood up in defense of the intellectuals. "Now before everybody gets carried away here, I'd like to remind you they *are* expanding our tax base. And they're taking the bad, tough jobs that nobody else wants, like being teachers, scientists, and engineers. They're not taking the good, high-paying jobs like bankers, salesmen, insurance agents, and football coaches. So we need to exercise a little restraint before we all get too worked up over this. Now, does anyone have anything else they'd like to add?"

A woman stood up and spoke. "My name is Norma Jones and I have lived here my whole life, just like my mother and father before me. I'm getting tired of the invasion of the *Young'uns*! You never used to see them and you only heard them when they were spoken to. Now they've over-run the mall, the town park, and the diner. There's no place for us life-long natural citizens to walk in peace! They don't even speak English! They're always talking in letters and codes, like OMG and FYI. And they use fake names that don't sound natural, like Njones1745 and Sjones345. If they are going to live here they at least need to learn to speak our language! And start paying taxes too! I'm sick and tired of supporting these free-loaders!"

Again there was a murmur of approval from the crowd.

The Chairman stood back up. "Okay, we've heard enough. All those in support of a very strongly enforced Invasive Species provision say I."

There was a chorus of I's.

"Anyone against this measure, don't say I."

There was silence.

"Adopted!" The Chairman banged his gavel on the podium, and then continued. "Another important issue is that of Erosion. There is a lot of eroding going on around us: family values, the use of the English language, our job market, and our way of life in general. This is *all* due to the invasive species, so I think our stringent and uncompromising stance on that issue will cover the Erosion issue. All in agreement say I."

There was another chorus of I's.

The Chairman carried on. "The other issues brought forward don't affect us. We have clean water and air, and have never had a toxic spill. We don't have any deforestation issues, and I don't expect any. Our government *has always* protected our right to log our land as we see fit. And there is no mining or drilling going on here. In fact, I recently met with a representative from EcoCo, a Mr. Big, who I found to be a very upstanding and trustworthy man, a true patriot. He has assured me there are no plans to ever drill or mine on our land, as long as no new restrictions are placed on mining and drilling at the EcoSummit. He explained that the clean drilling they are already doing in other places will meet the needs of all the Federated Lands for many years to come, provided no new restrictions or regulations are put forth."

The crowd nodded in approval.

"So is everyone in agreement that we will fight vigorously for very stringent new laws restricting invasive species, and that we vote for no new restrictions on any of the other issues at the EcoSummit?"

A chorus of I's came from the crowd.

"Then I would like to end this caucus by nominating Elroy and Norma to vote on our behalf at the EcoSummit. Does anyone second this motion?"

There came another chorus of I's.

"Then this concludes this caucus of the Southrightmost County, District 1. Goodnight and thanks for attending."

JJ and Izzy sensed they were being sized up by the crowd, so they slipped back out of the meeting as quickly and inconspicuously as possible, lest they be mistaken for invasive intellectuals. They agreed they'd best get back to camp before discussing what had just transpired. After a brisk moonlit walk, they arrived to find Frank and Statistic asleep. Yucca was in a vegetative state as well. The fire was dying out and there were just enough snacks left for the two of them. They stayed up for a few minutes, enjoying the last glowing embers of the fire.

"What do you think we should do in the morning?" JJ asked.

"Well we could get out of here and get back to our campsite and continue with our vacation as planned. We've gotten in plenty of hiking, but we haven't gone tubing yet."

"Or we could keep exploring these Federated Lands," JJ countered. "The politics and the wildlife here are crazy. We'll never get a chance to see anything like this again."

"Or we could also get back to camp and pack up and head to Myrtle Beach," replied Izzy. "I know the wildlife there would fascinate Frank, plus I'm not sure how safe this place is. We may be sticking our noses somewhere they don't belong. But it's ok with me if we stay here. Before I found you guys I walked a few hundred yards into a rain forest not too far from here. It looked a lot more intriguing than the woods here at our campsite. Maybe we could get up in the morning and go eat breakfast in District 1. I'm sure the locals will be calmed down by then. They'll be cordial to us if we explain we're just passing through and that we're not intellectuals."

"That'll be easy. We'll just let Frank do all the talking." JJ said.

"Then after breakfast we could go explore the rain forest if Frank doesn't complain too much," Izzy continued. "He'll be fine, as long as he's eaten."

"That sounds like the plan to me," agreed JJ. "But seriously, we do need to be careful. You're right to be worried about safety. But then again, it's not like we didn't get into trouble at our campsite either." JJ let out a large yawn and said, "It's been a long day. Let's get some sleep."

Last Night

9

Left Turn

The friends drifted off to sleep as the fire burnt out. Eight hours of sleep went by quickly and in the morning they all set off for town. As the group was walking they discussed the meeting from last night. The three that hadn't attended were anxious to hear what had happened.

"The locals were quite opinionated about some things, especially new people settling in their town," JJ explained. "They don't want to be burdened by outsiders or other peoples' problems. I'm sure they'll be calmed down by now, but we need to be careful what we say in town."

Then Izzy explained to Frank, "I saw a really interesting rain forest near here on my way in yesterday. JJ and I figured we'd go into town for a good breakfast, and then go explore the rain forest. We'll do that on our way back to the campsite, of course."

"Any plan sounds great to me when it starts with a good breakfast," Frank said agreeably. "While we're exploring the rain forest we can hash out our exit strategy and hopefully our plans for Myrtle Beach."

By that time they had entered the village. As they were walking across the town commons, they overheard bits of a conversation coming from a group seated at a picnic table: "That's what I said. We weren't invited."

"I know, I didn't even know about the meeting."

"Me neither. There was no mention of it in the newspaper."

"No, I mean at the meeting they said we weren't invited to be here at all. For some reason the Joneses are keeping track of us and don't like us being in their neighborhood."

The friends didn't want to be seen too close to the intellectuals, so they walked by quickly. They found a good café and ate breakfast without incident. No one even gawked at Yucca. When it was time to pay for their meal, they realized they didn't have any local money to pay the tab. JJ asked the waitress, "Do you take US dollars, by any chance?"

The waitress answered, "Here in Wrightsboro, we honor all foreign currencies, with one provision: When you've spent all of it you have, you need to go back home. You can't stay here."

"That works for me," said Izzy.

"Me too!" agreed Frank and Statistic simultaneously.

When JJ handed her the exact change, plus a generous tip in US dollars, the waitress remarked, "Your land's money sure is bland. Couldn't your leaders have used some prettier colors of ink? There's nothing noteworthy about them at all."

It was still early when they exited the cafe, so there weren't many people downtown yet. Apparently, since the town caucus had run so late last night, the locals were slow to rise. On the way out of town they passed through the town commons, and right back by the picnic table. The group of intellectuals had indeed multiplied, just as the Joneses had predicted, and they were now engaged in a spirited debate on anthropology.

Once the group left town, they took a pleasant walk through the woods. The path was well marked and their spirits were high. It took them ten minutes to get to the cave, and they followed Izzy through the entrance. They were becoming accustomed to the cave travel, so it wasn't as eerie as the day before. Statistic's lantern lit the way on the short walk through the winding cave. After just a few minutes they came to the exit into the rain forest, actually more of a jungle really, and walked in. The vegetation was very dense and it was quite hot and humid. There was a large, well-traveled main path blazed directly from the mouth of the cave, which they followed for a few more minutes until it began splitting up into smaller paths. One of the paths on the left led towards a large mountain that loomed in the near distance. That's the path they chose.

It took them fifteen minutes to get to the base of the mountain. The foliage was really interesting and foreign to everyone in the group. The trees were massive and had huge vines growing all over them. The trees were all grown tightly together, and the ground level vegetation was also thick and lush. The group really needed to stay on the beaten trail just to navigate their way through the jungle. They came upon a path that went a few hundred feet uphill, and appeared to end in a clearing. It was a fairly well worn path with tree roots exposed all the way up, forming built-in stairs. They figured there must be something up in the clearing, or the path wouldn't be so well worn, so they decided to climb up and explore. As they got closer and closer to the top, they could hear a chorus of whistling and many voices all talking at once. It grew louder and louder until they reached the clearing, where they saw a most amazing sight.

Right in front of them was an arc of huge gnarled jungle trees surrounding the edge of a small clearing. The trees had thick, low branches and formed a half circle, which faced a sheer rock mountain wall. Perched on the branches were thousands of tropical birds. They saw mynas, macaws, parrots, hornbills, cockatoos, and many other brightly colored exotic birds. And the birds *were all* intently looking down into the middle of the clearing at a lone toucan. The toucan was pacing back and forth on a log, looking up at the crowd, and *orating*!

"As I have said, ladies and gentleman, this summit is of historical proportions! The time to act is now, I say. And act we will!"

The crowd reacted boisterously. Half whistled shrilly while the other half repeated, "Act we will, Act we will," in unison.

The toucan went on. "This will be our moment on the world's stage! We *will* be heard!"

The crowd whistled again, with at least half of them repeating, "We will be heard. We will be heard."

The toucan continued. " The issues at hand shake us to our primeval core. These issues concern the fundamental building blocks that support life as we know it. Yes, ladies and gentlemen, this debate will decide our very survival!"

There was a cascade of whistles and caws from the crowd. "Primeval core. Primeval Core. Very Survival. Very survival."

JJ whispered, "This orator sure is charismatic. Talk about rapt attention."

The toucan paced back and forth a few extra times, paused, and then continued. "At this summit there will be three topics of the utmost concern to us all. I'm talking about air pollution, water pollution, and deforestation. I have carefully constructed our stance on each issue. Now listen closely, because what I am about to say will be our mantra, and none of us can forget it. Number one: Clean air is only fair, dirty air, say a prayer."

The crowd began a cascading whistle and chimed in unison, "Clean air is only fair, dirty air, say a prayer."

"Number two," continued the toucan, "Acid rain is a pain, acid rain is insane."

The crowd chimed even louder "Acid rain is a pain, acid rain is insane."

"Which brings us to number three: No trees, help us please. Trees, trees, we need these!"

Now the crowd was deafening. "Trees, Trees, we need these! Trees, trees we need these!" They chanted it over and over again. "Trees, trees. We need these! Trees, trees. We need these!"

The chant built into one big cacophonic, yet singular roar. The booming sound started biting into the eardrums of JJ and his friends. And then as the noise began subsiding, the birds started flying down and swarming the toucan, one by one shaking his hand and then flying off in their own directions.

"That was a great speech!" Frank said excitedly, obviously quite inspired. "I'd like to go meet that toucan myself."

"Yeah, he really had that crowd behind him 100%. But it was kind of odd, though," noted JJ. "It didn't really seem like the birds were taking time to digest what the toucan was saying. They seemed to be just mindlessly repeating everything they heard, without actually *listening*. It was almost like they were just mimicking him."

Izzy agreed. "Kind of like those people that listen to daily am talk radio back home."

"Exactly," continued JJ. "But still, maybe that toucan could give some pointers to the critters. They need somebody with that kind of charisma and focus to become more unified. Otherwise they're going to get slaughtered at the EcoSummit. You saw how fervent those people in the village were last night. They only care about the issues that affect *themselves* directly, and don't care at all about the issues that only affect their distant neighbors. It's the same with these birds. They probably won't care about mining and drilling either."

They watched for a few minutes as the crowd thinned out, and then walked into the clearing, which in itself cleared out most of the rest of the birds. They went up to the toucan and introduced themselves.

"It's a pleasure to meet you. I am Yucan the Toucan," the orator replied.

As he was shaking Yucan's hand, JJ asked, "How long have you been the leader of the birds? Do you go by, mayor, governor, or what other title should we call you?"

"I'm not the leader. I'm just a freelance motivational speaker. I called that meeting because if I hadn't, no one else would have."

"Actually, I think that *does* make you a leader," Izzy observed.

"Well since you freelance, would you be interested in meeting with some friends of ours, the Critters, and give them some advice on how to prepare for the EcoSummit?" asked JJ.

"Perhaps. I would need to learn more about these critters and figure out their angle in order to determine if I can be of any help. Where are you heading now? Perhaps I could walk with you and talk about it."

"We're just exploring right now, and we'd love for you to come along. We were going to walk further into the jungle to see what's here. Ultimately we need to head back to our campground, though. But we're on vacation for a week, so who knows, maybe we'll stick around for the EcoSummit."

Frank, who was so inspired by the speech that he had forgotten all about Myrtle Beach, frowned and said to JJ, "I don't know about that. I like the idea of last night being our last night here, wherever here is. I'd like to get back to our vacation. Don't forget the game will be on tv this weekend."

"I know," said JJ. "We're just going to explore the jungle a little and talk to Yucan the Toucan while we walk. You have to admit, you've never seen anything like this, Frank."

So JJ, Frank, Izzy, Yucca, Statistic, and Yucan the Toucan began walking and talking deep into the jungle. Yucan spent a while explaining the bird's eye view of the upcoming Ecosummit and how it affected his environment. And JJ gave Yucan the Toucan a detailed accounting of what was going on in Critterland. Then they walked quietly for a few minutes, just admiring the grand beauty of the jungle. Eventually, Yucca broke the silence.

"JJ, I've been thinking about something you said yesterday, that drug possession is a crime in your world. I'm troubled by what you meant, and don't think I understand correctly. Why do people get put in jail just for possessing something? Is it because they intend to harm other people with the drugs? Is this a preventive measure? And aren't drugs supposed to be good for you?"

"Those are tricky questions," replied JJ. "Where I live, some drugs are illegal to own because they are bad for your health if you use them. Some people call these street drugs and people take them recreationally. Some of these are definitely really bad for people's health, and can even kill them. Others probably aren't really bad at all if used in moderation, but they carry a bad social stigma, so the government selectively outlawed some of them. Medical drugs help sick people, but it's illegal for people to use them without a prescription. These drugs need to be taken in proper doses and can be harmful if not used properly. Large pharmaceutical companies design and manufacture these drugs. The government approves of their use to help sick people, and even awards the drug companies large financial incentives to develop and manufacture them. Many of these drugs are proprietary and are highly profitable for the manufacturers. But again, people need legal permission from a doctor to take them. If they take them illegally, then it's a crime punishable by going to jail."

"To answer your other questions, drug use can directly hurt the user. Or help. That distinction is apparently up to our government to decide. Doctors write the prescriptions, but the government sanctions the doctors. Apparently the government feels it's protecting the greater good by putting some of it's citizens in jail, presumably so they don't hurt themselves, while allowing others to use those same drugs because a doctor is paid to sanction the use. Each of us has a guaranteed right to pursue happiness in our society, but apparently we don't have a right to pursue unhappiness. More specifically, we don't have the right to pursue happiness if the government feels we might hurt ourselves in the process."

They walked for at least another half hour and didn't find anything of note, just more breathtakingly beautiful jungle. Perhaps the talking may have distracted them because they were busy just soaking it all in, and weren't heading in any predetermined direction. Then all of a sudden they stopped in their tracks and looked at each other, stunned. Right there in the middle of the jungle, up ahead, was a large, shockingly pink building. It had a big, bright neon sign hanging in front. Speaking for them all, Izzy said, "What in the world is *that* and what is it doing in the middle of the jungle?'

JJ answered in a measured, mystified tone, "It looks like a cantina to me."

"This is odd. I've never seen that here before," commented Yucan the Toucan. "I wonder when they built it?"

As they got closer they realized it *was* a cantina and the sign read "The Whole Tamale!" They looked at each other with varying degrees of puzzlement and excitement. They walked up to the front door, and went in. The cantina had a large wait staff, and they were all standing in the back. But JJ and his five friends were the only customers. The hostess stepped forward to greet them.

"Could we have a table for six please, preferably a window booth overlooking the jungle?" asked JJ.

"Of course, but you have your choice of waiters. We have the most qualified staff in this jungle. We have Wilma, who has 10 years waiting experience and a bachelor's degree in education. We have Walter, who has 12 years experience and a master's degree in ancient history. We have Winona, who has 13 years experience and a master's degree in psychology. And we have Percy, our headwaiter, who has twenty years experience and a doctorate in philosophy. Who would you prefer?"

Frank emphatically replied, "More importantly, are the cooks well qualified too?"

"Not really," replied the Hostess. "They're just a bunch of ex-journalists looking for a paycheck."

"Since you're not busy, we'd like the head waiter, please," JJ requested.

So the hostess sat them at a long table right in the front window. Chips and salsa and beverages were served. The waiter approached the guests and asked, "What may I do for you gentlemen?"

Yucca impulsively blurted out, "Has the Economist been here?"

"Not to my knowledge. Why? Who is the Economist? I took several classes in economics myself."

"He's just someone we know who may have mentioned this place," JJ said. "It's just a coincidence, I'm sure."

"In what context did he mention it?" the waiter wondered. "We don't get many word-of-mouth customers here, just walk-ins."

"I'm not really sure," Statistic responded. "He never really expounded much. He would always just say one sentence at a time. Each sentence didn't really mean much to me. I'm sure it meant something important, though. He has a doctorate, like yourself."

The waiter, on the other hand, *did* know how to expound, "It's really more about adding up everything a person has ever said, and taking it as one big answer. Just because someone says one thing that doesn't make much sense taken by its self, doesn't mean it's nonsensical. When you look at everything else they have said, and factor in their latest statement, then you can figure out where they actually stand on the issues. I find that most people say many things earlier in the day, and earlier in previous months, and even in their lives, that don't in themselves add up. But if you look at their whole body of work, it usually does evolve into a complete picture. But these opinions don't evolve *much* over a lifetime, though, no matter how much more eloquent that person may become with age."

"But what if someone has 27 lifetime achievement awards, would they evolve over their lifetimes?" asked Yucca.

Izzy peered at Yucca, quizzically. "What are you talking about, Yucca? Did you have a bad dream about a three-headed cat or something?"

"Izzy, we'll explain later," whispered JJ.

The waiter continued, "And something else to consider: You need to look hard at people's actual actions, not just their words. Sometimes a person will express themselves with words very eloquently, with an argument that makes total sense to everyone listening. But then that same person will do things that are completely inconsistent with what they have said."

The waiter paused for a moment, deep in thought, then proceeded, "But one thing to remember: If that person, or anyone else, for that matter, says something or believes in a concept that *you* disagree with, you need to be very careful how you respond to him. If he believes in a cause very deeply, it could prove to be quite difficult, if not impossible, to convince him to consider the other side of the issue. This is especially true if that person has developed these opinions over his whole life, and while in his own indigenous environment. Your attempts to share your alternate version of the truth will probably anger the believer, and could even be construed as an all-out assault on his way of life. That person may be incapable of examining rival philosophies, no matter how much better *you* think your position is on the matter. Sometimes it's best to say nothing and go on about your own business. But if you *do* try to sway someone's opinion, it won't be as easy as just outlining your position, no matter how sensible it is. You'll need to chip away slowly at that person's core set of beliefs if you want to truly change them. And it will probably take the use of both logical and metaphorical examples to do so."

As the waiter paused, lost in thought again, Frank was thinking, "What is this guy talking about? How can we sway him to take our food order?" Yucca and Yucan the Toucan were glued to every word the waiter was saying, and the other three were humored enough by their drinks and chips and salsa, that they were at least paying *some* attention.

The waiter dramatically raised his finger in the air and went on, "Pay attention to this very closely, my friends, because most people never achieve this understanding: You must make a distinction between true believers of an institution, and the institution itself. *You must never* attack a true believer. A person who has faith in just about anything must be personally respected, plus you won't get anywhere tearing that person down or arguing with him anyway. What you must attack is the institution itself and it's messengers, not it's devoted followers. Institutions with bad ideas and the individuals who deliver those messages are worthy of contempt. But those individuals who have been conditioned to believe in the bad ideas are not." The waiter paused and looked over his audience, and then said, "Do any of you have any questions?"

Izzy raised his hand and asked, with a sly grin, "Do you mean, for example, that if we think members of certain religious organizations are nuts, we shouldn't argue with them individually. Rather, we should respect their personal beliefs, and just ridicule their entire faiths publicly?"

The waiter looked shocked, and emphatically said, "No! Don't ever touch on the subject of religion with anyone. Ever!" He looked nervously around the restaurant, and then added in a hushed tone, "Actually that is what I meant, but religion is the exception to the rule. Every *other* institution is fair game for the critic's tongue. Don't ever attack or even mention the word religion in a negative vein. It's a bad idea."

Yucca was next to question the waiter, "I think I understand. Do you mean for example, that in JJ's world, an individual who is addicted to an illegal drug, like JJ was telling me about earlier, shouldn't be persecuted and thrown in jail, especially if it's not hurting them? But rather the drug seller that provided the drug illegally and the government, judges, and police who outlaw selected drugs to begin with, and who enact the bad, stringent laws, and enforce them, should be questioned and held accountable?"

The waiter mused for a second, then replied, "That's not exactly what I meant, but yes, if that is what you or JJ believe, it does apply, I suppose."

JJ was quick to clarify Yucca's question, "I wouldn't actually attack our police individually anyway. Most of them are good, well-intentioned people. I just question the sheer size of our entire law enforcement institution itself. I think the government has created too many unnecessary crimes, and too many harsh punishments to go with them. The *government* is the institution that I hold in contempt."

The waiter replied, "*That* is the point I was making, although I wasn't considering or suggesting such grandiose subjects to assault."

Next Frank weighed in, "I think I get it now too. Do you mean, for example, that if we have been waiting for way too long to order Mexican food, that we shouldn't personally attack the individual waiter or the cook? Do you suggest that we should instead hold the entire Mexican food industry at fault for the delay? Because if that's what you're saying, I'm not buying the malarkey you're serving up."

The waiter nodded his head 'yes', and then shook his head 'no', looking very worried and perplexed. He quickly pulled out his pen and pad, but before he could start taking orders, Yucca blurted out to him again, "What you've been telling us is all very interesting, but you still haven't answered my question about the Economist. Why, exactly, would the Economist be interested in tamales? What can you tell us about the economy that is applicable here?"

"Yeah, come to think of it, I've never really understood the concept of deflation," added Frank.

The waiter stashed his pen and pad back in his apron, and went on. "Well first of all, most people know all about *inflation*. It's the rise of the cost of goods and services over a period of time. Inflation is bad because it reduces the purchasing power of everyone. Each dollar becomes worth less and less and purchases fewer goods as each day passes. The most likely causes of inflation are supply chain and demand fluctuations, and the over-printing of money by the government. In extreme cases, inflation can begin spiraling out of control, creating hyperinflation. This would result in a total collapse of the monetary system, and the loss of everyone's savings. Deflation is the opposite, and can be even worse than inflation. With deflation the cost of goods and services declines steadily."

"That doesn't sound so bad," Frank reasoned.

"But it is. When the prices go down steadily, it makes people and businesses put off making purchases because they know the longer they wait, the more money they'll save. While purchases are being delayed, the businesses that manufacture and import goods have to slow down production, lay off workers, and possibly go out of business altogether.

This creates large-scale unemployment and shortages of goods, and could develop into a catastrophic deflationary spiral."

Statistic raised his hand and asked a specific question. "Concerning deflation, I realize you're giving us clinical definitions, but you kind of make it sound like people would be *choosing* to put off purchases just to save money. What if they *can't afford* to make purchases they need to make? And what if the reason they can't afford to do it is that they don't make as much money as they used to, and the cost of the goods they need to purchase are caught in an inflationary spiral, due to rising global demands, perhaps? What is it called if we're in a period of runaway inflation and deflation at the same time?"

"To my knowledge there are no known models to suggest that is possible. To be sure, though, I'll need to confer with the barista. He was an economics major. I'll be back in a second." The waiter went to the bar area, then came back. "I'm sorry, but the barista didn't show up for work today. But I'm fairly certain the scenario you described is impossible."

Then Yucca asked, "But if it was possible what would it be called?"

"How about "hyperdereinflation?" Statistic suggested.

"How about "The Whole Tamale!" Yucca decided.

With that, the waiter had been through enough. "Ok, your hour is up now. That will be $400 plus an automatic 18% gratuity for a party of 6 or more."

"But we haven't even ordered yet!" cried Frank.

"Look, buddy, the rates are posted on the menus. $400 an hour minimum for group sessions of 6 or more, no split checks. You've been eating complimentary chips and salsa the whole session. What else do you want? My next appointment is waiting. How would you like to pay?"

"Do you take US dollars?" asked JJ.

"We honor *any* dollars from all lands," answered the waiter. "Just as long as they're crisp and freshly printed. We don't want any old money around here. We strive to get rid of old money as soon as it has been around for too long."

So JJ and Izzy both chipped in some cash, and handed it to Frank. He grudgingly handed the waiter $500 in crisp US currency, and muttered, "I guess they don't believe in food as therapy around here."

The waiter counted out their change, minus gratuity. He handed Frank back two identical Federated Lands $10 bills, which were printed in vibrant orange and teal inks, and eight $1 notes, which were all different. There was one English pound, one old German mark, one old Italian Lira, one Canadian dollar, one Mexican Peso, and one American dollar, and those banknotes were all tattered and worn out, plus two crisp, new Federated dollars, which were printed in bright purple and yellow.

Statistic immediately pointed out, "I don't think the exchange rates on all those notes actually work out correctly."

"Who cares?" replied the waiter. "The governments are all only printing the money anyway. We're all just hypnotized by the pretty colors of the cash." He paused for a moment, and then added, "The monies' only values are the public trust in them. Personally, I don't have faith in any one of them, but that being the case, I just have to trust in all of them. I mean, a man has to believe in *something*, right?" He paused again, smiled, and said, "Thanks for your patronage. Come see us again!"

As they were leaving, Yucca said, "Well I think it was worth $500, but I sure hope the Economist isn't very hungry if he finds this place." So the group left The Whole Tamale that much wiser, yet still hungry for more.

"Yucan, what else is in the jungle?" asked JJ, as they were walking away from the cantina. "Is there anything else of interest we should go see?"

"No. There's just more jungle as far as I know. But there is a city called Seaside at the other end of the nearest cave from here. It's a port town with a beautiful harbor on the Great Sea. It's in a neighboring land known as 'Oceanea.' I've had several speaking engagements there. It is quite interesting to see, and the folks that live there are a very diverse group and are enlightening to talk with. There are some outlying islands off the harbor that are very picturesque. There are also plenty of restaurants there, and the town has a vibrant night life."

They quickly agreed to take the next cave to the city.

"Come to think of it," said Yucan the Toucan. "We could take the underground river to get there faster. There's an entrance near here, and an exit near Seaside."

"What's the underground river?" asked Izzy.

"It's basically another whole cave system that has a river flowing through it. It's underground, beneath the caves you've been walking through. It follows a different course than the foot caves, essentially a long meandering figure eight that spreads throughout the Federated Lands, with plenty of offshoots flowing out to the more remote areas. River boats taxi up and down the river to give travelers rides."

They all agreed that sounded interesting, plus easier than walking the whole way. They followed Yucan the Toucan back towards the mountain, retracing their path. They weren't talking so much now. After experiencing such unusual sights as they had seen this morning, they were all deep in their own thoughts. Yucan the Toucan was thinking, "This sure is an unusual and intriguing group I'm traveling with: Thoughtful, yet collectively scatter-brained; Genuinely caring, but do they know about what? I think I *can* help the Critters. This job falls exactly within my area of expertise." Frank was thinking, "What a rip-off The Whole Tamale was. I sure hope Yucan's right about this Seaside place. Darn, this rainforest is hot." JJ was thinking, "This is *my* idea of a vacation! I wonder what else we'll see? I hope Yucan the Toucan can help the Critters." Statistic was thinking, "I'm not buying that waiter's story about deflation. And I don't know why JJ is so gung-ho about looking at the bright side, but I do know one thing: I *am* starting to see a few things in a whole new light." There's no telling what Izzy was thinking. He had always been really hard to read. And Yucca was thinking about what JJ had told him earlier about drugs, jail, and the pursuit of unhappiness.

After pondering over it a little longer, Yucca said, "JJ, your government makes a lot of personal decisions for you that I get to make myself. I wouldn't feel comfortable with that, personally. I'm beginning to understand your frustration with your congress you were talking about earlier. It doesn't make any sense to pay governors to make your personal decisions for you if you can't even talk to them at all. It seems like people and their families should be able to make these lifestyle decisions on their own, for free. I'm surprised that even the wealthy, who you said *do* get to talk to your congress, would put up with getting sent to jail if they use a drug the way they see fit."

"Actually," JJ continued. "The wealthy people in our world don't typically go to jail for drug possession and other nonviolent crimes. Only the poor do. The wealthy can afford good lawyers. But it's a much larger issue than that. Our correctional system, the prison industrial complex, is one massive, profitable industry, involving billions of dollars. Millions of our citizens are locked up in our prisons, and over ninety percent of them committed nonviolent crimes. And close to a million people, almost half as many as those that are behind bars, have jobs as lawyers, policemen, judges, jail keepers, policy makers, bail bondsman, and other associated professions. The construction companies that build the prisons and police stations make money, and so do those facilities' service contractors. The states themselves contract out the construction and operation of the prisons, and of the prison labor, to private companies owned by wealthy, connected cronies that in turn kick some of the profits back to the entities, states and politicians that awarded them their contracts. All of these workers involved, except the two million prisoners who are effectively forced into slavery, make their profits and livings off of the system. And the government decides who makes the profits and who gets shackled in chains. And guess what group gives the money to the judges and the members of government that help get them voted into office to begin with? The wealthy."

JJ seemed to be done talking, but then remembered one more point. "And here's the kicker: Our government pays the private prison owners $60 a day for each prisoner, but the prisons only pay the inmates 25 cents an hour to work, eight hours a day. Then the prisons double-dip on their profits by charging market rates for the services of the prison labor, and for the products the prison labor is manufacturing. The prisons don't pay medical insurance, and the prisoners don't get vacation time. If they refuse to work they get thrown in isolation. Our government ceremoniously pays lip service to fixing the high unemployment rates we have, but at the same time has created and funded this entire slave labor manufacturing workforce. Consequently, over 90% of the manufacturing jobs in many leading industries are now filled with prison labor. And up to two million law-abiding citizens that would otherwise be employed, earning real salaries that included benefits, no longer have these jobs. Wall Street is making money hand over fist on this. And guess who has no say in any of it, since they're not even allowed to vote? The felons, that's who. Even the ones who have paid their debts to society have no vote. Some say this is the government's underhanded way of taking the vote away from a segment of our society."

"It sounds like your society should do a better job of paying its debts to the felons," observed Yucca. He thought about it for a minute, but was still puzzled. "Now I'm back to thinking you need a system fixer or new system maker. The more I hear about your systems, the more confused I become. Why is everything so complicated? Do your systems really need to be so complex and convoluted?"

No one really had an answer for Yucca's rhetorical questions. It was beginning to appear that Yucca was going to win "Do Ask, Do Tell" in a runaway victory, but he wasn't feeling very settled about it.

Then Frank pleaded, "Yucca, can you stop asking JJ questions for a while? Listening to his politics is starting to give me indigestion, and I haven't even eaten anything except chips and salsa."

"But you did eat a *lot* of hot salsa, Frank," JJ pointed out. "Maybe it's the jalapeños making you sick to your stomach, even though it *should* be the politics. But I'll take it down a notch, I guess. After all, we're on vacation. I won't bring up politics again the rest of the trip."

Frank and Izzy both rolled their eyes at JJ's promise. Frank nudged Izzy and whispered, "I'll bet he gets through the rest of the day, and that's about it."

"I doubt he even gets that far," replied Izzy. "Don't forget he has Yucca egging him on."

"I heard you two," JJ said. "I said I *promised*. But Izzy, I'll be counting on you to pick up some of the slack. Statistic, you could help me out here too, if you wanted. But who knows, I probably won't need any help anyway. Bad politics have a way of exposing themselves most of the time."

They walked on in silence for a few minutes. They were just arriving at the base of the mountain when Yucan the Toucan announced, "We're here!"

This cave entrance was different than the rest of the openings they had passed through. There was a split log fence encircling a round hole in the ground, about six feet wide. A crudely painted sign read "River Cave." A ladder stuck out of the dark hole and went straight down.

Yucan the Toucan went down the ladder first, with everyone else following him. At the bottom of the fifty-foot ladder was a large cave with a river flowing through, just as Yucan had described. The ladder landed down on top of a patch of sand and river rocks about twenty feet wide by forty feet long. The landing formed a bulkhead on the river, with a row of burning torches running the whole length. The river ran wall-to-wall in the cave, so that other than the twenty by forty foot landing, there was no place to walk. This cave was larger than the caves they had been walking through, about twenty-five feet wide not including the landing. There was a good twenty feet of head clearance also. The walls of the cave were wet and JJ and his friends could hear the constant dripping of water around them. It was much chillier than it had been out in the rainforest, and there was a damp draft in the air.

Luckily, moored to the bulkhead, was a large river raft, which also was lined with torches. Seated on the deck was the skipper, who jumped right up and welcomed his new passengers. "Come onboard, everyone. I'm Skipper Zack. Where are you heading today? Let me guess... Seaside, the vacationers' paradise!"

When Frank heard "paradise", he felt himself edging a little closer to the bright side, and answered, "Yes, Seaside." Everyone quickly climbed aboard. The raft cast off and headed down the river, the leaping flames of the torches lighting the way. As everyone's eyes became accustomed to the dark, they could see the ancient walls of the cave glistening in the torchlight. They could make out occasional batches of hieroglyphics and graffiti on the cave walls as they floated by. Some of the paintings were very crude, and some of them looked like art. The old ones were the hieroglyphics, and the recent ones were the graffiti. They knew which ones were the art when they saw it. The passengers were really enjoying the aura of it all. The sight of the flickering torchlight glowing off of the ancient cave walls was mesmerizing. It made the old drawings on the cave walls seem to jump back to life.

Everyone on board the raft was so spellbound by the surreal scenery that no one was talking. They were just taking it all in. Izzy, in particular, was entranced by the images adorning the walls of the ancient cave. The raft was drifting lazily down the river, so there was plenty of time to study each work of art. Izzy took a pen and notebook out of his backpack and sketched as many of the hieroglyphics as he had time to draw. He copied down some of the graffiti too. He noticed in particular one intricate cave drawing that appeared to be a detailed ancient map. He copied that down as quickly as he could possibly scribble, and even after the boat had drifted all the way past, was still trying to fill in the rest of the map from memory.

Skipper Zack, who was used to entertaining tourists with tales of local lore, could see how interested his passengers all were in the cave, so had been biting his tongue for a while. But he now felt a need to start earning his tip by being the entertainer, so he began to speak. "If only these walls could sing, they'd sing the songs of love and heartache. They'd sing the songs of great triumphs and of broken…"

Izzy cut him off and said, "That sounds like a great story, or maybe the words to a hit song or bad greeting card, but I'm trying to concentrate here. This ambiance doesn't need any help."

JJ glanced over at Izzy, who was frantically scribbling, and who was not typically so snippy, and walked over to the skipper. "Please forgive our friend for snapping at you. He's very preoccupied right now. Izzy's a graphic artist, and is clearly very inspired by the art in the cave. I am too, but I'm also wondering about the bottom of the river. The water is so clear that even in the torchlight I can see the bottom just below us. There are a lot of glinting minerals, mica maybe? And I can see the historical water line on the cave walls is much higher than it is today. This raft seems to be just making it by. A larger boat would bottom out, wouldn't it?"

"You've just brought up a big problem," replied Skipper Zack, who was excited that he now had an audience. "See, I used to have a larger boat, but it couldn't navigate the river any longer. The water level has receded so far in recent years, that it's scary. During prime tourist season, I used to make boatfuls of money. Now I only make rafts of money. It's a big difference. At the end of last season I had to take the old boat all the way around the river and dock it where the river flows out into the Great Sea. I bought this raft to replace it."

The skipper paused for a moment, surveyed his clientele, and realized these weren't his regular tourists. He looked back at JJ and continued his story. "The water level started going down a few months after EcoCo started their fricking and fracking in the far reaches of Critterland. No one knows they're doing it yet, because nobody lives there except a few critters. And to make matters worse, the river is starting to smell a little like diesel fuel. *You* may not detect it, but to someone like me that's lived on the river for many years, it's noticeable. I've read the propaganda, and I realize fracking is a big business that creates jobs and energy independence. But independence from *what*? Right now it's hard for me to fathom. And it's the exact opposite of profitable to *me*. Plus I'm a little nervous about drinking the water anymore."

The skipper took a pause as if he were done talking, but then added, "The ironic thing is, now that the water level is so low, EcoCo can't use the river effectively to transport the gas back from Critterland. Who knows what they're going to do with all that gas they're pulling out of the ground? I sure hope this issue is addressed at the big EcoSummit everybody's been talking about. I'm just a simple man of the river, a drifter, not a citizen of any particular land. So there won't be any delegation at the summit looking out for *my* interests."

"I'll try to work that in on the Critter's platform if I can," volunteered Yucan the Toucan. "Since the fracking is going on in their land, they should be aware of the side affects it's having elsewhere."

By that time Izzy had finished recording everything he remembered about the map and was gazing around the cave again. There hadn't been much graffiti on the cave walls in a while, but up ahead, through the flickering torchlight, he could see what appeared to be a very old stone landing on the right side of the cave. There was no daylight streaming down over top of the landing, but there was a large array of cave art painted all around it, including a few scattered works that looked quite old. Izzy asked Skipper Jack, "Why is there a landing here in the middle of the cave, with no exit? Why would someone have built it to begin with?"

"It's a mystery," answered the Skipper. "There are a handful of them scattered throughout the underground river. They are all of the same construction and are very old. They're also in between exits, so maybe they are just rest points. Sometimes I'll pass rafts moored at them."

After a few more minutes they saw sunlight beaming down through a six-foot hole in the cave ceiling. It was on the left, and it had a small dock below. This dock was only large enough to moor several rafts. A ladder stretched down from the cave exit to the dock. Painted on the wall of the cave above the dock was a ten-foot tall question mark. It was painted, somewhat crudely, in a dark blue color.

JJ looked at Skipper Zack and asked, "Where does that ladder go? Why is there a question mark?"

Yucan the Toucan volunteered, "That is a small mountainous land. I'm not sure if the area has a name, but you can also get to it through a pass on the other side of the jungle mountain where you met me. An eccentric mystic who goes by the title 'The Sayer ?' lives there. He fashions himself to be a sort of guru or sage. People sojourn to his compound from afar to listen to his opinions and to meditate with him. I've never visited the guru myself."

"I've dropped off and picked up passengers here before," added Skipper Zack. "About half of them said they were greatly enlightened during their stay, and the rest said The Sayer was just a quack. My suspicion is the place is just one big tourist trap."

They continued to drift down the river for another fifteen minutes, and they could tell they were getting close to their destination because they could now see a hint of natural light peeking through the cave. The glistening cave walls began displaying another spike of wall art, and soon they were easing in to the dock at the Seaside exit. Izzy put his notebook away, and they all got ready to disembark. The cave was a little wider at this point, and the dock had room for at least fifteen boats to moor. This was clearly a popular destination, but it wasn't currently very busy at all. Maybe on the weekends things pick up a lot, or it may have been the offseason. There was a souvenir and refreshment stand at the end of the dock. Frank started to perk up in particular, but they were all anxious with anticipation to see Seaside, or any civilization for that matter. They all thanked Skipper Zach for the ride, and everyone except Izzy got off the raft and headed down the pier towards the daylight. Izzy stayed behind for a couple extra minutes to ask the skipper some questions about the history of the underground river and the cave art. And he also wanted to learn the protocol for scheduling the raft, just in case they found the time to take the underground river taxi again.

This station had a small, open cage elevator that lifted everyone up to the surface. They had to go up two at a time, except for Yucca, who needed his own turn. When they arrived at the surface, everyone's eyes needed to adjust to the daylight again. Izzy couldn't resist baiting Frank *and* JJ by asking Frank, "Here you go again. Looking right into the bright side. Are you going to be grumpy again the rest of the day? Or are you going to snap out of the doldrums of your post recessionary hangovers?"

"No, I'm good," replied Frank.

"I'm over it too," said JJ, who then sarcastically added, "Thanks for asking." Then in a more earnest tone, JJ said, "I'd like to see that map you copied. What do you think it is?"

"I need to study it some more. I think it may be an ancient map of the Federated Lands, but long before they were federated. I think I recognized where we've been so far, too. There were some really good drawings down there, too. Even some of the modern graffiti had an unusual perspective and edge that I haven't seen before. I'd like to spend more time in that cave if we have time."

Yucca was the last one to reach the ground in the elevator, and everyone gathered together in great anticipation of exploring the new destination. As they adjusted to the bright sunlight and warmer temperature, they realized they could already make out Seaside's outline off in the near distance. The group wasted no time setting off for town, with Yucan the Toucan leading the way. After a short walk, they came to the city limit sign. It read 'City of Seaside, Land of Oceania.'

Last Night

10

The Turning Point

JJ and his friends entered Seaside through a residential district. The neighborhood was made up of several square blocks of two and three story dwellings. The homes were brightly painted in pastel colors and were of an old colonial architecture. When the group came upon the heart of the city, Yucan the Toucan explained that they were in the municipal area. The port was a few blocks straight ahead. To the east was the commercial district with the bistros, shops, inns, and saloons. It was comprised of many square blocks of three story buildings with residences above. The buildings were of an ornate old architecture and had decorative wrought iron balconies on the upper floors overlooking the streets. The west side of town was residential and had beautiful parks and schools.

The streets were all clean and well maintained. The main avenues all headed directly into the municipal zone in the center of town and terminated into a large roundabout. The group arrived at the Town Hall, which was situated in the center of the grand circle. A large lawn surrounded the building, and the grounds were clearly a gathering place for the community, the equivalent of a town park. People were spread out on the grass, picnicking and reading books. There were plenty of stately shade trees to sit under, and kids were running around playing. It was obviously a very peaceful and happy town. On a placard outside of the Town Hall, there was a sign announcing Seaside's meeting to discuss the EcoSummit: This afternoon Six o'clock. Special Meeting of the Seaside District Town Council to discuss the EcoSummit. The Mayor requests the presence of all concerned citizens.

JJ proposed that they go to see the waterfront first, then eat in the bistro district, and later go to the Town Council meeting. They all agreed, except Frank kind of preferred to head straight to the bistro district.

From the Town Hall it was a short walk to the harbor, and the view was indeed spectacular and panoramic. Scores of boats lined the docks, and there were many busy people bustling back and forth along the wharf. There were blocks and blocks of waterfront shops and seafood markets stretching around the waterfront. The whole group of friends was intrigued by the sight of three tropical islands on the outlying edge of the harbor. All three islands were overflowing with palm trees and thick vegetation and looked very inviting. They began to stroll down the boardwalk and shortly came upon a tourist information stand, which was staffed by a concierge.

JJ asked the concierge, "We're only visiting for the day. Can you recommend the key points of interest?"

"Preferably with restaurants nearby," added Frank.

"Most tourists concentrate on the bistro and shopping district," answered the concierge. "There are plenty of good local eateries and souvenir shops there. But you guys look more adventurous, so I would recommend taking Gruzzly's Ferry to Taboo Island. It's a sparsely inhabited tropical paradise right across the harbor." The concierge pointed out to the water while she was explaining. "It's the middle island right over there. The island has a tiki hut called the 'Sand-Witch Doctor' that serves food and spirits. It's popular with the more daring tourists. While you're dining the Witch Doctor tells spooky tales of local lore. Captain Gruzzly is a local eccentric with some odd stories of his own."

That sounded perfect, so they walked over to Gruzzly's Ferry. Captain Gruzzly was indeed eccentric, and he looked just like a veteran captain should look. He welcomed the group on board, and then shoved off for Taboo Island. The scenery was spectacular. The water was a clear blue-green, and from a distance their destination was a picture straight from a tropical travel brochure, a perfect palm-lined paradise. They were most of the way across the harbor when the captain began to speak. "You're the only six visitors to Taboo Island today. You can't stay long, either. I need to knock off early today. I guess I should have told you guys that already, but it's too late to turn back now. We're almost there. You'll be the Witch Doctor's only guests of the day, so he'll be trying his best to scare you."

"What kind of stories does he tell?" asked Yucca curiously.

"Local tales of lore, mostly, but who knows? He has plenty of knowledge. I'm one of the only other people around that knows some of his tales are true."

The ferry docked and everyone thanked Captain Gruzzly for the ride. The group disembarked, and followed the main path into the interior of the island. The island was covered in very thick vegetation, with many palm trees. It was completely uninhabited, except for the Witch Doctor, so it was a great tropical nature walk. They came to a fork in the trail that had crude signs with arrows pointing each way. One pointed to the left and read "Sand-Witch Doctor's Hut." The other sign pointed to the right and had "Cave" written on it. They headed towards the tiki hut, of course. They followed the path, which from that point forward was lined with burning tiki torches, and arrived within a minute or two. It was a large hut with a thatched roof, but was kind of run-down. Just as the captain had predicted, they were the only visitors there. Judging from the lack of customers and the hut's state of disrepair, it seemed like it must have been a more popular destination years ago. But maybe it was just the off-season.

The cook came out of the kitchen door to the rear of the hut, carrying menus. "Hello guys, welcome to Taboo Island, home of the Sand-Witch Doctor. I'll take your drink orders while you look at the menus. It will take me a few minutes. I'm working both the kitchen and the bar today. The barista quit the other day. Something about the job conflicting with his doctorate work."

"It must be hard on you doing both jobs at the same time," offered Yucca. "My friend here, Statistic, has two jobs, but he gets to do them at different times."

"Actually, working the bar too gives me more to write about. I need all the material I can get. Yesterday the only party was a group of bureaucrats and scientists. What a boring party! But it's hard to judge people anymore. I've noticed most of the tourists are getting more and more loose lately, letting their guards down more easily than the tourists of 20 years ago. But some are getting much more close-lipped than ever before. Those tourists can't have any fun on their vacation at all. It seems like all they do is worry about the work they left at home. (Frank glanced knowingly at JJ for a moment, shaking his head.) I can't believe some of them, like the scientists yesterday, are even on a vacation at all. But those guys yesterday did leave a sizable tip in bright, crisp $10 bills. I'll be back in a minute to take your orders."

The cook came back with the drinks and took their orders. Of course, the hut was known for its special, the sandwitch with voodoo fries, so that was what everyone except Yucca ordered. As the cook walked back to the kitchen, the Sand-Witch Doctor appeared from behind the tropical brush. His outfit was a sight to behold, complete with a vest made of bones, a thatched loincloth, and a crazy hat with feathers and beads. His eyes and mouth were accented with red and black paint. He danced towards the table, shimmying and shaking and chanting strange words. When he got up to the table he took one look at JJ, Frank, Izzy, Statistic, Yucca, and Yucan the Toucan and quit the act.

He said matter-of-factly, "I can see you're not normal tourists, and are probably astute tippers, so I won't waste your time with the regular act. I'm the Sand-Witch Doctor, but you can call me by my real name, Wilbur, if you'd like. What is it that you *really* want to hear about?"

JJ spoke up. "We saw the sign pointing to the cave on the way in. Is that part of the same cave system that we've been traveling through on our visit to the Federated Lands? Or is it just another tourist trap?"

"Yes, they're all connected, but yes it could be a tourist trap. Some tourists fall into the trap of thinking they're welcome everywhere they go, and then they go *too far* for their own good. So be careful in your travels."

"Is it possible to get a map of the entire cave system, then? We're thinking about traveling to the Ecosummit as outside observers."

"I doubt the governor even knows where all the caves lead. There are stories of new lands being discovered at the edges of the system just in recent days. But one thing *is* known, and hear me carefully."

The tone of the Witch Doctor's voice began to grow more hushed, but more sure just the same. And everybody felt a new sense of eeriness in the air they hadn't noticed before. The Witch Doctor continued, "All the caves end up in one central location. There, in the center, is one towering state built entirely of stone. It is the central state, the one that the most aspiring individuals of every society wish to see with their own eyes. The entire state is nothing but one massive building of stone!"

Izzy pulled out his notebook and opened it to his map. He began studying it while The Witch Doctor spoke. Everyone's attention was fixed on Wilbur, although they were taking his words with varying degrees of seriousness.

The Witch Doctor went on. "Many people live there, too. But they have no industry of their own, and no apparent real means of support, by any decent definition. They will not be affected by the results of the EcoSummit, because they have no ecological ramifications there whatsoever. They can't grow crops there. They can't drill for oil or mine there. They can't deforest it any more because its 100% stone. They don't need to worry about air pollution because the entire state is indoors. But strangely enough, *this* is where all the laws are made that govern the Federated lands, including the ecological statutes."

JJ was mystified. "But how can they have such a large, thriving metropolis, all in one big building with no means of production?"

"It's magic! Some say it's voodoo magic. They need to import every building block of life into the state, just like they imported all the stone building blocks that built the place to begin with! Everything. But some people believe it's evil magic. *Even though it's built entirely of stone, they say it has an organic constitution at its very core!* As the legend goes, this organic constitution was cemented into the foundation of the building by its original architects. The larger and larger the building grows over the years, the more and more imprisoned the spirit of the organic constitution becomes! It is now buried under so many layers of cold hard stone, that it is no longer close to nature or humanity, the very descendants of the building's architects."

The Witch Doctor looked around as if to make sure no one else was nearby listening in, then continued. "Now what I am about to tell you can only be spoken in private, and never repeated to strangers. Some people believe that one day a lone man or woman will start a movement to free this spirit from its imprisonment. The movement would be secret and localized at first, but would spread slowly to all corners of the Federated Lands. More and more citizens would come to believe they could escape the bondage in which their families have become ensnared through so many years of government-imposed hardships. And specifically, they will believe that the way to do it will be to raze the building down to its' very foundation, releasing the spirit of the organic constitution from its imprisonment. These people will believe that if the spirit is freed, everyone would be unchained of the constraints that have been placed on their families for so long."

The Witch Doctor gazed around the table to make sure he still had everyone's attention, and then continued. "This movement would need to spread to almost unimaginable levels of support to accomplish that mission. And the government knows this. See, being in the government is a very profitable venture. The members of government control all the money and all the laws affecting money. They share their laws with the wealthy, and the wealthy share their profits with the governors. The government knows there are a lot more citizens than there are governors and administrators, so the last thing it wants is a movement of *any* kind."

Yucca instantly grew curious to hear more about movements. But everyone was listening with a growing degree of attention now, and The Witch Doctor was getting more excited and spooky as he told his story.

"The wealthy that control the governors know this as well. That is why every once in a while the government starts new initiatives to keep some communities happy in the short term. This is only to deter any unrest from the masses. Each of these programs is passed with much debate. At first each seems controversial, but the controversy always somehow magically morphs into hyperbole and accolades. The government will then act slightly and slowly on the results of each pseudo-debate. They will give money to various groups of people through these grandiose programs in order to keep those people suppressed. These beneficiaries of the government's money *think* they are being helped, and think the government is concerned about their welfare. But the opposite is true. The recipients are in actuality being *declawed* by their own government. They lose the drive and ability to learn to do things for themselves, outside the realm of the government. They forget how to survive on their own in the wild, and begin depending on the government for all guidance. And even worse, they lose the innate ability to teach their children and their grandchildren how to learn, work, and fight for themselves. This is all in the government's interest, of course."

The Witch Doctor was becoming even more animated and excited as he went on. "Another trick the government uses to keep people suppressed is this: It invites select members from all the districts to join in the Federated Legislature. The "cream of the crop" of citizens from every district in the Federated Lands strives to be invited to fill these honorary, yet lucrative posts. Then once they arrive, they get brainwashed by the same evil magic that has imprisoned the spirit of the organic constitution. And when each of these individuals returns to their homelands, they are not the same people they once were. They are only a shell of their former selves. And the longer they're in the District, the more likely it is they are permanently damaged. *And* the more contagious they become, spreading their brainwashed lies to their neighbors." The Witch Doctor paused and eerily peered over the table at each of the diners for dramatic effect, and to catch his breath.

"Does this state have a name?" JJ asked.

"It has several aliases, but most people use the official name when they're in polite company. Its title is 'The District of Concrete,' aka 'DC.' The Witch Doctor then looked back towards the kitchen and could see that the cook was just putting the finished sandwiches on the plates, but he had one last thing to say. He crouched down and looked over his audience again, and then hushed into an even lower, exponentially more spooky tone of voice, and uttered, "Here's the *really* scary thing. The people of the Federated Lands *created* this government to *protect and serve.* But once DC was born, it grew a mind of its own. It started to feed off of its own creators so it could spawn and multiply. And now it's just a gigantic unstoppable malignant growth, leeching off of its creators' children. And the people no longer have any power to escape its deadly, grisly grasp."

At that point the cook showed up with the sandwiches and chips. JJ announced, "Well that settles the question of 'which came first, the chicken or the egg?' It was the chicken, but she laid a rotten egg."

The Witch Doctor had finished his story, so he thanked his guests for their patronage, and then danced back into the brush. Their meals tasted terrible, but there was plenty of ketchup and hot sauce on the table with which to doctor their sandwiches, so they made the best of it. When they were done eating, they thanked the cook and the Witch Doctor, who had walked back from the brush to the hostess stand. Frank requested their check. He also asked the Witch Doctor, "Wilbur, you do take US dollars, don't you?"

"We'll take any brands of dollars you have," replied the Witch Doctor. "Who cares where they're from? As long as I can pass them off on someone else, I don't care who's printing them. Try to pay with the prettiest colored notes you have though, please. It doesn't take a voodoo curse to entrance most people with the prettiest colors of money."

Frank paid the tab, plus generous gratuities as usual, in US dollars, which were the only larger bills any of them had. The cook gave him back his $15 change in three $5 dollar bills. Frank looked at the notes, and two of them were Federated Lands issues, and the other one was a pastel hued piece of play money from a board game. Frank winced at the sight of the play money, but didn't want to appear rude, so he tucked it in his wallet and silently thought, "I'll just pass it on to the next guy, I guess. That looks like the way it works around here."

They all thanked the Witch Doctor again for his hospitality and stories, and headed back towards Seaside. When they reached the dock, there was a sign nailed to a pylon from Captain Gruzzly, explaining that he was done for the day, so they'd better take the cave back to Seaside. Which is exactly what they did.

They had just enough time to get to the town hall by six o'clock and claim their seats near the back of the packed auditorium. There were a lot more people at this meeting than at the first caucus JJ and Izzy had attended. This was a very diverse group of citizens in attendance. The Mayor came to the podium and began the meeting.

"The Town Council has called this meeting to get feedback from the citizens of Seaside concerning the upcoming EcoSummit. The council will adopt a platform of our town's stances on each of the Eco-Summit issues, and we would like to get all of the opinions and input each of you wish to share. Each of the summit's topics is outlined in your leaflets. If you don't have a leaflet, they are on the table next to the entrance. Does anyone here have any points of particular interest they'd like to make on any of the issues?"

No one volunteered any opinions, so the mayor continued.

"Well I think we can all agree that we have a beautiful town that is blessed with wonderful picturesque views of the harbor and of the sea. Our port has always been our livelihood and is the anchor industry that our city is built around. But tourism is now our number one revenue stream. The ecology laws that will be debated at the summit are very important to Seaside. The tourists come here because of the natural beauty of our scenery and the quirky lore of our town's seafaring history. The quality of the water is also vital to our backbone, seafaring itself."

"It is of the utmost importance to all of us that we preserve the unpolluted air and water that we have now. Some of the issues on the EcoSummit agenda don't directly apply to us. But they are important to other lands in the same way that clean air and water are important to us. I believe we should support our neighboring cultures' positions on issues such as deforestation and drilling. The ecology laws should make the lives of all the creatures in these Federated Lands better, not just ours'. I believe it is our ethical responsibility to throw our support behind legislation that protects these neighboring habitats, remembering that some of our neighbors are less fortunate than us. Don't forget many of these neighbors are also the visiting tourists we rely upon for our own livelihoods."

The Mayor took an extra second to look over his audience before adding, "Furthermore, we haven't had a problem yet with invasions of foreign species in our port, but I believe we need to vote for strong laws regarding this issue. The Federated Lands has become much more industrious of late. Foreign ships could start using our port soon, and bring with them invasive species that could harm our native species."

There was a strong voice of support from the crowd on everything the mayor had just said, so he pressed on. "Since we're all in agreement, I'll form a committee tomorrow and draft our positions on all the EcoSummit issues. We'll post a completed copy of our platform at the town hall tomorrow afternoon for all to read and comment on. Is there anything else anyone would like to discuss while so many of us are gathered here together?"

Mr. Chester, the town banker, stood up and spoke, "The owners of several of the islands are in default on their mortgages. The bank has received a conditional offer to buy this real estate. The offer is contingent on gaining new zoning status and use permits. This will require a referendum vote from the citizens of Seaside, and I'd like to explain how beneficial these new improvements will be to the lives of all of us."

"Mr. Chester," the mayor sternly rebuked, "That business should be saved for Monday's Zoning Board hearing. We won't discuss those issues today."

And then suddenly a clanging of loud noises came from the back of the room. The auditorium doors had burst open and there was a collective gasp in the crowd. Through the entrance came a huge antique bathtub on wheels. In the bathtub were sea creatures. There was a dolphin, a starfish, a crab, and a lobster. And who was pushing the tub into the meeting? None other than Captain Gruzzly and the Witch Doctor!

Captain Gruzzly loudly announced to the Mayor and the rest of the audience, "What kind of railroad-job of a meeting are you running here? How can you have an EcoSummit meeting without hearing the opinions of our neighbors and friends from the sea?"

The mayor was trying to hold in a laugh and scold the two eccentrics at the same time, when he choked out, "Captain Gruzzly and Witch Doctor *and* friends, you've missed the whole meeting. But don't worry. We'll be protecting the welfare of the sea creatures on our platform. You can read the whole thing tomorrow afternoon when we post it at Town Hall."

The Mayor, who was still smiling, shook his head and thought, "I haven't heard 'railroad job' in many years. I wonder where that expression comes from? It must be an old seafaring term." Then another idea came to him as he watched Captain Gruzzly and the Witch Doctor look and shrug at each other.

The Witch Doctor and Captain Gruzzly nodded their heads at the mayor and they turned the tub around and headed right back down the aisle towards the door.

"Captain!" the lobster loudly insisted, as they were leaving, "Don't let them off this easy. I want my say. I want my rightful place at the table too."

"Be careful what you wish for lobster," warned the crab. "Let's just get out of here. These humans are making me nervous."

The Mayor quickly called out to them, "Wait, before you go, let me ask you two a question. Captain Gruzzly and Witch Doctor, would you be interested in joining the Seaside delegation at the EcoSummit? We could use some local characters like you two on the panel. I know we can all count on both of you to fight for our common good, and you would help display the diversity of Seaside's citizens."

Captain Gruzzly and The Witch Doctor were a third of the way back down the aisle and had turned around to face The Mayor while he spoke. They both eagerly accepted the invitation.

The Mayor said, "Great! I'm glad to have you on board. By the way, you will both want to be *on time* for Monday's Zoning Board meeting."

As the eccentric pair wheeled the bathtub back out of the entrance, the crab and the lobster could be heard saying in unison, "Can I go too? Can I go too?"

The meeting was quickly adjourned amid a collective laugh from the humored crowd. While JJ was leaving with his friends, he said, "*That* was an interesting meeting. Let's head over to the bistro district. We can discuss everything over dinner."

Frank said, "Let's find a place to stay tonight first. I think we should check in somewhere before we eat."

Yucca was quick to say, "I liked where we camped last night."

Frank felt very strongly to the contrary. "No, we're already here. Let's look for an inn in the bistro district. After two nights of camping, I could use a good hot shower, and a good hot meal."

Everyone wholeheartedly agreed except for Yucca, but he decided he could rough it for one night and sleep at a hotel. The restaurants and shops weren't very crowded and there were a lot of options. After walking two blocks they came upon The Seaside Inn, a quaint boutique hotel with a street-front bistro. They checked into two rooms for the night. Izzy and JJ split a room, because they were early risers. Frank and Statistic bunked together, and Yucca got permission to stay in a corner of the courtyard. Yucan the Toucan said not worry about him, that he'd be fine just hanging out with Yucca. After getting settled into their rooms, they met back down in the outdoor bistro. It was dark out by then, but there were candles on the table, and dim patio lights, making for a nice comfortable ambiance.

While they were being served their drinks and dinner they began reflecting on the day's events and the agenda for the next morning. They started by discussing their next move.

"Statistic," JJ asked. "What other lands did the Economist take you to? Are there any near here we'd find interesting to visit?

"I can't think of any off hand. He didn't take me to that many different places, and I think you've seen all but two of them now. But I understand there are quite a few other lands here. One of the places I've been is 'The Outpost'. It's just inside a cave exit between the Jungle and Seaside. We would have passed it if we had taken the cave instead of the underground river to get here. I don't recommend going there for recreational purposes. It's a convenient stopping point for travelers, but that's about it. They have a small assortment of cheap restaurants and fleabag hotels. In fact, that's where I had the Chinese food. Now that I think about it though, they don't have a Mexican restaurant. I wonder why the Economist was talking about tamales?"

"By fleabag, do you mean the kind of cigarette-stinking, small hotels like we have at desolate exit ramps back home, complete with bed bugs?" Frank asked. "That doesn't sound enticing at all."

"Yes, exactly. The bedbugs at the Crossroads hotels *are* intolerable.

But they don't bite. They just ask incessant rhetorical and philosophical questions all night. It's impossible to get any sleep over the chatter." Statistic paused to take a deep breath, and then warned, "You definitely don't want to go to the other land I've visited. It's called Boomtown."

"Yucan the Toucan spoke up, "I believe there are about one hundred territories in the Federated Lands altogether, and each has its own distinctive character. And I agree with Statistic. Don't go to Boomtown, whatever you do. You're probably best off staying around Seaside. There is a lot to do around here, and the scenery is unparalleled."

Now they were all curious, so JJ asked Statistic, "What's so bad about Boomtown?"

"A few months ago I spent three days there with the Economist while he completed some studies. It's a large industrialized land that is dominated by one sprawling metropolis, Boomtown City. It calls itself 'The Safest Place to Live in the Federated Lands.' Boomtown is the Federated Lands' largest business center. It's also the only district in The Federacy where civilians are allowed to own guns. And most of them do. Personally, back at home, I'm not a gun owner, although I do believe in our second amendment rights. I'm just not comfortable around guns. But I did buy one while I was in Boomtown City, just so I could feel safe too. It didn't work, though. I was a nervous wreck the whole time I was there. There were guns going off constantly. It may have made the shooters feel safer, but not me."

Frank and JJ were looking at each other, cringing too. "That must be where we were when the police chased us away from the bears and the gators. That was frightening," said Frank.

"Yeah," agreed JJ, glancing back at Frank. "That was a chilling experience." Then he faced Statistic and said, "I'm not fond of guns either, and I don't own any myself. But I do believe in our ownership rights too. The precise wording of the second amendment has always bewildered me, and I've wondered why the framers felt a need to specifically spell out their reasoning for granting this right in the amendment itself. I don't think they did that anywhere else. The rest of the document was self-evident. The way it reads to me, it seems that it guarantees our rights to own guns so that we can form militias to fight against invasive governments. It doesn't really appear to guarantee our rights to own guns for the purpose of sport or for self-protection from other citizens or for any other use than against government invasions. If I did own guns, I wouldn't like my chances if I ever had to use it against any invasive government, that's for sure."

Statistic listened to Frank and JJ, paused for a second, as if to rid the nervous feeling from his mind, and then continued his story about Boomtown, "While I was there I helped the Economist conduct a study in behalf of the Boomtown Chamber of Commerce. They wanted to prove their safety claim to be scientifically true. I surveyed a large representative sampling of the people living in Boomtown City and asked them if they felt safe. They overwhelmingly answered yes. But *I* think the final results were skewered. I just wish we could have asked the people who *used to live* in Boomtown what they thought. I'm sure the medium exists that could have made that communication possible. The Economist didn't want to put that much time into it, though. Plus I think he recognized the negative financial impact it would have had if he found to the contrary. In the end, the Economist concluded Boomtown is, in fact, the safest place to live in The Federated Lands. He cited the survey I helped with, plus the fact that they have the highest incarceration rate too, as the over-riding reasons. By the way, Boomtown City is where EcoCo's headquarters is located."

They still needed to decide a course of action for the morning, and Statistic's insight didn't help at all. Frank wanted to get back to their planned vacation, or even better yet, get straight to Myrtle Beach. JJ wanted to stay and see more of the Federated Lands, and Izzy wanted to study some more cave drawings. Statistic really just wanted to get home to his family, but didn't feel safe traveling alone through the caves, so he was along for the ride, no matter what was decided.

They argued back and forth for several minutes, before Yucca butted in, "You humans are very good at making obvious and easy thoughts become very confusing and complicated."

Izzy was quick to disagree, "Well actually I always know exactly what I want to do and how I'm going to do it. I know exactly how everyone else should do things too, if they are smart."

"Me too," agreed Frank

"Well why are you always so lost and confused then?" Yucca wanted to know.

Trying to explain, JJ reasoned, "I don't think any of us is individually confused. It's when we try to do things together that we get lost and start arguing about the right way to proceed. It seems we each have our own good ideas, but none of us really understands what the others are thinking."

"Perhaps there's a way you could form some kind of consensus of ideas or a joint plan?" wondered Yucca. "And maybe think about other things than yourselves? I was very peaceful and happy with no worries at all until you came to my home. I've only been traveling with you a short time, and now I'm lost and confused. I'm worried about my home too, and think I should get back and check on things. Can't you just form a committee and make a decision?"

"That *never* works," assured JJ. "Committees just form consensus indecisions that don't end up with real answers, just fragmented actions. We'd be better off just playing pen, sword, dollar to make decisions. Here's what *I* think we should do: We need to take Yucan the Toucan to meet the Critters to help them with their EcoSummit strategy."

Izzy was quick to remind JJ, "I wouldn't go back there if I were you, JJ. Mr. Big might still there. He had the police looking for you. He was very upset with you and Frank. I heard all about it from the critters. Do you have any other ideas?"

"Yes," answered JJ. "I know what we should do then. Izzy, *you* should travel with Yucan the Toucan to visit the critters. Don't you think you're better at diplomacy than me, anyway? Plus, since Mr. Big hasn't met you, he's not mad at you yet."

"'Yet' is the key word here. I don't know about being more diplomatic. It's just that I'm disciplined enough to keep my thoughts to myself long enough to decide if it's a good time to express them. That's the only reason I haven't left a string of people mad at me all the way from here back to Hillsville. But I am willing to go to Critterland as long as Yucan the Toucan is up for the challenge."

"I'm looking forward to the opportunity. I'm ready to tackle this job," Yucan the Toucan stated, accepting the challenge.

"Then JJ, you could travel with me back to my home, while Izzy and Yucan are in Critterland," suggested Yucca. "I'd like to check to see if everything is all right. Maybe we've been invited to the EcoSummit. If not, I think we should elect a delegation to send to it anyway. Even if we can't vote, our voices should be heard."

Frank cried, "Perfect! Then Statistic and I can just hang out here in the city tomorrow, and see what kind of trouble we can get into."

JJ wrapped up the plans by saying, "Then we could all meet back here tomorrow night and discuss how everything went. That's when we can decide whether to stay here or head to Myrtle Beach the next morning."

Yucca teased, "See, I told you so! I would call that a committee that worked. The fragmented results appear to be the best plan of action to me."

That seemed like a good place to end the discussion, so the group broke up for the evening. Yucan the Toucan guided Frank and Statistic on a walk around the tourist district. Yucca sat in with JJ and Izzy, who stayed seated in the courtyard for a while, discussing strategies for their excursions back to Critterland and Yucca's homeland.

Last Night

11

The U-Turn

JJ and Izzy got up early the next morning. They both knew they had a long day ahead of them. Yucan the Toucan and Yucca were already up and waiting in the lobby when JJ and Izzy came down from their room. All four were eager to get going, and were anxious, if not nervous, to see how successfully they would carry out their missions. They would all travel together most of the way since Yucca's forest was further down the same cave as Critterland. Yucan the Toucan had decided the night before to check in with his friends in the Jungle on the way to Critterland. He wanted to let them know what he had been doing yesterday and last night, and that he would be going to Critterland that day. He also planned on making it back to the Jungle later that night. He would need the rest of the week to pull together all the loose ends to prepare the birds for the EcoSummit.

It would be a long trip back to Critterland. Izzy had his notebook out, and had plotted the most direct course to Critterland, with the help of his map, which he was pretty sure was accurate. He was anxious to see how closely the map depicted their actual route. The plan was to follow the main cave system all the way from Seaside to Critterland. They had originally arrived at Seaside using the underground river from the jungle, which they had reached from a small side cave from the land of the villages. The new route would be much more direct, and would take them by the Outpost.

The group had hiked about halfway towards the Jungle when they arrived at the cave exit for the Outpost. Izzy could see from his map that this wasn't a very large land. It was clearly just more of a pit stop for the weary traveler.

"Why don't we make a quick run-through to see what's here and get some breakfast to go," suggested JJ.

They all agreed that was a good idea, except Yucca emphasized that they shouldn't dillydally. He was very anxious to get back home. When they exited the cave, they could see that the Outpost was just as Statistic had described it. There were three fleabag hotels and several cheap restaurants right inside the cave entrance. There was also a small village of older cape cod style homes on the main street, further down than the commercial strip. The houses weren't very big, and were presumably the residences of the employees and owners of the hospitality businesses. There was obviously no other commerce or other activities happening in that area, other than servicing travelers' needs. The area was so small that it was hard to say that it had any particular topography or geological characteristics. The rock walls encompassing this land could be seen in the near distance all the way around the landscape.

They headed towards the restaurants and passed the Chinese joint where Statistic had been, except that it had just closed down. Its old sign read "The Happy Dragon", but there was a big new banner hanging across the front of the restaurant that said, "Opening Soon by Popular Demand: The Happy Burrito. The Outpost's first Mexican cuisine establishment!" Walking past the Happy Burrito, they stepped into the closest diner actively serving breakfast, but Yucca decided to stay outside while they ordered, being too preoccupied with the politics of it all. While they were waiting for their breakfast sandwiches to be prepared, Izzy, JJ, and Yucan the Toucan sat down at the counter. Looking back outside through the glass, JJ could see Yucca talking to himself. He was talking almost nonstop and he looked agitated. JJ nodded towards Yucca, signaling Izzy and Yucan the Toucan to look over too. They too became immediately concerned, and Izzy said, "It looks like he's starting to crack up, he's so worried about his homeland. We need to get out of here ASAP."

"I'll go out and wait with him," Yucan volunteered. "He just needs a good pep talk." So Yucan the Toucan went out and started his uplifting chat, as JJ and Izzy watched through the window. But within two minutes, both Yucca *and* Yucan the Toucan were talking at the same time, and *both* were looking very perturbed. Something was going wrong. JJ and Izzy hadn't seen either Yucca or Yucan acting like that before. The sandwiches were ready to pick up, so Izzy grabbed the to-go bag, and he and JJ rushed out to see what was happening. When they opened the door to exit, they realized Yucca wasn't talking to himself after all. He and Yucan the Toucan were surrounded by at least thirty bedbugs, and they were all asking questions at the same time! The bugs were tiny, only standing about one inch tall, but they all had loud, shrill voices. It was hard to understand clearly what any one of them was asking, but Yucca and Yucan the Toucan were both trying to do their best to answer. There was no time for Yucca to really answer the barrage of rhetorical and philosophical questions being thrown at him, much less ask any of his own. But it just wasn't in Yucca's nature to be rude and not answer a question, so he was quite distressed.

Izzy quickly sized up the situation, so he shooed away the bedbugs and escorted, or more accurately, pushed, Yucca away, heading for the cave exit. JJ and Yucan the Toucan followed. When they had safely returned to the cave and were walking on, Yucca explained, "Thanks for bailing me out back there. That was the most frustrating game of 'Do Ask, Do Tell' I've ever been involved in. Those bedbugs had tons of questions, but none of them had any bite, and the questions were mostly nonsensical. And despite all the questions they asked, they didn't have any answers. It seemed like they were just trying to be a disruption rather than trying to contribute to any kind of meaningful dialogue. They wouldn't score many points in a real game of 'Do Ask, Do Tell, that's for sure.'

With the bedbug epidemic behind them, the group moved briskly along for the next half hour. They made the best use of their time walking through the cave by brushing up on what they would say to the critters and cactuses. They were feeling confident and mentally prepared by the time they reached the Jungle. Upon their arrival at the Jungle exit, Yucan the Toucan went to go run his errand. The other three took a break and waited patiently at the mouth of the cave for Yucan's return. They shared a moment of quiet solitude, all three deep in thought about what they would encounter that afternoon. Then to everyone's surprise, two stowaway bedbugs jumped off of Yucca's back and broke the peaceful silence.

The first bedbug looked at the second one and asked, "Haven't you been enjoying this lovely ride through the cave, Benjamin?"

"What's not to enjoy, Beatrice?" asked the second bedbug. "Don't you find this Yucca fellow interesting? Have you ever met a cactus so inquisitive in your life? I wonder if there are other cactuses so curious?" speculated Benjamin. "I wonder where Yucca is taking us next? Wouldn't it be great to see where he lives? Wouldn't it be interesting if all of the cactuses at Yucca's home all walk and talk? And what if they are all as adept at answering queries as Yucca seems to be? Wouldn't that be enlightening, dear?"

"Wouldn't *anyone* think so?" asked Beatrice. "How nice would it be if we lived with an acquaintance like Yucca that had the *answers* to our musings? Why don't you ask our gracious host what life is like in his land? Does he think it would be a good place for us to settle down and raise our family? Why did we ever move from Bigfoot's place to begin with? Why did we ever decide to seek a better life? I hate to say I told you so, but shouldn't you have listened to me to begin with? Wasn't that cigarette smell in our hotel room at the Outpost the most awful odor you've ever smelled? Who could tolerate that smell day in and day out? Is that any kind of environment to raise children? Why would anyone even want to smoke cigarettes to begin with?"

"But dear, how was I to know that we couldn't trust Logginoggin's advice?" asked Benjamin. "And do you remember me telling you that we just need to learn to look on the bright side sometimes? What if Logginoggin was right all along about the Outpost, and you and I just can't appreciate the good things we have when we have them?"

Next, Benjamin the Bedbug turned to face Yucca and asked him, "Where are we going now, Yucca? Would you be so kind as to call me by my nickname, Benny, and to likewise address my wife as Bea? How far a journey is it to your home? Do all the cactuses at your home answer questions as well as you were answering them back at the diner? What are the accommodations like where you live? Do you have comfortable mattresses? Would it be a good place to settle down? Can you tell that Beatrice is pregnant? Do you think she is showing yet?"

"Why did you have to ask Yucca *that*, Benjamin?" asked Beatrice. "Don't you think that was rude and embarrassing?"

"Can't you tell I'm just a proud parent, and wasn't meaning to be rude, dear?" answered Benjamin. "Isn't it important that you have a comfortable mattress to sleep on, being in your condition? How do you feel about the name Benny Jr. for one of the boys?"

JJ and Izzy were looking at the two bedbugs, shaking their heads. JJ silently thought, "A lot of people back home would just squish these annoying bugs, instead of attempting to tolerate them. But it's just not right to squish someone that is reaching out to have a friendly dialogue with you, is it? It doesn't matter how much bigger the squisher may be than the squishee. Especially when they are talking to you on a first name basis. As annoying as those bugs are, it's still clear that there is some common ground here. Benny even shares a goal of mine, to try to look on the bright side more often. They just want to raise their kids in the best way that they know how, just like the rest of us."

Yucca looked down at the bedbugs and said, "You two can't come home with me. You would drive the Elders crazy. We'll need to find somewhere else to drop you off."

Then, as JJ, Izzy, and Yucca were standing there contemplating the fate of Benny and Bea, the three saw a lantern weaving towards them through the cave. The light was coming from the direction they were heading. As the lone figure drew near, JJ, Izzy, and Yucca recognized the silhouette of the Economist emerging from the depths of the cave. Benny and Bea stepped back into the shadows, feeling more comfortable in the anonymity of the darkness.

Yucca warmly greeted the Economist and added, "I see you're still looking for the clues to the answers."

"Yes, my search is never ending. I'll dig as deep as need be to find that last missing piece of data. But I miss the help of Statistic. Have you seen him?"

"Yes. He's with Frank in Seaside," replied JJ.

"I'm heading in that direction. Perhaps I'll run into him. I'll bet I can glean some valuable information from him since we've been separated a few days."

"I wouldn't prod him too much this morning," warned JJ. "He was out with Frank late last night." JJ paused for a moment, then continued, "Economist, I've been wondering why you carry such an antiquated device as a lantern to light your way. Why wouldn't you use a modern flashlight, for example?"

"Because this light is easier on the eyes. Flashlights can blind somebody and make them squint. I'm just here to assess what I see, not to adversely affect the way other people see things. No one can appreciate the bright side when they're looking directly into it. And I, for one, would like to see more people looking on the bright side."

The Economist lingered for a minute, obviously contemplating something. He seemed to be searching for the right thing to say. Then he asked Yucca, "Are you headed home now? You *are* from the Land of Plateaus, just over to the right at the next fork, aren't you? It's curious that you can walk and talk. I've been there before and none of the cactuses I've seen there seem to have those talents."

"No," said Yucca, "Actually..."

JJ quickly interjected, "No, actually we're just exploring and enjoying the exercise of a good hike."

Then the Economist stared through the mouth of the cave and into the jungle, and then looked at JJ and asked, "What are you doing hanging around *this* boring area of the cave, then? I wouldn't waste your time going in this jungle if I were you. There's nothing there but a bunch of mindless tropical birds."

Yucca started to say something back, but JJ again butted in, "Thanks for letting us know. We weren't planning on going in. We're just resting right now."

"Well good luck in your travels," the Economist wished. "It was good seeing you again. I'm heading on to Seaside now. Hopefully I'll run into Statistic."

As the Economist turned away to leave, Benny and Bea emerged from the shadows and Benny whispered to Bea, "Doesn't Seaside sound like the perfect place for me to teach Benny Jr. the difference between rhetorical and philosophical questions, dear?"

"Wouldn't it be great if that opportunity came even sooner than you expected, Benjamin?" Bea whispered back.

"What are you trying to tell me, dear?" murmured a suddenly panicked Benny, as he and Bea quietly waived goodbye to Yucca, JJ, and Izzy. The two bed bugs hopped onto the Economist's back, and disappeared into the his backpack.

After the Economist was out of sight, Yucca asked JJ, "Why did you keep cutting me off?"

"I don't know for sure. I almost think the Economist and I were warning each other not to go to The Whole Tamale."

"I did sense a feeling of uneasiness coming from the Economist," Yucca noted. "And I think it *is* concerning the Whole Tamale. It seems to me that if he has found it, he knows there is something he doesn't understand about it and it scares him. Or maybe he hasn't even found it yet, and that is what he is *really* still looking for. Perhaps his 'clues for the answers' search is just his way of explaining that he's looking for the

Whole Tamale. Either way, he doesn't feel comfortable about it at all."

JJ thought about it and nodded. "I think you may be right, Yucca. That's probably why he wants to talk to Statistic again. He wants to see if we found it. Of course, it's probably just a coincidence that the restaurant was called The Whole Tamale, anyway. I doubt he was really looking for food. But then again, the restaurant *would* have been hard to find if one was actually looking for it."

"Well, at least there is *one* positive story line here," noted Yucca, who had a big smile on his face. "Seaside will be a *great* place for Benny and Bea to raise their kids."

"Yeah," agreed Izzy. "But for every happy ending, there's a corresponding bad ending for someone else. And we're sleeping in Seaside tonight, so we may not have heard the end of the bed bugs." Izzy paused for a second and added, "I wonder if the Economist will be able to help Benny and Bea learn any *answers?*"

A few minutes later Yucan the Toucan rejoined the group and they headed on. When they reached the cave entrance to the land of the villages, they paused for another break. While they were resting, Izzy remembered that Frank had left his "How to Spot Bigfoot" souvenir flashlight by the campfire the morning they left, and wanted to go retrieve it. The four all went in together. They found the campsite, but there was no flashlight. To their surprise, however, the embers were still hot in the fire pit!

A puzzled look spread across Izzy's face. "That's strange. It looks like someone else must have camped here last night."

JJ was perplexed as well. "This is such a remote area that I can't believe someone else would have just happened upon it. I wonder if someone has been following our footsteps?" They stayed for a few minutes looking for clues, but none were to be found. So they headed back to the cave, and onward in the direction of Critterland. They hadn't gone too far at all when they came to the fork in the cave the Economist had spoken of. They paused for a minute at this juncture.

Izzy studied his map, nodded, and said, "I'm pretty sure this is all lining up with my map. I believe Critterland is to the left of this fork, and not too much further up on the left. The Land of Plateaus that the Economist mentioned must be to the right side of the fork, just up on the right."

JJ thought about it for a moment, and then suggested, "Yucca, if it's not going to take us too far out of our way, maybe we should go take a look at the Land of Plateaus. If people are mistaking you for a resident of that land, we may find out something interesting if we visit. We could learn valuable information concerning their stances at the EcoSummit. They must have cactuses there. Perhaps there could be an angle for some collaboration or some other joint effort. Maybe they know something we don't. We won't know if we don't go."

Yucca hesitantly agreed, "I have to agree that it's a good idea, but I don't want to take long. I'm *very* concerned about what's happening at home, and we don't have much time to prepare for the EcoSummit as it is. Let's do it quickly, and if Izzy's guess is wrong, if it's not close by, or if it's not the Land of Plateaus, let's turn around and head home with due haste."

Yucan the Toucan spoke next, "I think it sounds like a very sound strategy. The more information you can garner, and the better prepared you are, the more likely your chances will become to have a successful presentation at the EcoSummit. But I believe you two should go alone. Izzy and I really need to press on to Critterland. We have our work cut out for us there, and we'll need all the time we have left. Plus, I need to complete my work at Critterland in time to rally my own delegation back in the Jungle."

Izzy agreed with Yucan the Toucan, and would have loved to see the plateaus too. But they all knew they had a job to do, so all four wished each other luck. JJ and Yucca headed to the right and Izzy and Yucan the Toucan headed to the left. And Izzy and JJ began looking forward to catching up with each other on the day's events and endeavors when they both got back to the Seaside Inn, which would hopefully be later on that night.

Izzy and Yucan reached their exit within twenty minutes and entered a much more subdued Critterland than they had previously encountered. There definitely wasn't as much turmoil as the last time Izzy was there. They went to the new critter condo complex looking for Critter 1 and Critter 2, and it didn't take long to find them. They were chattering away with a whole group of critters outside in the condo courtyard. They saw Izzy coming and scurried over to him.

Critter 2 looked very down. "What's wrong," asked Izzy, "Why the glum face?"

Critter 1 butted in and said, "He got fired yesterday."

Izzy was shocked, "I didn't know you even had a job."

Critter 2 started to perk up as he told his story, "Mr. Big hired five of us to work as EcoCo executives. On our first day, yesterday actually, we unionized. When we presented Mr. Big with our contract demands, he got really mad and fired all of us. He said he was scrapping the whole project. He went storming off, shaking his head, and we haven't seen him since. I don't know what made him so mad. I thought the demands were very reasonable. We just told him we didn't want to carry luggage or wear shoes."

Critter 1 asked, "Hey Izzy, Who is your bird friend? Where are JJ, Frank, Statistic, and the big cactus? I hope they didn't get arrested. The police were hot on their tails the last we saw them."

"They're fine, but thought it wouldn't be a good idea to come back here right now. This is our friend, Yucan the Toucan."

"It's safe now," Critter 2 said reassuringly. "The police are gone and so is Mr. Big. But the big rig keeps running all day and night. And the tanker trucks come and go at all hours. JJ said he might be able to help us organize and form a consensus for the EcoSummit. Do you think his offer is still good? We've been trying to do it on our own and all we do is argue louder and louder."

Yucan the Toucan stepped forward to properly introduced himself, and they all shook hands. "That's what I'm here for. My name is Yucan the Toucan and I'm a motivational speaker, a professional team-building specialist. I'm here to see if I can assist you. I'm an expert at bringing people together to support the common goal of self-betterment."

Looking somewhat relieved, Critter 1 said, "That's great! How do we get started?"

"I don't know about this." Critter 2 frowned suspiciously while he was talking. "Should we trust a bird to do this job? I think I could do it if the rest of you critters just listened to me."

"But your ideas are stupid. I think we should hear what the bird has to say," suggested Critter 1. "Let's listen to him."

Upon hearing that, Yucan the Toucan immediately took another step forward with authority and spoke. "Thanks for the vote of confidence. Now then, for starters, we need to call a meeting of all the critters in the condo complex as soon as possible. And I need you two to walk me around the neighborhood and explain to me exactly what is going on around here. JJ and Izzy have filled me in about your bad experiences with the drilling, but are you having any problems with the air or water?"

"There has definitely been something funny in the air lately," answered Critter 2. "And the water is murky too."

"Yeah, I've noticed that," agreed Critter 1. "I've been feeling queasy ever since Mr. Big and EcoCo showed up to begin with."

"Ok," said Izzy. "That input helps. Yucan the Toucan and I will canvass the crowd and go inspect the rig and generally look more closely at the whole situation for the next few hours. We'll see you at the meeting."

About two hundred critters showed up at the assembly, and they were bickering back and forth in one big wall of noise. Izzy and Yucan the Toucan walked up to the podium and Izzy addressed the crowd, "We called all of you together because we're trying to help you form a simple, unified position at the EcoSummit. I have witnessed three other communities' meetings and can assure you that the other communities in the Federated Lands are taking this quite seriously and will be very well prepared to argue their positions at the Summit. The other groups we have seen have organized cohesively and are sure of their positions. They have put aside their petty differences and are united in their beliefs. For *your* opinions to be taken seriously by the government, you'll need to do the same."

There was a general murmur in the crowd as Izzy continued, "These are the issues specifically targeted by the EcoSummit that affect you the most: Water Purity, Air Pollution, and of course, fricking and fracking. The problem is that the other communities don't really care about fricking. It's not happening in *their* neighborhood. There won't be any urgency to restrict the fricking laws unless it comes from you. You will need to come up with a way to seriously pull at everybody else's heartstrings to get any support."

Then one of the critters called out urgently, "I just want that big rig *gone!*"

Then the other critters all began loudly expressing their thoughts at the same time. It was hard to tell what any one individual was actually shouting, but it was clear to Izzy and Yucan that the gist of it was the critters wanted their lives back to normal.

As the critters started quieting down, one of them said, "Come to think of it, Mr. Big did tell me they were about to start some off-shore drilling somewhere else because there wasn't as much gas here as they thought there was.

Another critter added, "He promised *me* that when they were done fricking and fracking here they would restore our habitat back to normal."

"Maybe we don't have as much to worry about as we thought we did," Critter 1 observed. "EcoCo will move the rig, leave us alone, and destroy *somebody else's* homes. We can get *our* lives back to normal.

Maybe we should vote to leave the drilling law like it is. If new restrictions are passed, they may *never* move the big rig."

The crowd of critters all loudly voiced their support for that idea.

"But is it right for us to wish this mess on some other creatures? We *know* how bad it truly is," Critter 2 asked.

There was an awkward and unusual moment of silence from the opinionated critters. Then, after a few seconds, the bickering erupted again. When that round of noise subsided, one of them asked, "Offshore of where, exactly, would they drill? I wonder. It would surely disrupt the lives of the sea creatures and the shore creatures. *They* don't even use oil. How fair is that?"

"*But neither do we!*" reminded Critter 1.

The murmur from the crowd grew into a roar.

That's when Yucan the Toucan stepped to the podium, and loudly proclaimed, "That's it! You need to let everyone else in the Federated Lands know four simple words: *You could be next!* That is the clear message you need to carry with you to the EcoSummit. Several of you will need to draft a detailed account of your experiences with the big rig and EcoCo. And you'll need to print hundreds of copies to distribute to the other delegates at the Ecosummit. Don't forget to add your slogan, 'You could be next', in large font, at the top and the bottom of the page."

Yucan paused for a few seconds to add emphasis to what he had just said, then continued. "You'll also need to compose an official opinion on each of the topics being discussed at the summit. This is called your platform. Make each stance short winded and well defined. It will be best to be in favor of tight laws on everything. This will help you garner support from the other delegations for the tougher fricking legislation you're seeking. Don't forget that the reason each of these eco issues has been singled out for debate is probably because someone somewhere has complained about the problem. The other delegations obviously have their own eco problems to contend with, which are probably different than yours. If you help them, they'll probably help you. You can print your platform on the same page as your story about EcoCo to keep it succinct. Just remember to drive home the 'You could be next' message wherever and whenever possible during the summit."

Yucan the Toucan paused for a few moments for everything he had said to sink in, and for the few critters taking notes to catch up with their jotting. Then he continued. "And lastly, you'll need to select a delegation to send to the summit. Try to pick between four and eight of you who work well together and who have complimentary strengths. You need to elect a delegation leader who can channel all of your individual knowledge and opinions into a unified team effort. The critter you pick for that job will need to be able to side step and properly quell any petty internal arguing that any of you may become involved in."

There was a murmur in the crowd, but this time it represented a collective and cohesive understanding of what they needed to do next. Critter 1 stepped forward to tell Yucan that they understood now, and that they could handle the rest on their own, now that they had a plan. The meeting adjourned and many of the critters circled around to thank Yucan the Toucan and Izzy for their help, and to ask a few questions about the finer points of diplomacy. The critters began drafting their platform immediately. They didn't even squabble too much when they voted for their delegates.

Now that they had completed their mission of organizing the critters, Yucan the Toucan and Izzy headed to the cave and journeyed back to the Jungle together. When they reached the cave exit for the Jungle, it was time for Izzy to say goodbye to Yucan. He started off to shake Yucan's hand, but gave him a big, friendly hug instead.

Yucan told Izzy, "Hopefully I'll see you and your friends again at the summit. But if not, it has been a true pleasure working with you. I've learned a lot in two days and hope we get to do it again sometime."

"We all feel the same way, Yucan," Izzy confided. "JJ really wants to go to the summit, so don't be surprised if we show up. If we don't though, I know JJ wants to stop by on our way home to talk to you more about your motivational strategies."

And with that, Izzy was on his way back to Seaside. As he continued on through the cave, Izzy thought about everything that had been happening. He was proud of himself for his work aiding the Critters' organizational efforts, and he thought, "Hopefully they'll be able to help their cause at the summit. Hopefully they'll be able to stay unified and field a delegation that even makes it to the summit to begin with. And how are JJ and Yucca faring? It would be great if things went smoothly with the Cactuses. Surely, Frank will want to get to Myrtle Beach as soon as JJ and I get back to Seaside. But we've all come this far, so maybe we *should* stay and attend the EcoSummit. Guys like us don't get a chance to make a difference in other's lives very often. We can always go to Myrtle Beach on the next vacation."

"And another thing," Izzy thought. "This ancient map is definitely of the Federated Lands. We've only seen a small fraction of these places. I wonder what kinds of people and beings live in the rest of them? Come to think of it, I probably have enough time to double back and take a short look at the Land of Plateaus before heading back to Seaside."

12

No Return Policy

JJ and Yucca hadn't walked far when they came upon a cave exit on the right, just as Izzy had predicted. And just as the Economist had described, they exited the cave into a land of plateaus and cactuses. The climate was somewhat similar to Yucca's homeland, but the topography was not as dramatic and the colors were not as spectacular as the painted desert. This land lacked the sense of radiant energy that Yucca's land had, but it did have it's own distinctive aura. JJ and Yucca were looking out over a small desert plateau, more of a mesa, actually. The mesa was surrounded by steep-sloped ravines all the way around. On the far side of each ravine was another small mesa, and each of these was surrounded by ravines, which each had more mesas on all of the other sides. Basically, as far as the eye could see, were small plateaus. The network of ravines and gorges broke up the mesas, so they looked kind of like a panoramic series of islands. Cactuses were all over the tops of the mesas, including the one JJ and Yucca were standing on. Some of the cactuses looked like yuccas and prickly pears, which kind of freaked out Yucca, because these cactuses were not moving and talking, even though they looked a lot like Yucca's friends back home. There were hundreds of lizards lounging around, sunning themselves. They were perched on desert rocks, which were intermingled among the cactuses. The lizards were talking.

A lizard perched on the rock closest to Yucca and JJ moved his eyes a little, and said to the lizard next to him, "Hey, Louis123, look at that walking cactus! I've never seen one that walks. And he has a human with him!"

Louis123 answered back, without moving at all, "Me neither, Larry23456. Let's keep an eye on them."

Yucca overheard the lizards. He quickly walked a few long strides toward them, bent down to be closer, and asked, "So the cactuses here don't walk? That is very strange. My name is Yucca, and that is my friend, JJ. Can I call you Louis123 and Larry23456 also? Do you play "Do ask, Do tell, here? Like we do in my land?"

This verbal barrage of questions sent the lizards scurrying quickly off of their rocks, and they hid underneath a large boulder a few feet away. All of the hundreds of other lizards streaked back under their favorite large rocks also.

Louis123 stuck his head out from underneath the rock, poked his tongue in and out quickly, and replied to Yucca, "*No*, they don't walk, and they don't *talk* either!"

Then Larry23456 stuck his head out too and said, "No, we don't play 'Do Ask, Do Tell'. And no, I'm not Larry23456 right now. I'm Lizzyliz2014, so don't call me Larry23456 again, you big, scary, cactus monster." Then Lizzyliz2014 pulled his head back under the boulder.

Louis123 went back under the boulder too, and could be heard arguing with Lizzyliz2014. He then poked his head back from under the boulder and said to Yucca, "I'm not Louis123 right now, either. But you can call me Lattimore512. We're not sure what to make of all this. We've never seen a talking cactus before."

Yucca was very puzzled also. He said, "I don't know what I could have done that offended your friend, Lizzyliz2014, but I am not a monster. I may have acted over-aggressively, but I was just surprised the cactuses here can't walk like me."

Next Lattimore512 went back under the boulder and Lizzyliz2014's head reappeared. He looked over at the clump of cactuses next to the boulder, then at Yucca, then back to the stationary group of cactuses. He was clearly nervous, as if he had never considered that cactuses might be able to defend themselves or confront him. He said, "I didn't mean to offend you Yucca, but now I'm Larry23456 again, and I'm very friendly. When I'm Lizzyliz2014, I'm more mean and judgmental." Then he turned to the closest clump of cactuses, and apologetically said, "And I'm sorry I mistreat and make fun of you cactuses sometimes. I'm sure I never did it when I was Larry23456, but only when I was Lizzyliz2014, and *definitely* never when I was Leonardo789 or Ralph1076. So I hope you understand."

Then another lizard boldly slithered up to Yucca. He said, "A number of humans have stopped here lately, looking for talking cactuses. Apparently there is some secret you possess that some of the humans are interested in. What is *your* name? I couldn't hear what you told Louis123 and Larry23456 earlier. And what is your great secret?"

"My name is Yucca, but I didn't have a name until my human friends gave me one just recently," Yucca answered. "I've been thinking about what a name means since they gave it to me. I don't have any secrets that I can think of, nothing to hide at all. But if I did have something to hide, should I make up an extra name first? And what's your name?"

"My name is Leon the Lizard, but I also go by Stanley6789 and Lulu812. I can't imagine only having one name, much less no name at all. That would kind of make you *have* to answer for all of your actions, wouldn't it? *That* would be *very* inconvenient. It could make someone think twice before they spoke, and I believe in freedom of speech. If we only had one name, what would we ever do when we wanted to insult someone? Insults should always be anonymous, or else they would be even more hurtful. It could even be dangerous for the one doing the insulting. And what would politicians ever do if they couldn't hide behind names like governor, senator, or president?"

JJ concurred, saying, "Yeah, how would government officials ever defend themselves for some of their misuses of power?"

Leon the Lizard nodded in agreement and continued, "I'm glad you can see my point of view. I don't care much for politicians either.

I think they're corrupt, but I only believe *that* when I'm Stanley6789. When I'm Leon the Lizard and Lulu812, I have the utmost respect for those public servants. I wouldn't want the politicians or law enforcement to think that I believe anything less."

Yucca thought about everything that had been said, turned to JJ, and asked, "What do you think is in a name? I was just beginning to understand, or at least I thought I was beginning to understand, why a human needs *a* name. But these lizards believe they need three or four different names."

JJ answered, "It does remind me of some problems we have at home regarding acceptance of personal responsibility. It seems that the lizards, like some people in my world, want multiple names so they can avoid accountability for all of their actions. Some people adopt alternate egos so they can do things in secret. Many people in power adopt titles so they can commit acts of malice against their fellow man, and enrich themselves, without being held personally accountable. These people use their new names as legal corporate and political veils. All of these choices affect how these people reach out to the worlds around them. But humans also need to have a real *single* name so they can recognize when the world is reaching out to *them*."

"We don't have that need," replied Leon the Lizard. "But I'll tell you who does pull that off nicely, though. Loginnoggin, the terrapin. He stops by to visit occasionally, and I'm pretty good friends with him. Loginnoggin has the one master name, but he has four heads, and each of those has three other names that he uses on occasion. And each name has three distinctly different personalities as well: Nice, mean, and indifferent. He is usually socially disengaged, but once he signs on to a conversation, he becomes fully immersed in the thread of the dialogue at hand. When he talks, he keeps pulling in and poking out different sets of heads, and his heads keep flip-flopping the names and personalities back and forth between nice and mean. I can understand Loginnoggin, but most people become quite confused by him. *Every-*

body loves the nicest side of his nicest head, but we all dread enduring the wrath of the meanest side of Loginnoggin's meanest head."

Yucca looked even more bewildered, and sighed.

Lizzieliz2014 cautiously emerged from below the boulder and said to JJ, Yucca, and Leon the Lizard, "I'm not Lizzieliz2014 anymore. Now I'm Larry23456 again. I was listening to what you are all saying. I truly don't want to hurt anyone's feelings, but sometimes I want to say something mean or rude. And when I do, I'm doing it for *myself.* It makes *me* feel good to let off the steam. I never stop to consider how it makes the other lizard or cactus feel. So isn't it better that I do it under a different name? I would never want anyone to think that I would *intentionally* hurt him. Doesn't everyone hide a dark side that they don't want everyone else to see or hear? The choices are to suppress those feelings, or to adopt a new name and speak out. Wouldn't you agree?"

Yucca sighed again and responded, "Leon the lizard and Larry23456, I don't know the answers to the moral or ethical questions you're posing. But I'm glad you don't play 'Do Ask, Do Tell', because it would be tough to explain the score to an impartial observer with all these different name changes. I still look at myself as being one individual, and *I* would always view you as one entity, no matter how many times you changed your name. *I* would always know the true score, but I'm not sure that *you* would. In the end, it's all about the true score, not the false realities that any of us, including Loginnoggin, may use to try to explain ourselves to the rest of the world." When he was done sharing his thoughts, Yucca turned his back on JJ and the lizards, and strode over to a nearby outgrowth of prickly pears for a moment of solitude.

JJ kept a careful eye on Yucca, concerned that he might have become too overwhelmed with so much to worry about. JJ knew all about *that* problem, so he watched closely as Yucca stood next to the prickly pears, meditating.

After five minutes or so, Yucca turned around, and walked back over to face JJ, and said, "I can communicate with these cactuses. They told me how badly the lizards treat them, just because the lizards don't think they have any feelings or know who they are. They also told me that Mr. Big came here looking for a talking cactus, and the answer to some big secret. The Economist came a few days earlier, and *he* was searching for the whereabouts of something secretive as well. Maybe Mr. Big is looking for my land so he can exploit it, like he's doing in Critterland. And I suppose the Economist hasn't found the Whole Tamale yet either. They also explained to me that they know about the EcoSummit. The lizards have a committee that has met to discuss it, comprised of members representing all of the mesas. The cactuses are concerned that the lizards won't be looking out for their best interests, and are very worried."

As Yucca was talking, the three lizards gathered around closer to JJ, trying to be a part of the conversation. Leon the Lizard horned in and said, "I know all about our stances at the EcoSummit, and the cactuses have nothing to worry about. We *need* the cactuses. They are an important part of our way of life and survival. We both require the same protections of our environment. The leader of our delegation is named Leopold117, and lives nearby on Mesa 13, if you'd like to visit with him."

"That makes me feel a little better about the cactuses' welfare, but I'm still nervous about all this. I think we'd better get going, JJ. There may still be time to talk to Leopold117 later, just before the summit, but I need to get home now."

On the way back to the cave, Yucca stopped by the cactus patch and briefly shared with them what Leon the Lizard had said. He and JJ left the plateau and hiked as quickly as they could hike back towards Yucca's home. They talked about a lot of issues as they headed on.

Yucca did most of the talking. "JJ, I'm very grateful for the opportunity you gave me to come on your journey. We haven't made it to *your* land yet, but I did get to see a lot else that I never would have seen otherwise. I experienced things that I never would have known even existed if it wasn't for you. If it hadn't been for the good luck of you and Frank visiting, I never would have known about the Federated Lands or about the EcoSummit. And more importantly, I wouldn't have been aware of the imperialism that is spreading in our direction. I'm going to need to go speak with the elders as soon as I get back. I'm sure some of them have heard about the Federated Lands. But they probably have no idea what Mr. Big is up to right now."

Yucca took a minute to think, clearly very troubled by the idea that the Federated Lands might invade his land. After collecting his thoughts, he continued. "JJ, now that I've seen everything going on out there, I think I'll need to stay home with my family and community for the immediate future. I hope you don't take this personally, but I won't be able to travel on with you to see your world right now. I'm not sure I even want to anymore anyway. You humans have some serious problems, and I know what you mean now about getting arrested for being a lot different. I wish I could have helped you figure out a way to talk to your congress. But I'm sure you'll find a way to get the attention of congress on your own some day. Maybe you'll become the most successful cabinetmaker out there and become wealthy enough that *they* take an interest in you."

Yucca and JJ finally arrived. Peppy was thrilled and relieved to see Yucca. He rushed over to greet him and JJ. "Back so soon? It must not have been much fun in JJ's world. Did you finish the game? Who won round three?"

JJ answered first. "I kind of forgot about the game. So I wasn't keeping score, but I don't think either of us feel like we lost."

Looking at JJ, Yucca smiled and said, "I know who won. I was keeping score, but I'm not saying anything. It's my secret." Then he admitted to Peppy, "We never made it to JJ's world. Instead we traveled through the cave into some other fascinating places. They are all part of a world called the Federated Lands."

"The Federated Lands? They're in the cave? What kind of lands? Can you tell me all about them? Who lives in them?"

"Yes, they're all in the cave. Actually I think we may be part of them and didn't even know it. I'm looking forward to telling you all about them, but it will need to wait until later. I need to go talk to the Elders first."

"Well the humans haven't had any trouble finding *us* since you left. Two groups have visited over the last two days. And a third is here now, somewhere."

Yucca looked at JJ nervously, and then turned back to Peppy and cautiously implored, "What kinds of questions did they ask?"

"The first two groups didn't ask any questions, or try to talk to any of us at all. They ignored us, even when I tried to talk to them. They were using some scientific instruments to measure the land. The new guys are talking a lot right now, but I don't think they're here to play any games. There they are, right over there." Peppy pointed over to a crowd of cactuses all gathered around listening to someone giving a speech.

Yucca and JJ walked over to listen in, and to their utter dismay, it was Mr. Big doing the talking. Mr. Big glanced at Yucca and JJ joining the crowd, paused, and started over, "As I was trying to explain, I bring great news! Our scientists have discovered large deposits of copper and silver on this mountain. That means the Federated Lands is going to annex your community. Now you'll be able to enjoy the benefits shared by all the members of the Federacy."

"What kind of benefits?" inquired one of the cactuses.

"Most importantly, you'll have the full protection of the Federated Justice Department, which will protect you from all of your enemies. Secondly, you will gain the stability of law and order. We'll build an entire infrastructure from the ground up. We'll install courthouses, police precincts, and jails to protect you from criminals."

Yucca stepped closer to the center of the crowd and rebuffed Mr.

Big, "We don't have any enemies and we don't have any crime. At least not before you showed up."

"And there certainly won't be any once we get the police here," continued Mr. Big. "We have ways of catching criminals before they even commit a crime. We'll arrest them just for thinking about it. You will never have felt so safe. And that's not all. We'll build schools of higher learning so you can give your youth a modern education."

"But we already have a learning system that works for us. We don't need modern teachers," Yucca asserted.

"I didn't say anything about teachers. We don't have a budget for teacher's jobs. You'll need to hire them on your own. But we'll build the schools. Construction projects are great for job creation. Of course, you'll all need to move to the next valley over. It won't be an imposition, I'm sure, since your species has the innate ability to pick up your roots and live off the land somewhere else."

Peppy burst into tears. "But I don't want to move to the next valley. These are my favorite rocks right here."

"Perfect!" bellowed Mr. Big. "The next valley is where these rocks will land when we blow up the mountain. Now, if someone of authority can just sign this disclosure statement, I'll be on my way."

Yucca was glowering as he pushed his way through the crowd and stepped all the way up to Mr. Big and replied, "We're not signing anything until after the EcoSummit."

"How did you hear about *that?*" Mr. Big asked, surprised. "Oh wait, you're that insubordinate cactus from Critterland, aren't you? You cactuses all look so much alike. Very well, we can do this the hard way." And with that bit of intemperance, Mr. Big stormed off.

Once Mr. Big was gone, the cactuses all gathered closer together to discuss what had just transpired. One cactus suggested the obvious, "Let's just seal off all the cave entrances we know about so the humans can't get back in." The other isolationist ideas proposed became exponentially more complicated.

After listening to the other ideas, Yucca shook his head and explained, "The time for all that has passed. The humans know our land is here now and they have the power to do whatever they feel like doing. They would only blow open a new cave entrance if they wanted to get in. We'll have to send a delegation to the summit, I'm sure. But we need to go explain everything to the Elders. They'll know what to do."

Then JJ weighed in, "You might consider sending an ambassador to the District of Concrete to establish diplomatic relations. Maybe through negotiations the Federated Lands will recognize your sovereignty. I doubt it, but it's worth a try." JJ knew that idea was kind of a reach, so he added, "Yucca, would you like me to go with you to talk to the elders?'

"That might be a good idea. Follow me." Yucca took JJ on a short walk through the cactus forest. They came upon a large clearing with a group of very tall cactus trees in the center. These old cactuses were the Elders. Yucca told them his story while JJ stood next to him. It was important for them to understand how large a force they were up against, and also to explain to them that the other cultures seemed to be having troubles of their own. The Elders looked very concerned, but not panicked. Several minutes of silence elapsed while the Elders contemplated.

Finally, Elder 1 spoke. "We will need to send representatives to this EcoSummit."

"And I suppose it's too late to just seal the cave entrances off," sighed Elder 2.

"No, it's definitely too late to hide," acknowledger Elder 3. "We will need to send a delegation to the summit. We will also need to send an ambassador to the District of Concrete to establish diplomatic relations. We need to find out what the human's designs are on our land. Are they really going to try to annex and exploit us, as appears to be the case? Or will they recognize our sovereignty? We need to find this out before we decide how and if we should expend our weapons."

Another minute of silence elapsed. Presumably the Elders were thinking about the consequences of using whatever weapons it was that Elder 3 spoke of. Then Elder 2 spoke again. "As you know, during the intemperance of my youth, I traveled to the District of Concrete. I wanted to see if the legend was true. I can only imagine this will be an even more treacherous endeavor now than it was back then."

Yucca excitedly asked, "Do you mean you explored the caves too? What was it like back then? Did you meet critters and toucans and witch doctors?" Yucca realized he was blurting again, and sheepishly added, "Does this mean I'm not in trouble, since you did it too?"

"No you're not in trouble, but you *should* be," replied Elder 1. "As chance would have it, you may have helped save us all by stumbling onto the Federated Lands' evil designs. In fact, *you will* accompany our delegation to the summit. The good rapport you have developed with this human and his friends can only be of help. So will the knowledge you've gained by visiting some of the other lands and meeting their delegations." He seemed to be done speaking, but then peered over at JJ, then nodded towards Yucca, and asked, "He did handle himself in a cordial and befitting manner, didn't he?"

"Yes, he was very friendly and liked by everyone we met," replied JJ. "Except by Mr. Big, but he was quite snippy with everybody. It took a little while for Frank to warm up to Yucca too, but that's just Frank. You know, humans aren't used to playing 'Do Ask, Do Tell', and guys like Mr. Big don't like being questioned. Personally, I was proud to have Yucca on my side when we confronted Mr. Big. But I think I made Mr. Big madder than Yucca did."

Elders 1,2, and 3 all chuckled when they heard *that*.

Yucca stepped forward quickly while the Elders were humored, and announced, "I'd be honored to accept that invitation. But we don't have much time to prepare." Yucca looked urgently at the Elders, who were still winding down their chuckle. "The summit is in two days."

Next JJ stepped forward and addressed the Elders. "I sat in on more meetings than Yucca. I'd be glad to share with you what I've learned. I have some ideas for strategy."

"Thank you JJ," answered Elder 3. "We would like to hear everything you have learned on the subject. But leave the strategy to us. We will know what to do."

JJ and Yucca stayed with the Elders for two more hours recounting their travels. And JJ explained how he had come to this land to begin with. When they were done with the Elders, they headed back to Yucca's grove, where Peppy and the other cactuses were waiting. The Elders began speaking amongst themselves.

JJ was wondering about something the Elders had said. On the walk back, he asked Yucca, "What did the Elder mean when he said 'how to expend our weapons?' What kind of weapons do you have?"

"I guess he was referring to the various diplomatic channels we may be able to explore. But I wouldn't be surprised if they have something else in mind. They are quite sure of themselves, and they didn't seem as nervous as I would have expected. They always answer all of our questions we ask, but I've always had the feeling that they know something they won't tell us about."

They arrived back at Yucca's grove, and Peppy and the other cactuses gathered around anxiously to hear what the Elders had said. But first it was time to say goodbye to JJ. It had been a long day and he needed to start his trek back to Seaside before it got any later.

"Good luck at the summit, Yucca," wished JJ. "I would like to stay longer, but I can see you have a lot of catching up to do with Peppy and your other friends. If I don't see you again, I want you to know that it has been a genuine pleasure. I'll never forget the looks on the faces of Frank, Izzy, and Statistic when you said some of the things you said. Not to mention the way you stood toe to toe, so to speak, with Mr. Big. But don't be surprised if I show up at the EcoSummit. I just need to talk Frank into it. But he's pretty easy to sway."

JJ started walking towards the cave and he could hear Yucca, in a very animated voice, begin to tell the other cactuses the story about the Witch Doctor and the sandwiches. He imagined Yucca's eyes lighting up as he talked. The other cactuses were all laughing. They had never heard of such a thing. But Peppy tagged along with JJ, as he walked slowly towards the cave.

"JJ, thanks for bringing Yucca back safely. And thanks for helping him learn about Mr. Big and the EcoSummit. Why wouldn't he tell me who won 'Do Ask, Do Tell?' What happened in round three? You know he's never lost before."

They had reached the cave entrance, and JJ smiled and knelt down to look Peppy eye to eye, and replied, "'I'll tell you a secret, but you can't tell Yucca. I know who won too, but I'm not saying either. I *will* say, though, that I learned something important from Yucca. Sometimes when you come face to face with someone that is so foreign to you that at first you can't relate to them at all, and maybe you're even scared of them, just asking each other a few simple questions can change everything. We're all more alike than we are different, no matter how different we are. I enjoyed meeting you too, Peppy. I have to go now. Goodbye."

JJ stood up, and walked through the cave entrance. As he was disappearing into the cave, Peppy called out, "Thanks for giving me a name! I really like it!"

As Peppy was walking back to hear Yucca's stories, he thought, "If they closed off the entrance it probably wouldn't keep the bad guys out. They could still force their way in. But it *would* keep out the friendly people, and those are the ones we don't meet often enough as it is. I think tomorrow I'll go down to the valley and pick out a new perfect pile of rocks. Just in case."

Earlier in the day, back at Seaside, Frank and Statistic had finally woken up just in time for a late lunch. They decided to eat at the Seaside Inn's courtyard bistro. As they were passing by the front desk on the way out, the receptionist called out to them, "Mr. Statistic, Mr.

Frank, you have guests waiting to see you. Mr. Frank, your guest is seated right over there in the lobby. Mr. Statistic, your guest is in the courtyard."

"That's strange. I'm *certainly* not expecting any visitors," said Statistic.

Frank gave Statistic a strange look and agreed, "Me neither." The guest in the lobby overheard the exchange and quickly strode over to Frank. As soon as he heard the man's voice, Frank's shoulders slumped and a sour expression flashed across his face. He had heard that voice on the phone many times before.

"Mr. Frank, this is an attempt to collect a debt. I'm with AAA Debt Collectors. As you know, you're extraordinarily delinquent on your student loan. How will you be making that payment today?"

"How in the heck did you find me here? I'm lost. *I don't even know where I am!* I'm short this week. Don't call me, I'll call you." Frank abruptly turned around and rushed to catch up with Statistic, who was headed out to the courtyard to meet *his* guest.

The Economist was patiently waiting, seated in the bistro, and drinking a cup of tea. He had his notebook open and his pen ready when he spied Statistic walking towards him. The Economist warmly greeted his former cohort, "Hello, old friend, it's great to see you again! Please sit down and join me." He waved at Frank and said, "It's Frank, right? Will you pull up a chair and join me as well?"

Frank and Statistic both pulled up chairs and explained that they were ordering lunch. The waitress was right behind them, and took their orders. The Economist went on to ask Statistic, "I was hoping you could spend some time answering some questions. I'll bet you've seen and learned quite a lot, since you've been exploring the Federated Lands with Frank and his adventurous friends. I ran across the rest of your new comrades in the cave earlier and JJ told me you were here. I met Izzy." The Economist looked over at Frank and asked, "Frank, wasn't he the one you and JJ were looking for when we first met? It looks like *he* found *you*! But weren't you just trying to find your way back to your campsite? What did you find here in the Federated Lands that made you want to stay?"

Frank answered, "You're asking the wrong person. I've just wanted to get out of here since we got here. For some reason JJ and Izzy *want* to stay and explore."

Then Statistic apologetically said to the Economist, "Actually, Frank and I have a 2:00 tee time at the Seaside Golf Club. So we don't have enough time for a full interview. Maybe we could schedule a session for next week, when I'm back home in Virginia."

The Economist looked pained over the fact that he wasn't getting the information he was *really* looking for. "I suppose my studies can wait that long. As long as I'm here, though, and while you're still waiting for your lunch, can you recommend any of the restaurants you went to last night?" The Economist was scribbling notes while he was talking.

"Sure. We went to The Rowdy Crab, The Ruddy Crab, The Crabby Rudder, and The Cruddy Crab. They were all fun. Frank, what was the name of that last place we went?"

"Bad Captain Billy's."

"Great!" exclaimed the Economist, while continuing to scribble. "And where did you go yesterday afternoon?"

Before Statistic could answer, a young woman stepped forward to shake his hand and introduced herself. "My name is Nan100." She pointed over to a nearby bistro table while she was talking. "My friends over there, and I, couldn't help but overhear you. We're here on vacation too. What were the names of the good places to go?" She pulled out her own pad of paper and a pen. As Statistic repeated the names of the establishments he and Frank had been to, Nan100 drew her jottings into her pad, all along peering at the Economist's jottings over his shoulder, as if she were cheating on a test.

"Thanks!" said Nan100 as she turned away and walked back to her friends at their table. At that point, the waitress delivered Frank and Statistic's drinks and burger plates, and they dove in. Neither Statistic, Frank, Nan100, nor the Economist, noticed that the whole time Nan100 was asking questions, all four of them were being scoped out by a table of three teenaged young men who were seated nearby. The young men were listening in on the conversation and one of them had his own pad of paper and was making his own notes.

Statistic, after eating a few bites, got back to the Economist's question and answered, "We spent a few hours on Taboo Island with the Witch Doctor. That was entertaining and very spooky. I wouldn't go there on an empty stomach."

The Economist finished his writing, put his notebook away, and said, "Ok, one last question. All the restaurants you mentioned sound like typical tourist raw bar type establishments. I'm not really in the mood for seafood tonight. Did you eat any *Mexican* cuisine in your travels, by chance?"

Frank roared, "No!"

The Economist smiled, but kind of frowned at the same time, as if that wasn't the answer he expected. He then stood up to leave. "Well thanks for all the recommendations, gentleman. I'll leave you alone to finish your lunches. I'll see you back home in Virginia, Statistic."

As the Economist turned his back to leave, seven bed bugs jumped out of his traveling bag onto the dinner table. Frank and Statistic watched the bugs hop out and land right in front of them as the Economist was walking away.

Benny the Bed Bug looked at Bea and asked, "Beatrice, dear, would you mind finding a good, comfortable room at this wonderful hotel? And can you take the children with you? But would you mind if Benny Jr. stays with me? Don't you think it's time I started teaching him 'the ropes'?"

"Wasn't that our plan all along, dear?" responded Bea. "Why are you even asking? Shouldn't I just pick a room number now? Wouldn't that be the least problematic means of reconnecting later? How does room number 113 sound, for example?"

"Wouldn't you know better than I, dear?" asked Benny. "Haven't you always been in charge of these types of arrangements? Shouldn't Benny Jr. and I just join you and the rest of the kids later in room 113?"

Bea and four of the bedbug children went hopping off to room 113. But Benny Sr. and Benny Jr. stayed behind on the table. Frank was at first taken aback, as he had never seen or heard a family of talking bedbugs before. Frank looked down at both Bennies, and said, "I have to say that my first inclination was to squash all of you bugs as soon as I saw you on our table. But once I listened to you talk, I realized we have something in common. My son's name is Benjamin. My wife and I named him after myself and Benjamin Franklin."

Very distressed looks had spread across the faces of both Bennies. Benny Jr. stepped closer to Frank and asked, "But why would you want to squash us to begin with?"

Benny Sr. rushed to step in front of Benny Jr. and beseeched Frank, "It just wouldn't be right to squash both of us Benjamins, then, would it?" And then Benny Sr. looked back at his son and asked, "Do you know what kind of trouble I would be in if your mother found out that we got squashed?"

But Benny Jr. asked, "Dad, did I ask you to butt in? Can't you see that I can handle this? Does it look like I was born yesterday? Can't you just look on the bright side for once?"

Frank butted into the bugs' argument and explained, "Look, you two can relax. I don't squash living things. I'd just like to warn you that most humans *do* squash living things."

While Frank was talking, Benny Jr. looked at the reflection of himself in Statistic's water glass and realized how small he was. Then he looked up at Frank and asked, "But *why* would people want to squash other living things?"

Frank looked at Statistic for help, but they both shrugged at each other, even though Statistic was trying to come up with something quick. Frank was on his own this time. Usually JJ or Izzy would be around to answer this kind of question, so he didn't have to. Frank thought about it and replied, "I guess I don't have a good answer to that question. I'm six and a half feet tall. I could squash most *men* if I was so inclined, much less a tiny bug. But I'm just a big softie. I don't want to hurt anybody or any thing. I know how badly it feels to get hurt, and I know how badly it hurts when someone loses a loved one who got squashed."

Frank paused for a second to self-reflect on his own experiences, and then went on. "But you need to remember that the reasons most people do things doesn't need to make sense to *you*. You just can't put yourself in the wrong position. Others may decide to squash you just because they *can*. They may have no good reason for their actions. They might just do it because they have the power to do it. The fact of the matter is, that if I were back home right now, the social norms would dictate that I squash both of you and any other bugs that hop onto the dinner table. People would think I wasn't doing my job if I didn't. You need to understand your parameters and stay within them. You two bugs should get back to the rest of your family now. I'll do my part to help by overlooking this entire incident. I hope I was of some help to you." Both Bennies hopped off quickly, soaking in Frank's advice along the way.

Frank and Statistic quickly ate the rest of their lunches so they could rush off to catch their tee time. When they paid their check, the waitress gave them their change in eight $1 bills. One was another pastel play money note, another was a colorful $1 Federated bill, and the other six were $1 Bad Captain Billy's doubloons. They were printed in bright gold and silver inks, and had an ornately engraved pirate on the front, and a galleon on the back.

"These doubloons are my favorite money we've seen so far," remarked Statistic.

As they were walking out of the bistro, they passed by the table where the three silent young men were seated. Frank noticed a "How to Spot Bigfoot" souvenir flashlight sitting on their table, and thought to himself, "Man, that Bigfoot is making a killing on those flashlights. I hope theirs' worked longer than ours did!" Then as Frank continued to walk, he thought, "It actually felt pretty good to answer the bugs' questions back there. It made me feel a lot bigger than I would have felt squashing something smaller than me, not that I would have done any squashing anyway. Maybe there is more to 'Do Ask, Do Tell' than I thought there was."

As Frank was strutting along, quietly proud of himself, Statistic looked at him and remarked, "You exercised some extraordinary over-sight back there with the bedbugs, Frank. Do you remember that 113 is *our* room?"

After the hours spent playing eighteen holes, Frank and Statistic would take the scenic route back to the bistro, stopping at several nine-teenth holes along the way, and taking in another wallet full of oddball paper money in change.

It was just reaching dusk at the bistro courtyard, and Izzy was the first to make it back from the day's endeavors. He took a seat and opened his notebook to the map. He studied it carefully and thought, "Ok, so the entrance to the Land of Plateaus is right where it was supposed to be too. Everything lines up just right. The bold lines are the main cave system. This lighter, but wider, figure eight line is definitely the underground river, with all of it's offshoots drifting out, just as Yucan the Toucan described it. I just can't figure out what these dotted lines represent." Izzy peered at the map for five more minutes, then a perplexed expression crossed his face. I'll need to keep studying this as we go along."

Izzy looked up because he heard Frank's booming voice joking around with Statistic as the two walked in from the street. He put his map away, making room at the table for Frank and Statistic. The three friends shared stories about what they had done all day. They ordered appetizers and drinks and awaited JJ's return. They had been sitting at the bistro for an hour and a half when JJ finally got in. It was getting late. JJ was completely exhausted from his trek, and Izzy was fading fast too. Frank and Statistic were pretty drained also, but were actually just getting warmed up for the evening.

JJ and Izzy decided to forego the talk about the day's events until morning. They were too tired to think about complicated issues. The discussion drifted towards the plans for the next day instead.

"Well it's too late now to get back to camp and head to Myrtle Beach," Frank grudgingly admitted. "Statistic and I are really enjoying Seaside, though. Why don't we just stay here for the rest of the trip? We can't wait to take you guys to our favorite new spots tonight! Then we could get up and play a round at the club tomorrow."

Wearily, Izzy replied, "I might be able to stay up a little longer, but I'm pretty tired." Then he perked up, looked over at JJ, and said, "My map is definitely a very old detailing of the Federated Lands, probably from before they were federated, and I understand its scale now. This is a large world we're in. I can make out each of the lands we've been to. Assuming Yucca's land is where you describe it to be, its ancient name was Omni Potencea. And I can see where the District of Concrete is located, assuming The Witch Doctor's story is accurate. It's pretty far from here, but not *too* far.

"That's very exciting," JJ replied. "How long would it take us to get there, I wonder? Yucca and I found the Land of Plateaus, except the lizards there told me they call their home 'Boulder Gulch'. The plateaus are more like mesas, and each has a number."

"I know," said Izzy. "I went there briefly myself, just to check the map. The lizards have numbers too! At least three or four each. Maybe their land has four names too, but I like Boulder Gulch."

Then Frank abruptly broke in, "Look, we're wasting time here. Are you coming with us or not, JJ?"

"I'm not JJ anymore, I'm Kaput4321. And I'm just too tired. I'd only slow you down."

"That's too bad," Frank said disappointedly. "You said yourself that all you do is work. Then you go on vacation and invent work to do. I say let's *vacation* for the rest of this vacation."

"I guess you're right. I'll be the same old JJ tomorrow. But as long as we've lost the option to get to Myrtle Beach, I want to stay for the EcoSummit. We'll have just enough time to fit it in before heading home.

"I'm on board with that plan. I don't want to miss it either," agreed Izzy.

Frank rose from his seat to leave, and said, "Ok, Kaput4321, you can hide, but you can't run. We'll see you tomorrow, and be ready to vacation." Izzy and Statistic stood up to leave too.

Last Night

13

The Wrong Turn

As JJ was nodding off to sleep he was thinking about tomorrow. Frank and Statistic would be sleeping in again until early afternoon, most likely. That should give him and Izzy just enough time to go explore *The District of Concrete*!

JJ slept well and woke up Izzy early the next morning. They had a lot of cave to cover if they were to make it back to Seaside by mid afternoon. "Are you sure you're up for this?" asked JJ, looking for some reassurance that this was a good idea.

"That's *why* I'm up. Let's get going. But I don't think we should take the cave. Let's try to catch a raft at the underground river. I've studied my map, and there's a river exit very near the main cave junction where I'm sure the District of Concrete is located."

They took the short walk out of Seaside to the underground river cave junction, and rode the elevator down to the river. Luckily, moored to the dock was the same raft they had taken from the jungle, with all of its torches flickering. Skipper Zack was sitting on his raft and said, "Where's the rest of the crew? Couldn't get up this early, eh? And where are you going today?"

Izzy told him, and the Skipper let out a whistle, and said, "You'd have more fun today if you just stayed here. But the District of Concrete *is* worth seeing. Once. Make yourselves comfortable. This will be a fairly long voyage. We'll pass under five other lands on the way, including Boomtown. The Boomtown station is the closest exit to the District of Concrete. It's a very short walk away from there."

So JJ and Izzy made themselves comfortable in a pair of deck chairs and settled in for the ride. Izzy was hoping to see more of the river walls, and had his notebook out, ready to draw what he would see. Once again Izzy and JJ were dazzled by the scene of the flickering torches' light dancing off the glistening, age-old walls of the cave. The cool, moist air seemed particularly chilly. The wall art was concentrated most densely near the cave opening, and the further they drifted through the cave, the sparser it would become. The first two cave exits they passed were both small bulk headed landings, like the jungle station. No one was at either one. The next two were more bustling and larger, like the Seaside junction. It was also getting to be a more reasonable hour of the morning. Both of these stations had docks that could moor up to ten boats.

Finally they arrived at the Boomtown exit. It had the largest dock they had seen yet. At least one hundred boats fit at the docks. Clearly, this underground port was not natural. Dynamite had been used to blow out a large amount of rock to create a subterranean mini-bay. There were armed guards standing all over the place on the docks. JJ and Izzy could see a row of three small stone buildings at the far end of the dock. There was a large ramp behind the buildings that led up to the ground. The ramp had been carved into the stone.

The Skipper pulled the raft up to an open slip at the dock, and as he did so, an armed guard paced right up to them and barked, "What is your business here? Who are these passengers? Did you get permission to moor here? Where is your paperwork?"

Skipper Zack scowled at the guard, but in a polite tone of voice that belied his deep distain for the port authority, replied, "These passengers are here to visit the District of Concrete. My Commercial Raft License is posted outside the pilot's cabin. That's all the paperwork I should need, and I don't need permission to dock here."

The guard stepped onto the boat and inspected the Skipper's license. He frowned and approached the Skipper. "It's a class A Commercial Boat License. That's the highest classification, but this is just a raft. Why is that?"

"The license is transferrable. I'm allowed to operate a raft with that license. If you want to know the reason, go ask your buddies at EcoCo. You know, the ones that probably sign your paycheck. Please stop over-stepping your bounds with me. And leave my passengers alone too."

"The Boomtown Port Authority signs my paycheck. I'm just doing the job I'm paid to do."

"Well then, go ask the heads of the Port Authority who signs *their* paychecks! And leave us alone." With that, the guard went pacing straight back to the center of the three stone buildings. The sign atop that one said, "Boomtown Port Authority."

Skipper Zack turned back to JJ and Izzy, and warned, " You two had better get going. The path to The District is short. You'll see the signs. It's very safe, and heavily guarded. But don't stray away from the path. Boomtown is an entire land of under-educated paranoid vigilantes, who all think they're smarter than the next guy. They're armed and dangerous. Don't take anything I say personally, but you guys act kind of funny, so I'd be careful if I were you.

JJ and Izzy exited the boat. Both were already questioning their wisdom in deciding to make this trek to begin with. They walked past the three stone buildings. Flanking the Port Authority was a Federated Lands Official Substation to the right, and the Boomtown Customs Department to the left. They walked up the stone ramp, which was on the left of the buildings, wondering what they were getting into. At the top of the walkway they had to walk under two large signs hanging from overhead. The rectangular sign on the left said "Welcome to Boomtown." The sign on the right was round and had a logo in the center, which was just a large, stylized 'BC'. Circling around the outer edge of the sign was the motto, "Boomtown City - The Safest Place to Live in The Federated Lands." As they were walking out into the direct daylight, they were both bracing their eyes for the bright side. But when they reached the surface, there was thick smog in the air that deflected the light, making it much easier to clearly see the big picture.

Everywhere else they had been so far seemed to be natural environments. But this was a metropolis of stone buildings. At the top of the ramp was an official overhead sign with an arrow that pointed to their right. It read "District of Concrete Boulevard." There were armed police and guards posted all up and down the street. As they passed the first intersection, they could hear gunfire blazing off in the distance. Izzy glanced nervously at one of the cops standing guard at the crossroads. The policeman looked at Izzy, and said, "Don't worry about the gunshots. That's just one of BC's finest reigning in one of BC's roughest. We're here to protect our citizens."

Izzy and JJ stepped up their pace. It was only a few city blocks to the District of Concrete. The final two blocks they walked through was the financial district. Both sides of the street were lined mostly with tall stone banks and the offices for lobby groups. The buildings were not of traditional architecture, but were instead flashy, like the Las Vegas strip. Neon lights abounded. Each bank had a flashing billboard in front advertising all of the brands of paper money they carried, and each lobby group had the same. JJ and Izzy passed in succession the Tenth, Ninth, Eighth, and so on, down to the First Bank of Boomtown. The largest building on the block was the Federated Stock Exchange, which was also the last building they passed before arriving at the District of Concrete.

JJ and Izzy reached the cave, but it wasn't really a cave any longer. The walls of the cave were completely blown out on both sides. The two explorers were now facing a massive gaping hole. It had an ornate stone arch built around it, forming a grand portal that Caesar would have been proud to pass through. The dramatic archway had been erected as an entrance from the cave and the District of Concrete into Boomtown. But in this case it was a welcome exit from Boomtown. It was a sight to behold. Looking through the arch, they could see the caves were all merging into this central location.

Right there, where all the caves came together there was indeed a colossal stone building the size of a whole state! They walked through what used to be the cave, and right up to the building. The entrance they approached was very imposing. It had a massive set of steps going up to a row of eight huge iron doors. Each door was over twelve feet tall, and would be impenetrable when they were closed, no matter how badly someone wanted to get in. Or out. There were dozens of serious looking guards standing outside.

Izzy saw an information desk, and talked to the woman working as the information officer. "Excuse me ma'am. How many entrances are there into the state?"

"Thirteen. Each entrance is identical," she replied.

"Are they all so heavily guarded?" asked Izzy.

"I said they were all identical," answered the officer.

Izzy walked back over to JJ and said, "I don't think we'll be able to sneak in. Security is very tight here."

"We don't need to. I was talking to the guards, and everyone is allowed in. Why is it that guys like us always just assume that we need to *sneak* into the best places? I think we're actually welcome here."

"I don't know about in, but I'm usually pretty sure why we're sneaking back out," replied Izzy.

So JJ and Izzy walked right into the stone building. When they reached the lobby, there were so many signs with arrows that it was overwhelming. The Bureau of Trade was this way, the Bureau of the Interior was that way, and the Bureau of National Monuments was that way too. There were hundreds of bureaus and departments and literary omens and foreshadows. It was all so collectively overwhelming that none of it registered to JJ or Izzy. (As chance would have it, sometimes not registering is a good idea to not have.)

Izzy said, "I think I might just like to go to the Bureau of the Exterior and get back out of here!"

"No, we came this far. We should explore. Lets go down the main corridor for a while, past all the tourists, and then cut down some side hallways. That's where we'll find the *real* District of Concrete. Just follow me."

They walked down the corridor quite a while, probably a quarter of the way into the state. JJ saw a side door that didn't look used very often, so they went through the door and down three flights of stairs. At that point there was another large hallway running parallel to the previous corridor, which they took. There was a loud humming noise coming from further down the hall, so they walked towards it.

JJ walked slowly up to the door where the noise was coming from. "Izzy, What does that sign say next to the door? I can't find my glasses."

"Men's Room."

"No I see that one. I mean the one next to it, the one written in small writing. But I *do* need to use the bathroom. I'll be back in just a second."

Meanwhile, back in Seaside:

Frank slept in until the early afternoon again. Statistic wasn't too far ahead of him, but had time to go down to the bistro for brunch while waiting for Frank to wake up. He walked back up to the hotel room, by which time Frank was awake and getting ready for the day.

Statistic asked, "Have you heard from JJ and Izzy? The receptionist said they left at four this morning."

"No, but they should have left word at the desk if they went somewhere without us. I don't think we should cancel *our* tee times, though. We'll leave a message with the receptionist for them to meet us at the club. We need to hurry. I'll just catch breakfast on the go."

After 18 holes there was still no sign of JJ and Izzy. So they hung around the 19th hole for another hour or more, just in case the other half of their foursome showed up. When there was still no sign of them, Frank and Statistic went back to the inn. They sat waiting in the courtyard bistro for another hour. They were starting to get worried now. It would be getting dark soon. Frank noticed the inn receptionists were changing shifts, so he talked to the night shift woman who was working last night. She was just clocking in. "Did they say anything about where they were going when they left this morning?"

"No. I just overheard them talking about a story the Witch Doctor told them. Oh, and one of them was studying some drawings in his notebook while they were talking."

Frank looked at Statistic in dismay. "Oh great. Those boneheads tried to find the District of Concrete. There's no telling where they are now. Did you pay any attention to the directions the Witch Doctor gave, or anything else about the District of Concrete?"

"No, I wasn't really listening. The Witch Doctor didn't call me by name, so I didn't think he was talking to me specifically. I guess I was just zoning out."

Frank thought about it for a second and decided, "I think we need to go see the Witch Doctor right now. Maybe he can give us directions in case we need to go find them, or knows of some authority we can contact to aid in our search."

"That's a good idea. I hope Captain Gruzzly is still running the ferry this late. We'd better get on down to the port."

They arrived at the dock, but there was no ferry to be seen. "That's ok," Frank said. "We'll take the cave."

By the time they arrived at the Sand-Witch Hut, night had completely set in. The path was lit with tiki torches, as was the hut itself. The barista greeted them, "Can I get you gentlemen something to drink?"

"I thought you quit," Frank abruptly replied.

The barista explained, "The cook quit today, so the Witch Doctor asked me to come back. He gave me permission to work on my thesis in-between waiting on parties, which I have been doing for years anyway. But now I have to cook too. It's not as easy to keep three lines of thought going at the same time as I thought it would be. It hasn't been busy, though."

"We'll save the drinks for later," said Statistic. "We're looking for the Witch Doctor."

"He's down at the dock. Come back and join me when you're done talking to him."

They walked down to the dock, where there was a small boat moored. From the glow of the tiki torches, they could see the Captain and the Witch Doctor onboard the skiff. They were discussing something in dire tones.

"Witch Doctor," Frank said in a hushed, but urgent, tone that pierced through the night air. "It's us, Frank and Statistic, from the other day."

The Witch Doctor squinted into the dark towards them, trying to discern who was talking to him. "Oh, I recognize you now. I remember your friends JJ and Izzy, and Yucan the Toucan and Yucca too. But you two never told me your names, and seemed more focused on your food and drinks anyway."

Frank replied, with a serious tone in his voice, "JJ and Izzy are why we're here. They're missing. I'm pretty sure they tried to find the District of Concrete, today. To be honest, Statistic and I weren't paying attention to your story, so we're hoping you can tell it to us again, plus anything else you know that might help us find them."

"Uh-oh. That's not good. I warned them not to go too far. I know a lot about the pitfalls and the pratfalls of getting to the District. And I shudder to think of what they may have come up against if they found it. I hope they didn't get seduced and brainwashed by the evil magic. It's a long story, Frank and Statistic. I suggest you listen to every word. But you'll need to stow away with the Captain and I to hear it. We are just leaving for a short ride over to the other side of the island."

So Frank and Statistic jumped on board with Captain Gruzzly and the Witch Doctor. But now they were stuck on board for the trip. The Witch Doctor and Captain Gruzzly were fully immersed in their mission. Captain Gruzzly brought the boat to a stop and The Witch Doctor pointed at two boats anchored offshore of Taboo Island, and uttered, "There they are."

The Captain whispered in a hushed tone, "They've been there three days now. They carry the flag of EcoCo. Let's take a closer look."

"Don't get any closer, warned The Witch Doctor." "I don't think we should confront them yet. But if they're doing what we think they're doing, this will be a big problem for all of us. We should keep an eye on them until the zoning meeting Monday night. At the meeting we can act swiftly with whatever evidence we have."

Captain Gruzzly grudgingly agreed, and he turned the skiff around and headed back to Taboo Island. As they were pulling back up to the dock, the Witch Doctor realized he had forgotten to retell the story, so he turned to Frank and Statistic and said, "Now if you men will join me back at the Sand-Witch Hut, I'll tell you about the secret, evil magic of the District of Concrete again." Captain Gruzzly bade farewell, and sailed the skiff back to port.

The barista joined Frank, Statistic, and the Witch Doctor at a table back at the Sand-Witch Hut. He explained that he liked to hear the District of Concrete story as many times as he could hear the Witch Doctor tell it. In every recounting, the doctor would add or leave out more of the sinister details. But this time the Witch Doctor mostly retold the same story he had already shared with Frank and Izzy, except this time it was much spookier. Maybe that was just due to the eerie ambiance of the tiki torches flickering at night, or maybe it was because this time the Witch Doctor addressed Frank and Statistic by name, so they *listened*. Either way, the story made a deep and visible impression on its audience this time.

"What do you think we should do?" Frank asked the Witch Doctor nervously. "Can you tell us how to get to the District?"

The Witch Doctor answered, "The fastest way is to take the underground river from Seaside to Boomtown City. But you shouldn't go at night. It's too dangerous. If Boomtown City doesn't get you, those soul-snatchers at the District of Concrete will. It's best to wait until morning. Who knows, maybe JJ and Izzy found their way back already anyway."

The mere mention of Boomtown made Statistic feel uneasy, but the Witch Doctor was right. So he and Frank thanked the man of medicine, and headed back to the cave. Hopefully JJ and Izzy had made it back safely. After all, JJ *did* have Izzy and his map with him.

But getting back to earlier in the afternoon in the District of Concrete, JJ's and Izzy's curious quest continued:

JJ came back from the bathroom holding some trash he had found.

"The sign says 'Federated Division of Prisoner Opportunities.' But more importantly, look at the sign across the hall!" exclaimed Izzy.

JJ glanced across the hall, where a much larger sign on another door read, "Federated Bureau of Engraving." Then JJ said, "Look at this to-go food bag I found in the trash!" Printed on the side was "The Whole Tamale!" "We need to see what is going on around here. Let's take a quick peek in the Prison Opportunities Office, then we'll look across the hallway."

They opened the door and walked in. There was a long corridor running to their right, parallel with the main outer hallway. Directly in front of them was a glass window with a sign that read, "Everyone must check in here." But there was also a temporary sign hanging in the window that said, "Closed for lunch 12-1." There was nobody there. Extending down the hallway was a row of glass doors, which were pretty far apart, but stretched as far as the eye could see. JJ and Izzy walked down to the first door and looked in through the glass.

Through the door was an expansive room the length of a football field. It was filled with heavy manufacturing equipment. All of the machines were belching along, spewing out piles of products by the second. Each of the pieces of machinery was stamped with the EcoCo name and logo. And working behind all the machines were animals and humans wearing orange prisoner uniforms. Every imaginable animal was represented, and the smaller ones were working the equipment. The larger animals, like the bears, gators, and tigers, were pushing wheelbarrows full of completed products back towards the rear, as fast as the machines could spit them out.

On the left side wall, which was the front of the room, hung a row of huge round gauges, each about ten feet in circumference. The closest one read, "Federated Overall Incarceration Rate." The gauge had a big arrow that swiveled around to the headings that circled its face. The categories were "Grotesque Profit, Large Profit, Average Profit, Small Profit, Arrest a Few More, Arrest a Lot More, and Just Arrest Them All." The arrow was pointing towards the "Arrest a Few More" category. The next barometer down the wall was the "Federated Bear Incarceration Rate" Monitor. Its arrow was pointing at 6%. The next one after that was the "Federated Squirrel Incarceration Rate" meter, which was pointed at 2%. The fourth meter read, "Federated Crawdad Incarceration Rate," and it was hovering at 20%! There were at least one hundred more dials running all the way down the football field-long wall.

"I guess the crawdads are a lot easier to catch than the squirrels," noted Izzy. "Or maybe they can't afford good lawyers." Then to his horror, he spotted a new gauge being wheeled in. He pointed it out to JJ, who was crestfallen as well. It read, "Federated Talking Cactus Incarceration Rate." Thank goodness it was still pointed at 0%! And right behind that, another gauge was being rolled in that read, "Federated Yeti Incarceration Rate." That one was already pointing at 100%.

They walked down the hallway further, both visibly shaken. They looked through each of the other doors' windows, and each room was identical to the first, all filled with machines humming away, and all staffed by creatures wearing orange prisoner uniforms. They kept walking all the way down the corridor, because they could see an exit sign at the end of the hallway, heading back into the main corridor. They came to a halt directly in front of the last two doors in the row. The very last door did not have glass. It was made of solid wood and a sign on the front said, "Federated Prisons, Former Legends Division."

"That must be where Bigfoot is being held," noted JJ. "I wonder who else could be in there? I know I haven't seen Loginnoggin yet."

Upon hearing 'Bigfoot' and 'Loginnoggin', Benny and Bea, the bedbugs, instantly jumped out of Izzy's knapsack. Benny asked Bea, "Did you hear that, dear? Do you think Bigfoot is really behind those doors? Wouldn't it be great to be reunited with our old friend?"

"Wouldn't that be just marvelous?" asked Bea. "Don't you think we should get off here and go find Bigfoot? He can't possibly have much more time remaining on his jail sentence, can he?"

"Who cares?" asked Benny. "Didn't you notice that this joint has free room and board? Who wouldn't want three free square meals a day? Can't you imagine that this will be a comfortable place to stay until Bigfoot gets out?"

"But should we feel guilty about leaving Benny Jr. and the rest of the children on their own back in Seaside?" asked Bea.

"Don't you think we should be proud of how well we've done for the kids, raising them in such a quaint village as Seaside?" asked Benny. "And don't you realize that its time for them to be self sufficient and start their own families? And how great would it be if we could raise our *next* batch of kids back at Bigfoot's gift shop? I mean, what's there to think about? And Beatrice, dear, what do you think of the name 'Franklin' for our next son? I wonder if Loginnoggin is here too? Wouldn't it be great if I got the chance to give him a piece of my mind?"

"But if we did find Loginnoggin, how could you be sure you were scolding the correct head?" asked Bea. "What if you accidentally admonished the nice side of him? How damaging would that be to his egos? Don't you think you should swallow your pride lest you hurt innocent feelings? Weren't you the one saying we should look on the bright side of things from now on?"

Benny and Bea quietly waved goodbye to JJ and Izzy again, and they hopped right under the door to Bigfoot's cell. With *that* distraction over, Izzy and JJ peeked in through the second-to-last door's glass, and just as they did, a gator pushing a full wheelbarrow right inside the door, accidentally crashed it into a machine. The whole load spilled on the ground and the small cylindrical gadgets he was toting rolled all over the floor. Two of the objects rolled out under the outer door, and came to a rest at JJ's feet. He picked them up, and they were both surprised to see that they were "How to Spot Bigfoot" souvenir flashlights!

"That's ironic," marveled JJ. "I wonder if anybody knows the only guy that buys these things at a wholesale level is in custody now? Who are they going to sell them to?"

"Who knows?" said Izzy. "On one hand, the government never cross-references itself, but on the other hand, maybe the government is moving in on Bigfoot's product line, now that they've audited his books and have seen how profitable the venture is. I'm sure the government guys have shown their wealthy backers the bottom line. They've stamped out the competition by putting Bigfoot in jail. Come on, let's get out of here while everybody except the inmates are still on break."

They exited and walked back down the main corridor. No one seemed to be around, so they walked right into the Bureau of Engraving. They couldn't believe what they saw! There were rows and rows of machinery, each a city block long. The one closest to them was printing thousands of $100 banknotes a minute! As they walked further into the room they saw that the next five rows of machines were printing $50, $20, $10, $5, and $1 notes. The notes were being printed in a wide array of flashy, bright colors. The printing machines were huge and complicated, with many gauges, gears, belts, and gizmos all working in unison. At the front of the row of machines, overhead, there were two massive gauges at least ten feet in diameter each, very similar to the meters across the hall. One gauge was labeled RATE METER and had a big arrow that was fluctuating back and forth between the meter's three headings: INFLATION, ZERO, and DEFLATION. The other gauge was labeled TEMPERATURE METER. The arrow on it was fluctuating between its 6 categories: OVERHEATED, HOT, FLAT, RECESSION, DEPRESSION, and COLLAPSE. Across from the gauges was a glass cubicle with a sign that said CONTROL ROOM.

It was unmanned and hanging on the glass door there was a sign that read "Out To Lunch."

Unimaginably high piles of each note were being printed. But even more unbelievable, at least half of the piles of money were being ushered along a conveyer belt that did a *U-turn!* After making the U-turn, these bills were combined onto a conveyer belt that fed straight into the next machine immediately adjacent going in the opposite direction: *A Paper Shredder!* The printing machines and the shredder were clearly calibrated to slow down or speed up depending on the fluctuations of the rate and temperature gauges, but were not synchronized together. So the machinery was not humming along smoothly at all, but was rather running in jerky fits and stops of almost cosmic proportions. It was very disconcerting, frightening even, to be standing in the middle of it all.

When the huge wads of shredded money rolled off the conveyer belt out of the end of the shredder, the wads of former cash did yet another *U-turn,* and started heading into the third city block-long row of machines. It was a detonator-fuse making machine! Apparently too much unused money makes perfect fuses! The fuses were getting loaded straight into big trucks after leaving the machine. Engraved on the side of each truck was an EcoCo sign and logo.

JJ and Izzy realized they were in over their heads, but couldn't resist the temptation to explore further. About half of the originally printed banknotes were heading off on a separate conveyer towards the right. A smaller conveyor belt branched off even further to the right. A slim percentage of the money travelled down that channel, but it was still a ton of money. They decided to follow *that* paper trail to get out of the District of Concrete. They walked through a side door heading in that direction and came to a loading dock where two sedans were parked. The money was being loaded into the back of the sedans, which both had diplomatic license plates. And standing right next to one of the sedans was the Economist and Mr. Big.

Mr. Big exploded when he saw JJ and Izzy! "What are you two doing here? Guards, arrest these men. They are trespassing on government property! These men are criminals wanted in the Critterland District for felonious muckraking! I want them held indefinitely until we decide every crime they have committed."

The police swarmed in from all directions and surrounded them. One of them exclaimed "Hey, this is one of the guys wanted in The Hills for dangerous thought crimes! Two of the police grabbed JJ and two more grabbed Izzy. The officers started manhandling both of them back out of the door, past the printing presses, and right across the hallway to the "Federated Division of Prison Opportunities." The police dragged JJ and Izzy to the first office, where they were asked to stand against the wall as their paperwork was being prepared at the desk. JJ could see through the glass door of the first manufacturing room, and the "Federated Overall Incarceration Rate" gauge was easing ever so slightly back in the direction of Profit.

One of the officers sneered at JJ, and warned, "It's time you wake up and smell the roses, mister. You can't just walk around breaking the law everywhere you go. Eventually it's going to catch up with you." The cop then started yanking him towards the desk and added, "Like I said, it's time for you to wake up and smell the roses."

It looked like the predicament could only get bleaker. Izzy called out to JJ, "Remember what the Economist said?"

"He didn't say anything. And I thought he might help, too," JJ replied dejectedly.

"No, I mean back at the Jungle, about why he uses an old fashioned lantern," Izzy reminded.

"Oh yeah," realized JJ. He immediately pulled the two "How to Spot Bigfoot" souvenir flashlights out of his pocket and shone them right into both of the eyes of the arresting officer, then into the eyes of the cop shoving Izzy along. The police were temporarily blinded. Nothing had prepared the cops for looking directly at the bright side!

JJ and Izzy went running off, and zigzagged back and forth through the corridors, and straight out the front door of the District of Concrete.

14

A Turn Against the Tide

"Wake up," Izzy urged JJ. Wake up."

JJ sat up in bed. "What. What is it? I don't want to smell the roses. It's not time yet."

"What are you talking about?" Izzy asked. "You must have had a bad dream last night."

"Okay, I'm up, I'm up. I was having a really weird nightmare, I guess. It was all one big conspiracy with Mr. Big and the Economist and the District of Concrete. We both got arrested. Man, that would have been one bad chapter in our lives."

"That doesn't sound so far fetched to me," replied Izzy. "But I thought I was the only one who dreamt up those kinds of crazy theories and scenarios. I had my own dream like that last night."

"No, I do sometimes too, I suppose. So the last thing that really happened was meeting you and Frank and Statistic at the bistro after I got back from Yucca's homeland? Oh well, I'll get showered and be ready to go soon. Did you end up going out with the guys last night, then? I don't even remember."

"You don't remember anything at all since dinner in the court-yard?" A mischievous smile spread across Izzy's face. He chuckled for a moment, and then he explained, "That's because you were so wiped out you fell asleep early at the bistro table. Frank and I carried you upstairs, and I went out with them for a couple hours. I was too tired to stay out late. I came back to the inn, but there's no telling how late those two were up." Izzy paused for a moment, then said, "You can actually go back to sleep if you want. It's only six o'clock, and Frank and Statistic won't be up until noon, or even later. I'm going to use the morning to take the underground river back to study the map and that abandoned landing more closely. I should be back by noon. I figured you might want to go."

JJ eagerly got out of bed and jumped in the shower. While JJ was getting ready to go, Izzy went down to the lobby and left word at the desk for Frank and Statistic where they were headed and when they'd be back. The desk clerk had a message for Izzy from Skipper Zack, saying he would be waiting at the dock by 6:45. Izzy thanked the clerk, and then headed to the courtyard bistro to order their breakfast. Just as he had finished ordering, Statistic walked up to the bistro counter. Statistic tapped Izzy on the shoulder and said, "I see you couldn't sleep either."

"Actually, JJ and I are going on an early trip down the underground river," Izzy answered. "I want to see the cave drawings and map again. I just assumed you and Frank were still asleep or I would have called the room to see if you wanted to go. Is Frank awake too? Do you want to go?"

"I'd love to. Frank will be sleeping for a while, I'm sure. Last night was miserable. First the bedbugs kept us up half the night with their incessant questions, and then Frank finally fell asleep. Luckily, his snoring lulled the bedbugs into a deep snooze. But I couldn't sleep through any of it. Frank and the Benjamin family kids will be out cold for hours. Just give me a few minutes to go to the room to grab a few things. I'll be back down soon."

JJ and Statistic made it down to the lobby shortly, and the three made the brisk walk to the underground river. Skipper Zack was waiting with his raft to greet them, right on time. There were several other rafts moored at the pier, and a handful of other travelers and skippers milling around. When they approached the raft, Skipper Zack called out, "Welcome back aboard mates. I lined the raft with some extra torches this trip, so you could see all the writing on the wall."

Izzy stepped on the boat ahead of JJ and talked to the skipper in hushed tones about the itinerary. JJ, Statistic, and Izzy settled into their deck chairs for the ride. Izzy pulled out his notebook and pens, very excited to take a more in-depth look at the cave art. He'd have a lot more time to closely examine the ancient cave walls this time, since they were headed upriver. The river's current wasn't very strong at all, but they would still be navigating against it on the way back to the map. Luckily, Skipper Zack's raft had a nearly silent motorized propeller, so it wouldn't detract from the isolated ambiance of the cave. This time, Skipper Zack knew his passengers wanted him to remain silent so they could study the cave.

As they made their way up the river, Izzy feverishly drew renderings of everything he saw on both sides of the cave, which wasn't that much for long stretches. JJ was still pretty tired, so when they hit the periods without any wall art, he just relaxed and quietly zoned out, deep in thought. "I wonder why I'm so tired and sore?" he silently asked himself. "It's curious that Skipper Zack knew to be here at 6:45. It's as if Izzy had it prearranged, but when did he have time for that? Or maybe the Skipper just has a sixth sense."

They passed the abandoned landing, and the density of the art and graffiti picked up a lot. JJ noticed that the older writing on the walls was mostly in several different strange languages he didn't recognize. After a few more minutes, Izzy cried out, "There it is!" He pointed to it, and the skipper pulled the raft as tight as he could get to that side of the cave, and threw in the anchor, which only had to go down about two feet to hit the glittery, mica-lined floor of the river.

At closer inspection, the map was indeed very old. It had an aura about it that was stunning to behold. The torches flickering against the cave wall made the map seem to leap back to life, as if it was waking up from ages of hibernation. Izzy, JJ, Statistic, and Skipper Zack all stood silently at the edge of the raft, studying it up close. The irregularly shaped map was about eight feet tall and ten feet wide, but it didn't have any borders. The rendering just randomly stopped at the outer edges. It was somewhat faded by time, but was painted on the wall with green, blue, red, and yellow paints. The green lines divided it into at least fifty different areas, and each apparently were the various lands that comprised the modern day Federated Lands. Many of the lands had names etched in blue, and the names appeared to be written in ancient corruptions of various old, forgotten languages. At least twenty of the lands had these place names. Just above the center of the map there was a directional compass, indicating the top of the map was north, just like a modern map. Directly in the middle of the compass were the words, "Status Quo Ante Bellum." Izzy, JJ, and Statistic all shuddered when they read those words.

Most of the painted detail was in the lower part of the map. The northern half didn't have much information painted in at all, especially the further north the map stretched. There was just one large word stretched across the top, northernmost part of the map: Vangeolot. Izzy turned the pages of his notebook to his copy of the map, and held it up in the air, so he could study it alongside the original. Skipper Zack was very interested too. He had never paid too much attention to the ancient rendering previously.

"Look down here in the lower left area," said Izzy, while pointing to a particular section of the map. "See where it says 'Vasty Sward'? That's Critterland. If you follow the map clockwise from there, around the outer boundary, heading north, you can see Yucca's land, Omni Potencea. You can tell how remote it is by how far separated it is from the rest of the map. If you keep going north, you get to Hillsville on the left. It's titled Hylla on the map. What is now Boomtown is to Hillsville's right. See that split in the cave before Boomtown? JJ, that's the fork in the cave where you and Frank turned right to get to Bigfoot's place and Omni Potencea. It meets up with the fork, which coming from the other direction, took you and Yucca to Boulder Gulch. See, the map says 'Reptilia' where Boulder Gulch is now. Izzy hesitated for a moment to catch his breath, and then kept explaining, "Now, going back to Critterland, if you follow the outer cave counter-clockwise, you can see the Land of the Villages. It's name on the map is 'Shady Grove.' Then continuing on around, you get to the Jungle, then Seaside. I can't make out the name for the Jungle, but the map calls Seaside's land Oceanus. And the name of Seaside's harbor is Safe Haven. The harbor juts inland from the Great Sea. Look! There's a big sea serpent drawn offshore!"

JJ pointed to the center of the map where the caves came together. "That must be the District of Concrete. Except the map calls it 'Labyrinth'."

"You're right, JJ," agreed Izzy.

Skipper Zack pointed to a yellow line that made a big, roughly shaped, figure eight from top to bottom of the map, and said, "That's the underground river. It looks like it has dots where the exits are now." He scrutinized it for another few seconds, then added, "I wonder what the big red dotted line is for?" The red line formed a perfect giant circle, which was centrally transposed over two thirds of the map. It intersected the figure eight in four places. A bewildered look spread over Skipper Jack's face. He said, "That's strange. You know what? That circle intersects the river where four of the abandoned landings are. And see where the figure eight intersects itself just to the left of the center of the map? Well, that's where the other two abandoned landings are. There are six of them altogether. Of course, it's not really an intersection. The river flows very slowly, so if I had to guess, I'd say the lower part of the figure eight is only about two hundred feet below the upper section, even after the river sweeps all the way around through the north. But why would there be landings built, with no exits, in those places? It looks like someone at one time planned on connecting the river by elevator or some other means at the intersection."

JJ and Izzy looked at each other with mystified looks on their faces, and JJ remarked, "I'm much more interested in stopping at that landing on the way back now."

"Me too," Izzy quickly added.

The skipper said slowly. "I'm curious now too."

JJ had been studying the map and pondering the meanings of some of its words. He asked Skipper Zack, "Does everything you see on the map add up, as far as you know?"

"It all makes sense to me, but I grew up on the river. I know what it does. I know where it goes, and I know where it's been. There are a lot of things going on that won't add up if the math hasn't already been ingrained in your head, JJ."

They stayed anchored in front of the map while Izzy filled in every last detail into his notebook. JJ and Skipper Zack spent the time studying the map too, and speculating what the dotted line might represent. After twenty minutes, Izzy was done, and they drifted back down towards the abandoned landing.

Izzy was bursting with excitement. "Okay, JJ. I'm willing to admit that this does beat going to Myrtle Beach." They both laughed. Then Izzy said, "Next trip maybe we can explore the northern half of the river. There could be another map up there with more information."

"I'll start keeping my eyes out for one," promised Skipper Zack. "I don't navigate those waters as often, but when I do, I'll be looking. If you do come back to visit, be sure to seek me out. I'll be your personal tour guide. You know where to find me."

It wasn't long before they docked at the abandoned landing. Izzy, JJ, Statistic, and the skipper, each grabbed torches from the side of the raft, and began exploring. The pylons that the raft was moored to were made of hand-fitted masonry. In fact, the whole landing was made of stone. It looked like a lot of the landing was natural, but over half of it had been built by masons. Natural limestone deposits had accumulated on the landing, the result of the dripping water coming from the moist cave ceiling. This made it hard to tell how much of it was natural and how much was hand-built. The docking area was about forty feet wide and thirty feet deep, and was sunken into a large recess in the cave walls. The cave also widened at that juncture, so there was plenty of room to dock six to eight rafts without blocking the flow of traffic down the river. The rock floor was uniform and smooth, but didn't have any distinctive features. They noticed the cave ceiling was a little higher back in the recessed area. Other than that it was the same old cave ceiling, with a lot of very short, damp stalactites. The silence at the site was only broken by the occasional drop of water falling down from the stalactites on to the cave floor.

The striking feature of this "station to nowhere" was the writing on the wall. JJ and Izzy carried their torches over to the wall to examine it more closely. Unfortunately, it was mostly modern graffiti, left by the day-trippers and picnickers who obviously frequented the location. Surely some of this graffiti covered up older paintings. There were some older drawings visible. They looked around for a while and hadn't found anything noteworthy, or much in the way of clues at all, until JJ spotted a full paragraph worth of old words back in the recess. They were written high enough up the wall, that not even Bigfoot could have reached it to write over. It was comprised of large letters and symbols, painted in red, that didn't make any sense to JJ or Izzy. Skipper Zack noted that it looked like it was written in the same language as the map, just with a few symbols mixed in.

"It looks like some kind of official sign to me," JJ observed.

"Yeah, I'm going back to get my notebook," said Izzy. "This is important." Izzy brought his notebook and pens back over to the recess. JJ, Statistic, and Skipper Zack held the torches while Izzy copied down the old passage. Then the group walked around to the areas where there were snippets of old writing so Izzy could get those recorded too. When he was done, they re-boarded the raft and began the slow drift back to Seaside.

Izzy glanced over all of his drawings and notes for a few minutes, and then put his notebook away so he could enjoy the rest of the cave scenery. As he was stashing the drawings in his backpack, JJ walked across the raft and said, "You have a lot to study now before our next trip."

"I know. It will give me plenty to do in the evenings during the rest of baseball season. I'll study the map while I listen to the games on the radio after work. I'm very anxious to spread everything out side-by-side and start deciphering it all. Plus, I'll be able to use some of the paintings I recorded as inspiration for my own work too."

JJ nodded understandingly and said, "I'm curious about the reference to war on the map. It makes me wonder even more about something that has been gnawing at me. I've been thinking about that thought meter the border patrol was using back at the gate when Frank and I came in. It seemed to be very advanced technology, yet ancient or from another world. We haven't seen technology nearly as advanced as thought meters anywhere else since we've been here. Nor seen anything else that looked like them either. Could the meter have been a remnant from an earlier time? I wonder what happened in the war? Could the society here have been very technologically sophisticated at the time? The landings to nowhere and the connecting circle on the map could also be evidence of a scientifically advanced society. And another thing, when I think about war, I think about guns. I wonder why Boomtown is the only place in the Federated Lands that allows guns? Could there be any correlation? I wonder what happened exactly?"

"Those are things I'm thinking and wondering about too," replied Izzy. "It could very well be that we find clues on the map that we need to follow up on. I'm beginning to think Frank will be outvoted on what to do next vacation. I wonder how many people in our world know about this place?"

"Who knows? I've been wondering how many other entrances there are from our world. And do they all have thought meters guarding the gates? Maybe our entrance is the only one."

"It's not the only one. I know there is at least one more," volunteered Statistic, who had otherwise been listening silently to the conversation. "It's the one the Economist and I came in through. They had a thought meter there too. Come to think of it, I'm surprised the Economist didn't set it off."

"Well, there's one thing I know for sure," said JJ. "I'll definitely be coming over to listen to some of the games with you for the rest of the summer, Izzy. By the way, I wonder if we could fit in a winter get-away this year?" As JJ was finishing his thought, they could see that looming ahead was the dock and cave exit for The Sayer ?'s compound. "Hey, we're running a little early to meet Frank," JJ noted. "Why don't we stop and see what this mystic's place is all about?"

Izzy and Statistic agreed, so Skipper Zack pulled the raft up to the dock and tied it off. "You know, I've never been up there and this mysterious exploring is growing on me," admitted the skipper. "I think I'll come too."

They climbed the ladder and entered into a land that had the same topography and thick vegetation as Yucan's jungle, which made sense, as it was an extension of the Jungle anyway. There was a clear trail leading from the cave. Just outside the mouth of the cave stood a wood sign that simply had a large question mark painted on it. It also had an arrow that pointed down the trail away from the underground river. They wound their way around the path and within minutes had reached The Sayer ?'s compound. The grounds consisted of eight small residential buildings built of stone masonry, and they all had thatched roofs. Each was large enough to accommodate two guests. Apparently guests were welcome for extended stays. The eight buildings circled a large pagoda in the center of the compound. The grounds were thickly landscaped with flowering trees and bushes. It was more of a natural landscaping, not the kind that took much maintenance or manicuring. Surrounding the grounds was a low, two-foot wall, which was built of logs in most places, but stone in some sections. The wall was just there to define the grounds, not to keep anyone out. In front of the compound was a pair of stone pillars and an iron gate. There was a plaque in front of the entrance that read "Home of The Sayer ?. All those seeking enlightenment are welcome to enter."

As the group of four entered through the gates they saw a large chalkboard sitting on an easel. Its headline read "Parables of the day." Underneath that it listed "The Ant and the Grasshopper, The Goose and the Golden Egg, and Loginnoggin and the Hare." Underneath that list was another title heading, "Today at Noon. A symposium on yesterday's news: A frank discussion on the social conflicts and geopolitical impacts of the incidents surrounding the Princess, the Frog, and the Pea."

After reading the sign, they approached the pagoda. Seated immediately inside was an older woman who quietly greeted them, "The Sayer ? is meditating right now. I'll let him know you're here to see him. I'm ?'s wife, ~#%@&?. Please call me 'Tilda' for short. I'll be right back." Tilda walked over to The Sayer ?, who was seated towards the rear of the pagoda. She whispered to him and he responded by nodding back. Tilda strode back to JJ, Izzy, Statistic, and Skipper Zack, and announced, "? will see you now. Please go sit with him."

The group proceeded forward through the pagoda. They quietly sat cross-legged on a rug in front of the mystic. The guru stared silently at the group for two full minutes, then spoke in a soft, but even tone, "I am The Sayer ?. Thank you for traveling great distances to share in my wisdom. Today's lesson is the tale of 'The Ant and the Grasshopper.' He paused for another moment and then he began the story. "The Grasshopper was an inquisitive and fun-loving insect. He was quite charismatic. It was the Grasshopper's nature to yearn for new and exciting learning experiences at all times. He wanted to frolic with new friends each and every day and night. He strived to broaden his mind and see the whole world in all of its grandeur. The Grasshopper was a party animal, you see. He didn't like to perform mundane or arduous tasks, though, and the Ants saw a problem with this. The Ants *never* took time to socialize or explore the world around them. They instead chose to toil away every day, saving for the future. They lived their entire lives under spartan conditions, looking at the outside world with tunnel vision. They never splurged or had any fun at all. Their singular focus was upon the size of their holdings. The Ants would scold the Grasshopper for not saving as they did. 'What will you do when you get cold and weary?' the Ants would ask."

The Sayer paused for a moment, looking at his listeners in a wise sort of way. Then he continued, "Just as the Ants predicted, one day the winter set in. The Grasshopper became cold and hungry. So he visited the Ants, looking for refuge and shelter. He began to tell the Ants his stories of what he had seen and learned on his travels. His tales were so exciting that the bored and overtaxed Ants gladly gave him food to stay and entertain them. The Grasshopper became a celebrity. Once word spread through the insect world about the Grasshopper's wealth of knowledge and about his stories of fun and intrigue, all the other insects also began vying for the Grasshopper's presence."

Then The Sayer ? paused again, and was clearly deep in thought. After a full minute of silence, he finally went on to add, "In the end, the Ants saved up quite a bit, but became too old and feeble to fully enjoy the stockpiles of their labor. They passed away never having enjoyed life. The younger ants received all of their parents' savings. The Queen Ant took her cut too. The Grasshopper, on the other hand, lived a full and eventful life. The stories of his journeys became a fabric of local lore. In his later years he became impoverished and had to live off of a government assistance program. But he didn't care. He knew he had enjoyed more than his share of enriching experiences during his lifetime."

"So what is the moral of the story?" asked Statistic. "That it's better to goof off than work hard?"

"No," answered The Sayer ?. "The lesson to be learned is that it's better to do what interests you when you're young enough to do it. Toiling away your whole life doing hard labor may bring you riches, but it won't bring you comfort of the mind. Plus, you always have the government safety net to fall back on anyway."

JJ said to The Sayer, "I'm guessing that you must have travelled to the corners of the world in your youth, like the Grasshopper. Is that where you met Tilda?"

"Yes, as a matter of fact," answered the guru. "That is how I attained my wisdom. I have some old photographs from my youthful journeys to show you." He looked over towards Tilda and called out, "~#%@&?, dear. Would you come here for a second?"

Tilda walked over to the group and asked The Sayer, "What is it, dear?"

Her husband became immediately aghast and responded, "Are you *really* asking *me* what 'it' is?" The Sayer ? looked over at JJ and his group, then stared up at the sky, clearly entranced in deep thought. He eventually looked back at JJ and explained, "You see, the story of what 'it' is would take me all day to explain. 'It' is a word that means many different things to many different people. 'It' is one of the most provocative concepts known to man. 'It' is…"

At that point Tilda cut off the Sayer's thought. She looked him in the eyes with a peeved expression on her face, and said, "Look, save *it* for later. Why did you call me over? What do you want?" Then a sudden look of panic flashed across Tilda's face, and she added, "Your guests don't want to hear the stories of 'why' or 'what' either."

The mystic nodded his head in agreement and said, "~#%@&?, dear, you may be right. Will you *please* bring over our photo album from our journeys afar?"

While Tilda went off to find the album, Skipper Zack asked, "Will you tell us the story of 'The princess, the frog, and the pea'?"

"I don't have time to tell the whole tale before the symposium," answered The Sayer. "But you will learn a lot if you stay for the lesson.

In a nutshell, this is the way the story goes: A long time ago, a princess was so greedy that she used to tuck away all of her extra peas under her mattress. She wouldn't share her food with anyone else in her kingdom. Then one day an ugly frog hopped into her chamber. The princess was very annoyed to be bothered by the frog and told him, 'I suppose you're another charming prince that wants a kiss? Be gone with you.' To which the frog replied, 'I'm just hungry and want your extra peas. These peas are fruits of *my* labor. Why are you taxing me so much, only to hoard extra peas while your subjects are hungry? How can you possibly sleep comfortably at night? Whether or not I'm a prince doesn't matter. I don't find anything interesting about you and don't want your affections. I just want to eat enough of *my* peas to satisfy my hunger."

At this juncture the story didn't really seem to be finished, but The Sayer ? ended the narrative and drifted into a prolonged state of meditation nonetheless. JJ, Izzy, Statistic, and Skipper Zack all looked at each other wondering what to do next. They were mildly interested to hear the end of the story, but more importantly, needed to get going to meet Frank back at Seaside. It seemed rude to just stand up and leave while the guru was meditating before them. Three minutes of silence passed. Finally, Skipper Zack spoke up, "Excuse me Mr. ?, but what happened to the frog? Did he get the peas? Or did the princess eat frog legs that night? Or did the frog turn out to be a prince after all?"

The Sayer ? was startled out of his trance, and barked, "*No* he wasn't a prince. His *son* became the prince. You see, when the princess wouldn't share the peas, the frog led a coup d'etat and became king. He shared the peas with his whole hungry kingdom, even the dethroned princess. Her punishment was to sleep on a bed of boulders for a month in solitary confinement. The rocks were so heavy that there was no way she could lift them to hide peas underneath. Then the Frog King issued an edict that the farmers start growing peppers, corn and onions, because everyone was sick of boring old peas anyway. End of story." The guru peered over the group, and added, "You'll learn much more if you stay for the symposium, but I can see you are in a rush to leave. Just remember that if you ever want to come to a complete understanding of the world around you, you'll need to invest the time to contemplate all of its nuances. Thanks for visiting. That will be eighty bucks." The Sayer ? proceeded to look over at Tilda, who was on her way back with the photo album anyway, and bellowed, "~#%@&?, will you see these men out, and bring in the symposium guests?"

The group stood up and thanked the guru for all the wisdom he had imparted upon them. On the way out, they paid The Sayer's fee to Tilda in US dollars. She gave them their change in more of the gold and silver $1 Bad Captain Billy's pirate doubloons. They exited The Sayer ?'s compound and headed back to the raft, although they never passed any symposium guests coming in.

As they approached the underground river, JJ blurted out, "I need to go back. I forgot something."

Izzy glanced at JJ and said, "Oh yeah. Me too. I'm coming with you."

The two hurried back to The Sayer ?'s compound.

Skipper Zack shrugged at Statistic, as if to say, "I wonder what that is all about?"

They waited patiently for about sixty seconds before Statistic looked over at the skipper and said, "I'd better go with them to make sure they don't get sidetracked. Why don't you wait for us at the raft? I'll usher them along as quickly as possible."

Statistic went tearing off for the compound, all the way thinking, "I'm not sure what they forgot, but if they're asking the guru the questions I think they're going back to ask, I want to be there too!"

As Statistic came running up to the pagoda, Tilda waved him back to the guru. He joined JJ and Izzy just as they were sitting back down in front of The Sayer.

JJ asked the mystic, "I'm wondering what you know about the entrances into the Federated Lands. How many are there? And what is the story on the thought meters the guards had at the gate we came in through? I know you've travelled to all corners of the land. Can you shed any light on any of this?"

The Sayer ? smiled and nodded. "How many ways are there to get in, you ask? That I can't tell you with any certainty. But I *have* witnessed eight ways to get out. They're scattered around the lands. There are probably more. The exits are hard to find because they are more or less unmarked."

The guru took a deep breath and exhaled seemingly forever. He said, "You see, the Federated government doesn't want people coming in from outside the gates, and it doesn't want its citizens leaving either. That is why the guards are armed with the thought meters. It's to detect thoughts from outside our world. Alien thoughts. The meters are very old. They come from a time when these lands were first settled, centuries ago. The meters are the lone relics still in use that date back from before the war. The meters were necessary at that time, because our land had been infiltrated by alien invaders. These barbarians carried with them thoughts of greed and power. You see, these were not natural thoughts. They were an alien behavior. To this day, the gates are carefully guarded to ensure the protection of our citizens."

The Sayer ? paused again to let everything he had explained sink in. He could see the bewildered looks in the eyes of JJ, Izzy, and Statistic. After a moment of silence, the mystic went on, "Still, every once in a while someone gets by security. You gentlemen are examples of these breaches, although *I* feel safe near you. But there are some out there who believe that a few of these aliens have been able to secretly imbed themselves amongst us with evil agendas in mind. These people believe the intruders' unnatural thoughts have already infected our government. Personally, I don't know about that, but I *am* pretty sure that outsiders have taken over the brains of some of the leaders of the big businesses and banks in Boomtown."

The Sayer ? took another deep breath and said, "That is all I can really say about the questions you brought before me. I don't have any more time anyway. I *must* start preparing for the symposium now. That will be another fifty bucks. Please pay Tilda on your way out. Thank you and goodbye."

On the way back to the raft, the guys didn't talk much. And they still didn't pass any symposium guests coming in. They were all thinking to themselves about what the mystic had said. Within a few minutes they had reconvened with the skipper at the raft. The group soon drifted back into the Seaside station. JJ, Statistic, and Izzy talked to Skipper Zack for a few minutes while he moored at the dock. After settling up with the skipper, and bidding farewell, they quickly headed back to Seaside, running just a few minutes late.

15

A Turn of the Tables

When the group reached the Seaside Inn courtyard, Frank was seated at the bistro, waiting for them. He was enjoying a cup of coffee, and hadn't been sitting there for long. "So I understand you guys have already had a long day," Frank said as JJ, Izzy, and Statistic walked up.

"Yeah," said JJ. "The map was amazing up close, and the whole trip was very enlightening. Now that we're back, though, I'm ready to vacation the rest of the day! I'm ready to go all-out doing nothing but relaxing. Did you get a good night sleep? It sounds like you and the bedbugs have been getting along fine."

Frank acknowledged that he had slept well and was ready for a big day. He was happy to hear JJ was finally ready to separate himself from responsibility, even if it was only for half a day. They were all hungry, so they decided to stroll down to the waterfront and have brunch at a water front café at the marina. They were soon seated at a dock-front table, enjoying the view. They were surprised to see Captain Gruzzly at the dock, mooring a brand new ferryboat. The captain had christened it the "Grace II."

Izzy called out to the captain, "Hey Captain, come sit down with us and tell us about your new boat."

The captain walked over and joined them and said, "I only have a few minutes, mates."

"Captain Gruzzly, why did you buy a new ferry? The old one seemed perfectly seaworthy," asked JJ.

"It was very difficult to say goodbye to her. She was like family to me. We went through a lot, me and her, the peaceful seas and the rough storms. We sailed through them all together." The nostalgic thoughts were causing the captain to tear up a little. "She seemed just fine on the outside, but it turned out she was in bad, bad shape on the inside. By the time her inner mechanics stopped working regularly, it was too late. I towed her to the boat shop and they said there was nothing they could do."

"We're all sorry to hear about your loss," Izzy said in an understanding tone. At least you have a brand new boat now, though. Hopefully insurance paid for it. It looks expensive."

"Aye, the insurance company paid for it, but they were also the problem to begin with. They would rather pay claims for total losses and expensive, lengthy repairs, than pay a little bit up front for preventive maintenance. There's only one way to identify the problems on the inside, and it's not waiting until things start failing on the outside. If only they would have allowed me to take her in more often for regularly scheduled checkups and diagnostic tests," Captain Gruzzly shook his head and continued, "She'd still be with me today." The captain paused again, and added, "But that's the way the system works, so I just have to live with it."

JJ and Izzy glanced at each other because they noticed both Frank and Statistic were tearing up too, just a little. But no one wanted to talk about it, apparently. JJ asked, "Captain Gruzzly, can we travel with you and the rest of the Seaside delegation to the EcoSummit tomorrow? We've decided to stay for one more day so we can attend. I hear it's being held at a place called The Meadows."

"Of course you can come. It's a fair distance away, so be ready to leave early tomorrow. We're meeting at Town Hall at six in the morning. We'll see you there, mates." The captain stood up and headed back to his new ferry.

When they were done eating, JJ paid their check at the cafe. The cashier paid the change with a handful of colorful $1 notes, most of which were shiny gold and silver Bad Captain Billy's doubloons. JJ looked at the notes, and then looked at his friends, and said, "We should probably plan on hitting Bad Captain Billy's for dinner tonight, since this is our last night out. Between the four of us, we're accumulating quite a few of these doubloons. They may just be coupons redeemable for food and drinks."

"It doesn't really matter, does it?" asked Izzy. "As long as everybody honors them. I mean, food and drinks are more than our US dollars are backed by, so I'll take all the shiny doubloon coupons we can get. Bad Captain Billy's sounds good to me."

After brunch they headed off to play golf, and JJ and Izzy finally had a great time enjoying themselves all afternoon. When they were done with golf, they headed to the restaurant district. They went to souvenir shops and restaurants. They did all the things that tourists normally do on vacation.

While they were walking by the restaurants, Izzy said, "We all need to get plenty of souvenirs. I want to get my wife and kids some tee shirts. Hopefully they won't ask where any of them came from, though. It would be *very* hard to explain!"

"That's a great idea!" said Frank excitedly. "I hope Bad Captain Billy's has them in 2X."

"Yeah, let's go to The Rowdy Crab too," Statistic added. "I want a tee shirt and a baseball cap. And I'd also love to get a Sand-Witch Doctor tee shirt."

JJ seconded that idea. "I definitely want one of those. And on the way home I'd like to get one from that stupid mountain general store we couldn't find to begin with. I wanted to get some more postcards there too. I was looking at the store's shirts the night we got there. They had plenty of 2X's, Frank. One of them said "Lose Yourself at Cabin Mountain Park."

"Very funny. Do you mean they had resort cabins there to begin with? Now I'm really not laughing."

"Don't forget we still have one long day left," reminded JJ. "I, for one, am really looking forward to the EcoSummit tomorrow. I'll stay out late with you guys tonight, but not too late. We need to remember it will be a long hike back home after the EcoSummit."

"Yeah," Izzy agreed. "I want to make sure we still have time to see Yucca's land on the way home too."

They decided to head straight to Bad Captain Billy's, which was only a block up ahead. But when they approached the establishment, Frank and Statistic were surprised to see that the name had changed to "Bad Captain Billy's Mutiny." They were all very curious about what may have precipitated the abrupt name change. They walked in and seated themselves at a good spot next to the window.

As the waiter walked up to their table, Frank immediately ordered. "We'd like a full round of what Statistic and I were drinking last night, and a couple of those seafood appetizer platters to get started."

The waiter replied, "Are you sure it wasn't two nights ago? Anyway, you've got it. If you want to order entrees, though, we're only serving fried food tonight. The head cook had to leave early this evening."

"What made you decide to change your name to 'Bad Captain Billy's Mutiny'?" asked Statistic. "We were just here, and there was no 'Mutiny', just business as usual."

"I'll send over the new owner to explain," replied the waiter. He walked off, and could be seen talking with a professionally dressed woman seated at the bar. He pointed over towards JJ's table, and then walked back to the kitchen.

The new owner walked over to the friends' table, and asked, "Do you gentlemen mind if I join you for a minute? My name is Ms. Black. They're all calling me the new owner here, but I'm technically the new Chairwoman of the Board." They all welcomed her to sit down and join them, so she pulled up a chair. "I understand you are curious about our new name. Well, let me tell you the story. I have been a frequent customer here over the years, and this has always been my favorite eatery in Seaside. But the last few times I visited, the previous chairman and figurehead, Captain Billy III, was rude to me. He arrogantly treated me like just another tourist, which I actually was, of course, but he shouldn't have felt that way to begin with. I was a paying customer who made the choice to come here. But he acted like he chose me, not like I chose him. He talked down to me, and I overheard him doing the same to his own staff also, especially the cook. He seemed to only care about his own agenda, not caring about what should have been the real reason he was on the job: to serve his customers, the ones who put their faith in his restaurant, the ones who chose him. I was sitting at the bar, watching him behave badly, and thinking about how I would run things differently if I were in charge."

Ms. Black paused for a second, then continued, "That's when the barista explained to me that this was a publicly traded company. I've been looking to invest myself into something meaningful for a while, so I bought a majority of the stock in the company and performed a hostile takeover. All it took was 50.1%. I fired the old board of directors and brought in my own crew. The previous board was just a bunch of shriveled up old men who felt most comfortable with the status quo, happy with business as usual. It was almost as if they had been brainwashed through the years. The investors in the corporation were so profit-driven that they forgot what Bad Captain Billy's business even was, what had made it profitable to begin with, and why the generations of customers loved the place so much. I made Captain Billy walk the plank, so to speak, but I didn't keelhaul him. I knew he was just a grumpy old liberal stuck in his ways, and was unable to consider other points of view than his own. I was sure he'd adjust to life outside the public eye just fine. I knew he had a nice little treasure chest stashed away from his years at the helm, not to mention what his father, the original Bad Captain Billy, left him."

Chairwoman Black looked off into the distance briefly, and then went on, "You know, I've noticed something through the years. When a man is in a position of power, it twists his way of thinking about money. Wealth gravitates towards him. Many people who have earned their power forget that they got where they are by pursuing their wealth, which is the honest way to achieve it. When it's the other way around, when money pursues people, those lost souls have no understanding as to its true value, especially if their wealth is inherited to begin with."

Chairwoman Black paused again for a second, realizing she was ranting just a little. But she could also see the knowing smiles on the faces of JJ, Izzy, Statistic, and even Frank, as they listened to her story. She toned it down somewhat as she continued on with her story, "Anyway, when I took control, I wanted to add my own personal touches, while keeping the brand value in Bad Captain Billy's name. So accordingly, I tweaked the restaurant's name to set an edgy new tone for the business. I kept all of the original staff, and I'm leaving everything on the menu, but adding some daring new entrees and drinks. And we have some interesting new tee shirts to go with the traditional designs."

"Are you honoring the old Bad Captain Billy's $1 pirate doubloons?" asked JJ. "We have quite a few of them."

A pained expression swept across Ms. Black's face, and she answered, "Yes, they're still good. I'm not going to devalue them. You see, Captain Billy III liked flashy, gimmicky promotions, especially the trick of quantitative pleasing and teasing. He printed a large quantity of those pirate doubloon coupons. He said he did it to please the customers, but I think all it did was tease the board into thinking that our business was busier than it really should have been. All I know for sure is that it will take me years to clean up this mess." At that point the waiter came back with the drinks and was ready to take the orders for the entrees. Chairwoman Black got up to leave and said, "Thanks for asking me over, gentlemen. I hope you enjoy your meals, and thanks for choosing Bad Captain Billy's Mutiny."

Izzy spoke up. "Ms. Black, Please feel free to sit longer, if you'd like. We're not your normal tourists, and we'd be interested in hearing more.

It's not like we need our privacy or anything."

So Chairwoman Black delightedly sat back down, as JJ began reflecting on their journey. "It's actually been a fun vacation in a weird way, hasn't it? I'm choosing to look on the bright side. We met a new friend, Statistic. We met some interesting characters and helped them sort out some of their problems. We met the Economist, and Yucca, and Yucan the Toucan. And we got to see that the politics in other places are just as complicated as they are at home."

"Yeah, every bit as frictious," agreed Frank, who was finally warming up to the whole ordeal. "And we certainly fit in all your hiking too, JJ. You got a lot more walking out of me than I was planning on doing, that's for sure!"

Up until then, JJ and the guys had been somewhat oblivious to the parties seated next to them, but as soon as JJ and Izzy finished talking, members from the two adjacent tables, both three-tops, jumped up to greet them. The first to reach JJ's table was one of the three young men from the Seaside Inn bistro who had the Bigfoot flashlight. He reached out to shake everyone's hands and energetically said, "My brother and our friend and I would like to introduce our selves, and ask you a few questions."

But before he could continue, a young woman from the other table butted in and reached out in front of him to shake Statistic's hand, and said, "Hi. It's me again, Nan100. My two friends and I are here on vacation, and we're staying at the Seaside Inn." Nan100 looked at Statistic and then at Frank, and refreshed their memory, "I'm the one who overheard a conversation at the Seaside bistro you had with a man identifying himself as the 'Economist'. The questions he was asking didn't sound like normal questions. My friends felt the same way. The Economist kept jotting down what you were telling him, but he was treating you like just another statistic. It seemed like he didn't even know your name." Nan100 looked around suspiciously, then added, "Or even seemed to care."

The young man jumped back into the hand-shaking logjam, and said, "As I was beginning to explain, we've been shadowing the Economist, and we noticed the same oddities. I'm sorry that I can't give you our real names while we're working undercover. We'll have to use our aliases. I'm Assiduous1935, my brother is Impetuous1935, and our friend is Chum1313. We spied the Economist snooping around in our hometown, Port Manteaux, which is the town on the other side of the bay. He was asking our local residents strange questions and was looking for some sort of clues to a big mystery. His degree of complexion was of particular suspicion to me. He seemed edgy, but relaxed and calm, and yet he was sweating too, all at the same time. Very mysterious. We've been following the Economist for two days now, keeping an eye on him, and trying to figure out what this big mystery is all about. We've noticed that he has a keen interest in your group's actions. It seems he is most interested in your cactus friend who isn't with you tonight. And what's more, we think he may have been trying to retrace your path here to Seaside, possibly to find out where your cactus friend resides. We're also fairly certain that he's spreading bedbugs around as he travels, but so far the evidence for that is only circumstantial. Can you tell us anything about this Economist?"

Before anyone could answer, Nan100, who had been rolling her eyes as Assiduous1935 gave Frank his group's code names, interjected, "We arrived at the same conclusions. He also seems to be searching for a restaurant with good Mexican food."

Assiduous1935 blurted, "That part is not so suspicious to me. I'm tired of all this seafood. I'd like to find a good Mexican joint myself."

"Me too!" chimed in his jovial friend, who had ambled over next to him. Chum1313 looked at Frank and asked, "Perhaps if you and the ladies don't mind, we could all turn our tables together, so we can join you?" Everyone agreed, and they swiveled the tables side by side, so that all three groups were now seated together.

Frank excitedly surveyed everyone moving over to sit with them, and exclaimed, "Now, this is starting to look like my kind of dinner party!"

Chairwoman Black, who had been silently watching and listening as the conversations unfolded between the three parties, looked at Frank and said, "I'm not sure if I'd call it a dinner party just yet." Then she looked at everyone else at the table and said, "Thanks for asking me to join you, but I need to get back to work now. Thanks again for choosing Bad Captain Billy's Mutiny!" Then she stood up and walked back over to her original seat at the bar and began discussing business issues with the barista, while also keeping one eye on JJ's group.

After Ms. Black left the table, Frank looked over to Statistic, and said, "I hope you'll join us on our next vacation, which had better be to Myrtle Beach." But he noticed Statistic was looking sullen all of a sudden. "Is something the matter? You're acting quieter than normal."

"I'm okay. That sounds great. It's been an unexpected, but much needed, getaway for me too, and I'd love to go to Myrtle Beach with you," Statistic said, looking at Frank. He was quiet for a few seconds, and then continued, making it a point to speak to the new members of the party as well. "It's just that some of the things I've seen and heard since I've been with you guys has made me think about things in a different way than I had before, and it's really bothering me. There is something about being so far from home right now that has allowed me to see the big picture in sharp focus. And taken as a whole it's a frightening evolution."

"What do you mean, exactly?" asked JJ.

"Well, for example, is it possible that our government at home has inserted itself too far into our lives? And is it possible that this has happened over such a long period of time, over generations, that no one has even noticed it? Or thought it was peculiar? It's profound to a level I had never considered. I mean, we've all fussed about specific issues, like taxes. It's easy to complain about how much fairer the system is to everyone else. But is it possible that all of this government involvement in our lives is what in itself causes so much bickering between various classes and regions of people? Maybe the different segments of our society are all suffering from a government-imposed "The Grass is Always Greener Syndrome." Human nature is bound to take over when the government takes away trillions of dollars from us all, and then arbitrarily decides how to divvy it back up."

JJ, Frank, and Izzy were all looking at each other in a knowing kind of way. Nan100, Assiduous1935, and all of their young friends were all busily scribbling down notes. When they were done scribbling, they looked at Statistic, waiting for him to finish his lecture.

Statistic leaned forward and continued, "For example, Yucca's take on social security may have been absurd, but the fact is families, even entire communities, did used to take care of the elderly and the ill. And they did what they could for the poor and for their less fortunate neighbors. The strong and fortunate citizens didn't complain about the others not carrying their fair share, like they do today. They reached out their hands to help. And everyone, even the poor, knew they were expected to contribute whatever they were physically and mentally able to contribute to the community cause. The social norm being what it was, people were much more responsible with their actions. They kind of had to show the rest of the world that they were holding their own to the best of their abilities."

Statistic paused for a moment, and as Nan100 and Assiduous1935 caught up with their jotting, he continued, "I suspect there once existed a sense of human dignity that doesn't exist any longer. A dignity that folks wouldn't even understand today. A dignity that a person would have earned knowing there was no government safety net. A dignity that one's neighbors would have understood had been earned. I'm not saying it was easy living back then. It was a much harder life than we have now. I know it and you know it. But people did it on their own, making their decisions for themselves along the way. The government didn't think for them. People had their own ideas, and they elected government to act in their behalf, not to dictate or control their lives. Now government makes many of our decisions for us, and rules every facet of the way we live. We work to support the government now, not the other way around. They impose burdensome restrictions on us, even criminalizing citizens for exercising liberties that our founding fathers would have thought we'd be taking for granted now. In fact, I'll bet that if our founding fathers were alive today, they'd be leading the charge for a whole new revolution."

JJ and Izzy looked at each other, nodding their heads. Statistic's eyes surveyed the crowd listening in, and he silently wondered, "Did I just screw up, saying something that I believe, for once? Maybe if I have something of importance to say, people will listen even if I don't call them out by name."

After a minute of silence, Statistic's words had fully sunk in. JJ finished Statistic's speech, "But now the government has become our social safety net. It has become our family. And our family tree has been taken over by a small club of extremely greedy, wealthy uncles who only care about themselves. They know they can control the family by using the family tree itself to drive wedges between all of us. They intentionally create family rifts and feuds to keep us focused on anything but the big picture. When we disagree with them, they say we don't love our family. They have pulled off this "Grand Coup" right before the eyes of our selves, our parents, and our grandparents. And they never called any of us by name, so we weren't paying attention."

Everyone seated at the table looked at each other in an awkward silence, contemplating what had just been said. Eventually Nan100 stood up and announced, in a very indignant tone, "If what you are trying to imply is that my parents ever let anyone pull the wool over their eyes, then you'd better think again. My Dad is one of the best people around at analyzing the clues of nefarious behavior. Come on girls, let's get away from these nuts."

As Nan100 was finishing her scolding, one of the brothers immediately stood up and agreed, "I feel exactly the same way. Our Dad is one of the foremost detectives of dubious character around. He never would have let any of the villains you describe dupe him in such a large caper." At that point all of the new guests at the table were standing up and turning their backs to leave. The brothers' friend became the exact opposite of jovial and moved the other two tables as far away as he could from JJ, Frank, Izzy, and Statistic.

After another moment of silence, Frank jumped up and announced, "I guess they didn't realize you guys were talking about the world you live in, not the one they live in. I'm not sure I live in the same world as you either, because they're right, you know. You guys are nuts. But I already knew that, and I love you anyway. It's time to pick out the tee shirts. Come on, I'm buying. We're all going to take something home from this trip!"

They went over to the souvenir counter and chose their Bad Captain Billy's Mutiny tee shirts, and then returned to their seats. They spent another hour or more sitting at the table reminiscing about everything they had done and seen so far on their vacation. When the waiter brought the final check for the night, JJ and Frank fought over who got to pick up the tab. They decided it was only fitting to decide it by playing "pen, sword, dollar." Frank played a dollar and JJ played a pen.

"I think that means I win," Frank claimed. "Which way is the wind blowing?"

Izzy was the judge. "Tonight the dollar wins. So Frank, you get to pay. We'll see about tomorrow."

16

The Turn Signals

The next morning, JJ, Izzy, Frank, and Statistic were all up early and ready to go, as planned. They checked out of the Seaside Inn, grabbed an early breakfast, and headed down to Town Hall. Captain Gruzzly, the Witch Doctor, the Mayor, and the two others who comprised Seaside's delegation were waiting patiently for JJ's group. The friends arrived on time, and all ten embarked for the EcoSummit. Once they reached the cave, everyone pulled out their flashlights. Luckily, the previous guests in JJ's room at the Seaside Inn had left two extra "How to Spot Bigfoot" flashlights behind, so JJ now had three of them, which he shared with Frank and Statistic.

Not long after they had begun their trek, Izzy struck up a conversation with the Witch Doctor. "Doctor, I may have mentioned this before when we ate at your restaurant, but during our travels, I came upon an ancient map that details the Federated Lands. I think it dates back from before the lands were federated, before the war. Do you know anything about the war?"

This got the attention of the Mayor also, who was eager to listen to what the Witch Doctor might know about the matter. The Witch Doctor was startled at first, but then looked at Izzy with an eerie look in his eyes and replied, "The War is something that people don't know much about. It's the first paragraph in grade school books now, but the books don't explain what actually happened. Or why. All I know is the lore that was passed down to me from my granddad. He was also a man of medicine. The Witch Doctor thought about it for a moment, and then said, "I'd like to see your map with my own eyes."

"Me too," echoed the Mayor.

Izzy showed the Witch Doctor his map while they continued to walk. The doctor studied it intently for two full minutes, nodding his head the whole time. When he was done, he handed it to the Mayor. Izzy waited until the Witch Doctor was done looking, then asked, "Where would one go to learn more about the war? Can you tell me what you do know?"

"After the EcoSummit, I'll tell you the little bit that I know about it," replied the Witch Doctor. "The only place I can think to go is the library at the college. You might find something there, or someone that knows other things than I know. Some of the professors there are the types that remember everything they've ever heard, and more. The college is Oceania University in Port Manteaux. It's not far from Seaside."

As the Mayor was studying the map, the Witch Doctor continued to ponder the subject. When the Mayor handed the notebook back to Izzy, the Witch Doctor began to speak in a substantially eerier voice than he had used previously. "Izzy, I'm sure there are clues that will help you learn more about the war, even if you can't find a full accounting of it somewhere. See, every man and woman of substance leaves behind a piece of him or her self wherever they go. Usually this trace is so minute that it only becomes evident upon very close examination. Sometimes it is quite obvious. Either way, it's there. This trail is called their 'xyzacta'. All the people involved in the war left their xyzactas somewhere. You'll uncover the whole story if you look close enough for the clues." The Witch Doctor paused for a second, then continued, "The problem is this: Every great person leaves a great xyzacta behind them. And every great person is followed by a hoard of lesser men and women. Each of these lesser people takes it upon themselves to try to dissolve the great xyzactas of their predecessors and replace them with their own xyzactas. Izzy, your challenge will be to sort through the strata of xyzactas to get at the truth."

Everyone had been listening intently to the Witch Doctor. A minute of silence elapsed. Then Statistic asked the Witch Doctor, "So a xyzacta is the same thing as a legacy, isn't it?"

"No!" shot back the Witch Doctor. "A person's legacy is part of their xyzacta, but a legacy is written and spoken. A legacy is the fodder historians speak of. A *xyzacta* is more than a legacy. It's an energy sequence. It's a radiant signature that we all leave behind wherever we've been. A xyzacta is something you feel, something you *know*. It's not something to be read or heard. Sometimes you can see it, but often it's invisible. A xyzacta is a ghost and a ghost is a xyzacta."

Clearly, no one really had a clue what the Witch Doctor was talking about, no matter how closely they were listening. Most everyone in the group looked at each other and shrugged.

The Witch Doctor told Izzy, "Just because *they* don't get it, doesn't mean it's not true. I'll explain the xyzacta to you in more detail later, when I'm telling you about the war."

Izzy nodded and thanked the Witch Doctor for his efforts.

The delegation proceeded onward for at least another hour through the dark cave. Eventually a voice came from Captain Gruzzly's backpack, "Are we there yet? Are we there yet? It's quite uncomfortable back here."

The Mayor and the rest of the group all stopped and looked at Captain Gruzzly, who sheepishly explained, "They really wanted to be a part of things. Come on out guys." He opened the flap on his backpack, and the Crab and the Lobster both peeked out.

The mayor smiled, shook his head at Captain Gruzzly, and commented, "I asked for local characters, and characters is what I got. It's too late to turn back now, whether it's a good idea for them to come or not." The Mayor turned back around and kept walking, shaking his head.

They walked through the cave for the first half of the morning, and the cave started to get taller and more wide as they edged closer and closer to the summit. The walls of the cave were becoming increasingly full of graffiti too. There wasn't much older wall painting to be seen, mostly modern works that bordered more on being vandalism than art. They had to walk slower than normal due to quite a bit of congestion up ahead, even though the cave was now wide enough for three or four people to walk side by side, going in each direction. As the foot traffic became clogged up, some of the travelers were starting to become un-hinged and were bordering on a state of cave rage. They trudged along. The Mayor suggested, "Don't start tailgating. We left in plenty of time to get there on schedule. Let's all act respectful of our fellow travelers. The last thing we need today is any accidents or unfortunate incidents. We might get hassled by the police since we're from out-of-land."

They came to a long down grade and could finally see up ahead what was slowing everybody up: Left lane blockers!

Frank exclaimed, "Oh great! This is just what we need: People out for their weekend stroll. And they're walking right next to a group of right lane blockers!"

They could see the impatient cave traffic trying their best to weave around the lane blockers, and even the Mayor was getting antsy.

Finally they made it up to the lane blockers, but just as they were weaving around them, they came up on a row of turnstiles. The cave was now quite wide, at least twenty feet, and it was a good twelve feet high. Starting at this juncture there was also overhead lighting to il-luminate the whole cave, so the Seaside delegation was able to turn off their flashlights. There was a big sign overhead hanging from the cave ceiling that read "Cavepike", and another that read, "Last Exit Before Toll." They all looked at each other, puzzled.

Captain Gruzzly muttered, "There's got to be a side cave we can take. Maybe we should exit."

"No", The Mayor explained, "This will be faster. I'll put it on the city expense account, so don't worry about the Feds taking their toll."

But just as they had all passed through the turnstiles and taken their tickets, the local Division of Cave Transportation police inspectors pulled the group aside.

One of the DOCT inspectors asked, "You weren't thinking about avoiding inspection by taking the back caves around the cavepike, were you?" Next he pointed at JJ's boots and said, "Sir, do your shoes comply with section 1398a.bc of the Federated Footwear Safety Inspection Code? I'd like to see your logbook."

JJ meekly answered, "I don't know. What's a logbook?"

Frank reprimanded JJ, "I *told* you just to wear sneakers, but no, you *had* to have professional gear."

Another inspector pointed at The Witch Doctor and barked, "Are those bones on your vest indigenous, or are they from an exotic protected species? If they are from an endangered species, you're in big trouble, but if we've already killed the species off, then that's just fine."

"They're plastic! They're just replicas." he explained in an agitated voice.

The officer was steadfast and said in a monotone voice, "And you don't have a license to carry counterfeit bones into this jurisdiction, do you? We've dealt with your type before."

The Witch Doctor just glared back, a bevy of curses beginning to brew in his head.

"Ok, you two (the inspector motioned at JJ and The Witch Doctor) will need to come with me to the office. The rest of you are free to continue on."

"Lets go," said the Mayor. "They can catch up. We need to make sure most of us are there on time."

The inspectors escorted JJ and The Witch Doctor into the police office and up to the front desk. Seated behind the desk, a female officer was busy writing an important communiqué for her subordinate, who was standing and waiting. Looking past JJ and the Witch Doctor, she addressed the inspectors. "I'll be with you in just a minute, officers."

One of the inspectors replied, "Take your time, I'm on the clock."

"Me too," added the other inspector. "I only have one year and twelve days remaining until I retire with *my* pension. I can wait as long as you want."

The Witch Doctor was starting to twitch and rub his plastic beads anxiously. The desk officer smiled at the inspectors, nodded in solidarity, and handed the communiqué to her underling and asked, "Do you have any questions?"

The junior officer studied the communiqué carefully and replied, "I can't read your handwriting very well. Does this say toasted or roasted? And I *know* they're going to ask if you want fries or onion rings."

The desk officer angrily looked down over her glasses and tersely replied, "It's the same thing I get every day, you moron. Toasted, with onion rings. Now get going."

She was still shaking her head when she turned to the inspectors and said, "Can *you believe* what I have to put up with? It's getting harder to do this job every day, Inspector. I'm envious you're retiring next year. It's as if all these new guys think everything comes to them for free or something. Where do they think their paychecks come from, anyway? Can't they see I have a job to do here? They new ones are always thinking, that's the problem." She nodded towards JJ and The Witch Doctor and continued, "Now what do we have here?"

The inspectors explained the situations. The desk officer looked like she didn't feel like dealing with the tasks at hand, but was also clearly a professional. She looked stonily through JJ and said, "If you're guilty of these infractions, you're looking at one week's incarceration at best. If you don't want to be found in violation, you'll need to do the following legwork. You can't leave this precinct until you've done one or the other. To walk on, you'll need to take your shoes to the Department of Footwear Inspection, where you'll need to obtain a copy of form 21398A.BC and return an approved copy in triplicate. You'll also need a variance, form # 2355A.BC from the Customs Department. To get to The Department of Footwear Inspections, turn left at the next corridor, pass 13 doors on the right, and then turn left at the next corridor.

It will be the third office on the left. From there, turn right, go down eight doors on the left, and turn right again. The Customs Department will be the next door on the left. Bring those signed forms back to me and you'll be all set, assuming your footwear is in compliance."

The desk officer then turned to the Witch Doctor, and explained, "Now Mr. Doctor, the same scenario applies to you, except you're looking at two weeks in jail, or a $20,0000 fine. You'll need form #45732A. BC from the Federated Textile Inspections Department and form #24451A.BC from The Office of Trade Compliance. Both forms need to be signed off by the inspectors and returned to me in triplicate. To get to the Textile Inspections Department, turn left, then go to the end of the corridor. Then take a right and pass 12 doors on the right, then take your next left. It will be the second office on the left. From there, turn right and continue down the corridor until you get to the dead end, and then turn left. Take the first elevator you see to the second floor, turn right, then take your first left, and The Office of Trade Compliance will be the first office on the right."

JJ headed off to the Department of Footwear Inspection. Meanwhile, the Witch Doctor completed his first step at the Textile Inspections Department after a long wait. He was the only one in line, but had to sit while the officers completed a large batch of communiqués. Then he headed to The Office of Trade Compliance. He was thinking to himself, "Did she say 'take the elevator to the second floor, then turn right, then take the next left, or did she say take the second elevator on the right to the second floor, then turn left?" The Witch Doctor then proceeded to wander around the bureaucratic maze for thirty minutes until he found himself back at The Textile Inspections Department, where he stopped for directions. Just as he finally arrived at The Office of Trade Compliance, an inspector posted a sign on the door that read "Closed for Lunch 12-1"

"Damn!" exclaimed The Witch Doctor. He decided to go down and wait in the lobby for JJ so he could explain that he had to wait until one o'clock. JJ returned a few minutes later and handed his completed paperwork to the inspector at the desk. She took one look at the forms and said, "Oh I'm sorry. I see now that form 2355A.BC has an updated version, form 2355A.BC.AD. You'll need to go back to The Customs Department for the correct variance after lunch. They'll reopen at one. Oh, and you'll need a copy of your general liability certificate from your local agent as well."

JJ sat down in the lobby next to the Witch Doctor, thoroughly dejected. He was wracking his brain to come up with an idea to streamline his paperwork through inspections when he noticed the first door in the hall behind the desk officer's office. The sign on the door read, "Federated Prisons, Cavepike Substation." On the wall next to the door was a two foot round meter, which was identical to the Federated Incarceration Rate gauge he had dreamed about two nights earlier. The arrow was pointing towards the "Arrest a Few More" heading, and wavering a little. "Hey wait a minute," JJ was thinking. "I thought that was a dream. I wonder if Izzy..." He broke off his own thought and shook his head and muttered out loud, "That just *couldn't* be." But it certainly wasn't helping to ease his anxiety at all, either.

JJ looked beside himself, at the Witch Doctor specifically, who was busy deciding which evil voodoo curses to place on each of the government employees. The Doctor had overheard JJ mutter to himself, and said, "Strange things happen in government offices, JJ. I wouldn't be shocked about anything you see here. The truth is probably stranger than you can imagine."

But just then, JJ had an idea. He addressed the desk cop, "Ma'am, my friend, the Witch Doctor has a VIP Delegation pass for the Eco-Summit. Doesn't that give us diplomatic immunity?"

"Are you traveling with him?"

"Yes." JJ replied.

"Oh, in that case you can both travel freely and break any laws at all, just use your best discretion, of course. Goodbye."

JJ jumped out of his seat and urged The Witch Doctor along. "We need to hurry to get caught up with the rest of the group."

They rushed back out into the cavepike, and luckily the traffic flow was walking along smoothly. They were able to maintain a steady pace for ten minutes, which was putting them more at ease, and less worried about arriving late to the summit. They hit a long, straight downgrade, and JJ could see up ahead that several cavepike patrolmen had set up a speed trap. The policemen were pulling over travelers on a regular basis. As they got closer, they could see that each person that was pulled over had to go straight to a temporary police desk, which was positioned right at the side of the cave. Behind that desk was another temporary desk with a sign overhead that read "Clerk of Traffic Court Cashier." When they were about to reach the checkpoint, JJ saw that one of the patrolmen was counting each traveler as they passed, "One, two, three, ..."

The Witch Doctor got to the speed trap first, with JJ right behind him. The patrolman counted, "...thirteen." He pointed to the Witch Doctor and ordered, "Step aside sir. You're being charged with walking too fast or too slow. Go to the desk to receive your traffic ticket, then proceed to the cashier to pay your fine."

The Witch Doctor, who was already quite fed up with police in general, started cursing them. JJ jumped to the Witch Doctor's defense, "He didn't do anything wrong. We're just going with the flow of traffic. You just singled him out as number thirteen, for some reason."

The officer responded authoritatively, "Look buddy, every thirteenth traveler needs to plead guilty to walking too fast or too slow. He's obviously guilty of one or the other, or else he wouldn't be number thirteen. He has no defense, so he needs to step aside and pay his debt to society. And you'd better curb your insubordination, or I'll ticket you too. You should be respectful and appreciative of the job we public servants do protecting you citizens by upholding law and order. These court fines pay our salaries. What would you ever do without us here to protect you from the thieves?"

"I'm not being insubordinate," responded JJ, who was thinking to himself, "Contemptuous maybe, but not insubordinate." He nodded at the Witch Doctor, who had just finished his curses, and told the patrolman, "My friend has diplomatic immunity anyway."

The police officer became infuriated and said, "In that case, *you're* number thirteen!"

"No, I have diplomatic immunity too," JJ replied insolently.

The patrolman's face turned beet red, and he bellowed, "Just get out of here and stop wasting *my* time! Can't you see I have citizens to serve here!" Then he pulled over the next guy in line as JJ and the Witch Doctor hurried off.

Unfortunately they didn't get far before the cavepike became very backed up. After walking at a snail's pace for ten minutes, they hit a bottleneck and slowed down to a crawl. It took them ten more minutes to advance far enough to see what the problem was: They were stuck in a cave construction zone. The cave workers had coned off most of the path, so everybody had to walk through single file. But when they reached the cones, they could see no one was even working! JJ muttered, "Cave construction on a holiday. Typical government decision."

When they finally reached the group of construction workers, JJ and The Witch Doctor became incensed to see that the hardhats were just sitting cave side, playing cards. JJ cried out to the workers, "What are you thinking? It's a Federated holiday. Everybody's using the cave system today to get to the EcoSummit! And you're not even doing anything!"

The foreman gruffly barked back, "Take it easy, mister. We had to cone off the zone for the pavers coming in tomorrow."

"Couldn't you have waited until tomorrow for that?" asked JJ.

"Of course not. We get paid double time for working on holidays."

The Witch Doctor started fiddling with his beads again and softly chanting some mumbo-jumbo. JJ was quietly thinking, "I wonder what they get paid for *not* working on holidays?"

17

The Turn Out

JJ and the Witch Doctor eventually arrived at The Meadows not too much later than the rest of the Seaside group, who had also been stuck in the construction zone. A very large mob was building. Throngs of denizen from all of the Federated Lands were converging on the site of the EcoSummit. JJ and the Witch Doctor entered The Meadows through a large pair of ornate wrought iron gates at the top of the hill. They then fought through the crowd near the entrance until they could finally get a view of the landscape. The entrance was at the top of a gently sloping, grassy hill. It was a beautiful sunny day, so the scene developing below in the meadow was a particularly joyous sight to behold. The only buildings at The Meadows were a small, but stately, stone castle, and a large two story stone building. These structures were located to the left of the entrance and were built into the top of the hill, so that they overlooked the meadow. The building was to the right of the castle, and was apparently used as a conference center. JJ couldn't see the front of the castle, just its palladian window-lined backside. The two structures were attached, and formed an L shape.

A majestic stone veranda spanned the length of the castle's back wall and attached on the right to the conference building. In the center of the veranda there was a single lectern. Adjacent to the lectern was a small bleacher section, two rows high, which was large enough to seat about thirty dignitaries. Stretched over the veranda, raised high in the air, was a massive banner that read "Welcome to The EcoSummit." The lectern faced the spacious meadow, where there was room for thousands and thousands of guests. The meadow itself was fairly flat, so the elevated veranda formed a grand stage. The meadow was the size of four football fields put together, and the grounds had been freshly manicured for the event. It was lined most of the way around the edges with a forest of majestic old growth hardwoods, which were displaying their full array of green summer grandeur. Looking over the meadow, to the extreme left side, was a one hundred foot long break in the tree lining. Through that break was another massive meadow joining the main lawn. Directly in front of the pavilion there was a special section of seating with a sign next to it that read "VIP Delegation Seating." There were several hundred VIP seats, and behind this section was a twenty-foot wide pathway, with a temporary roped-off barrier separating it from the sprawling spectator gallery.

Thousands upon thousands of spectators were gathering in the gallery. The ones in front had probably been there since early morning. It was indeed a celebratory time. The buzz in the crowd was gleeful and incredulous. No one could believe that this day had actually come. The government was *finally* going to address the environmental issues that had plagued so many communities for so long! The crowd kept growing and growing. Critters and humans and birds and plants, hailing from all corners of the Federated Lands, were all crowding together. Down in the spectator gallery, they had to keep bunching closer and closer together as the mob continued to grow. Back at the top of the meadow, the throng became so large that the entrance gates were toppled! The police, who were trying to conduct an orderly attendance, gave up and retreated. No one, not even the Right Governor himself, could have ever envisioned *this* spirited of a turnout!

JJ and the Witch Doctor worked their way through the crowd, looking for the rest of the Seaside delegation. JJ had never seen such an array of creatures. But with everything he had been through all week, nothing would surprise him now. Gazing over the crowd, it appeared about half of those in attendance were human, but the other half most decidedly were not. JJ could see three-foot tall squirrels mingling with green flamingos. He saw five-foot tall praying mantises debating the issues with armadillos. There were even some creatures JJ had never seen the likes of before. He noticed the delegation from Boulder Gulch, which was just walking by. There were six lizards in the group, and one of them was Leon the Lizard.

JJ called out, "Hi Leon the Lizard! It's me, JJ. It's great to see you here! Which one of your friends is Leopold117 from Mesa 13?"

The lizard contingent stopped in front of JJ and the Witch Doctor, and Leon the Lizard answered, "I'm not Leon the Lizard right now. I'm Stanley6789." Then he pointed to Leopold117 and looked back at JJ and said, "But it's my pleasure to introduce you to the mastermind of our team, Leopold117."

Leopold117 cordially reached out to shake JJ's hand, but glanced back at Stanley6789 before turning back to face JJ, and said, "I'm not Leopold117 right now, I'm Leary4321. Stanley6789 and my other friends know this is the side of me that distrusts and questions authority. It's nice to meet you, JJ."

Stanley6789 replied to Leary4321, "I know the feeling. That's why I'm Stanley6789 today. I have diplomatic immunity today, so what the heck?"

After meeting the lizards, JJ and the Witch Doctor continued to fan through the crowd until the Witch Doctor stopped in his tracks and grabbed JJ's arm. He nodded towards a flamboyantly dressed group of eight sea gulls. The birds were much larger than the gulls JJ had ever seen before, standing a good four feet tall. They were walking parallel to JJ, about twenty feet away. Each was dressed in elaborate, brightly colored outfits, and each was dripping in flashy jewelry. The last one in line was wearing a gold crown. The Witch Doctor warned JJ, "Look out for those gulls. Be very careful what you do or say around them."

"Why?" asked JJ, who was shocked to see them so big, and walking instead of flying. "They're very large, but sea gulls are pretty harmless, aren't they? They can be annoying too, I guess. They do tend to flock around you at the beach if you pull some food out of your ice chest."

"Annoying would be putting it mildly," explained the Witch Doctor. "The sea gulls are the least imaginative beings around, but also the wealthiest. They've made a fortune by shamelessly copying other people's ideas. Whenever they see someone else enjoying a modicum of success with an original idea or endeavor, the gulls swoop in and mimic the concept detail for detail. Before you know it, they have mass-marketed the product at a lower cost and are racking up the profits. Most people try to shoo them away when they show up uninvited, but the gulls are very persistent. They just keep hovering around until they've amassed the numbers to swarm in and overwhelm their competition. They are quite proficient and prolific at their intellectual thievery. I'm sure they manufactured my fake bones, for example. And can you believe they opened a copy of my Sand-Witch Doctor's Hut in their land too? They came to my restaurant on a busy day last year, smelled the profits in the air, and then opened their own hut within days! The gull on the end wearing the gold crown is their leader, the Design Ferro."

Do you mean Design *Pharaoh*?" asked JJ.

"No, Ferro is what he calls himself," answered the Witch Doctor. "The gulls *are* good at inventing novel grammatical twists."

At that point, the first gull in line made an abrupt left turn, heading straight towards JJ. Each of the other gulls followed the lead bird, in perfect formation. The Witch Doctor panicked and grabbed JJ's arm again, urging him along in a different direction, out of the gulls' path. The Witch Doctor and JJ had only worked their way another thirty feet through the crowd before they bumped into the two gators from the swamp across the cave from Hillsville.

The gators were surprised to see JJ, and one of them said to the other, "Hey look Al, its one of those humans we scared the other day!"

Both gators started chuckling, but one turned to JJ and said, "You should have seen the look on your face! I'm sorry we scared you *that* bad, though. We realized after you ran off that you were probably from

Wacko World, and may not have been prepared for the shock. We're surprised you're here."

JJ, who was laughing himself, replied, "Frank and I had no idea what we had gotten ourselves into, that's for sure. But once we realized what was going on around here, we decided to stay and observe. What do you mean by 'Wacko World'?"

Gator 1 answered, "You *are* from outside the gate, right? Outside the gate is Wacko World. Nothing personal, but you guys are nuts! We sneak out every once in a while, and can't believe how archaic and il-logical *your* world is."

"I'll say!' added Gator 2, who began gnashing his teeth as he con-tinued. "We've noticed that the members of *your* society have a way of swallowing each other whole."

"I know what you mean," said JJ. "It's a dog-eat-dog world back home, that's for sure. But everything's relative, I guess. Where are the Bears?"

Gator 2 looked dejected, and answered, "They were arrested by a couple of revenuers that stopped by the swamp not long after you left. Those unlucky bears took all of our money playing poker. The revenuers walked up while the bears were counting it, and told them they had to pay taxes on their winnings. Suffice it to say, that when the Bears pulled their 'scare the humans routine,' it didn't set well with the revenuers. They came right back to our swamp with backup and took the bears away."

"Well I'm sorry to hear that about the bears, but good luck at the summit," wished JJ.

As he and the Witch Doctor wrapped up their conversation with the gators, Frank, Izzy, Statistic, and the Seaside delegation walked up. The Witch Doctor had been soaking up every word the gators were say-ing about Wacko World, and would have some questions for JJ about his world, once time allowed.

Upon reaching JJ, Izzy asked, "What happened with the police back in the cavepike? Apparently you thought your way through it."

"It was crazy. They have almost as much red tape and as many procedural hoops to jump through here as we have back home. I'll tell you about it later."

As JJ was answering, the Witch Doctor started murmuring and fidgeting with his bones again, just thinking about it.

The Joneses from Southrightmost County were marching in behind the Seaside delegation, and the Lobster and the Crab were bringing up Seaside's rear, right behind Captain Gruzzly. Mrs. Jones pointed to them and exclaimed to Mr. Jones, "Look at those cute, funny looking crawdads! I wonder if they play checkers too?"

The Lobster had a very indignant look splash across his face. He retorted, "*Crawdads*? *Checkers*? Ma'am, I am a Lobster. I am the most advanced crustacean in the family. Checkers is hardly befitting of someone with my intelligence. I play chess. And I certainly don't associate with *crawdads*."

The crab looked at the lobster and responded, "Stop bad-mouthing our southern cousins, you blue-blooded buffoon. You couldn't beat the crawdads or anybody else, at chess *or* checkers, even if they spotted you an extra king. Besides, cribbage is the true test of skill for distinguished seafaring gentlemen. I'll give you a lesson sometime."

Captain Gruzzly leaned down to the crab and lobster and said, "Will you two behave yourselves for once? This is an important event and we need to make a good impression."

Mrs. Jones wasn't amused by the antics of the lobster and crab. She turned to Mr. Jones and said, "Have you ever seen such unruly crawdads? And look at all of the odd looking creatures in this crowd. I hope none of them find out how quaint our town is and try to move in. We need to be careful what we say around here and we *really* need to press hard on the invasive species issue!" Then Mrs. Jones spotted some *real* crawdads working their way through the crowd. She pointed them out to Mr. Jones, and exclaimed, "Look how dignified *those* crawdads are.

They're even wearing cute matching orange suits!"

JJ and his friends looked over to where Mrs. Jones was pointing, and sure enough, there were eight crawdads walking in line two by two. The crawdads were following the two bears from the swamp, and they were all wearing orange prison suits, including the bears! The bears were clearly searching for the gators, and found them still standing near the Seaside delegation. JJ, nudged Frank, and said, "Come on, let's go hear what's going on."

The gators were relieved to see their friends, and one of the bears eagerly told them their story, "We were able to get out because we told the jailers we had diplomatic immunity since we're members of the Swamp delegation to the EcoSummit. As soon as we realized the ploy was actually working, we sprung eight of the crawdads with us. The jailers said ten was the size limit for delegations. But we're lucky they only arrested us for the tax issue, though."

The second bear took over the story from there. He looked at the gators and asked, "Remember the other night when we snuck out of the gate and had that party at the campground in Wacko World?"

Gators 1 and 2 both looked at each other nervously, glanced at JJ and Frank, and Gator 1 quickly muttered, "No, not really. It must have been some other gators you're thinking of."

The bear tried to refresh the gators' memory by adding, "Remember, we ate and drank everything in all the campground coolers? We danced on the picnic tables? While the possum played the accordion? Anything ring a bell?"

The gators both silently shook their heads "no."

"Yeah, right," said the bear. "Anyway, we heard through a jailhouse snitch that the Wacko World police pinned all that on Bigfoot!"

"And here's the kicker," the other bear said. "The Wacko World police arrested that camper that walked up and saw us do it. He's out on bail, but the police won't even consider his testimony! How lucky could we be?"

JJ had to apologize to Frank, "So you're off the hook from the other night. I guess Izzy and I should say we're sorry. You must have actually been very hungry the morning you got us lost. And you must not have been as hung-over, either. I guess you're just naturally inept at directions."

"Thanks for the apology, pal," Frank said, with a sarcastic grin, "You followed me, not Izzy, so think twice before you apologize for anything else."

Next, JJ turned to Izzy and Statistic, who had since joined him and Frank, and said, "Well guys, I guess we should leave the delegates alone now and start looking for some good seats where we can actually see what is going on when the summit starts."

Then JJ looked at the Mayor and the Seaside group and wished them the best of luck. As they were walking off, JJ said, "Lets go by the VIP section on the way down to the lawn. Maybe we'll see Yucca and Yucan the Toucan."

The Mayor rallied his delegation. They gathered together for a last minute pep talk. Once the Mayor had scoped out what a large event this was with his own eyes, a few last second ideas started to occur to him. He addressed his troops, "I think we should sit near the back. That way most of the delegations in front will have already spoken. That will give us time to figure out how the political winds are blowing before we speak. And another thing, in light of Seaside's recent bedbug infestation, we should probably take a more proactive stance on the invasive species issue than we had originally planned."

By that time, down below in the meadow, the spectator gallery was becoming so packed that there was barely room for anyone else to cram in. Then, within that sea of living beings, something unforeseeable began happening. Being in such close quarters, the spectators had no choice but to participate in *inter-special empathy!* Birds explained to humans why they need the trees. Trees explained to humans why they need clean soil and air. Humans explained to critters why they shouldn't poop on their lawns.

Meanwhile the VIP seating area began filling up as well. JJ, Frank, Izzy, and Statistic were nearing that section when they recognized Chairwoman Black walking next to them. She was wearing a VIP Delegate pass. "What are you doing here, Ms. Black?" JJ asked, surprised.

Ms. Black stopped and politely answered, "I sit on the board of a small eco-friendly startup company based out of Boomtown City. Boomtown opted to not field a delegation at the EcoSummit. I wouldn't call it a boycott. It's more like sheer arrogance. In fact, I think they may be the only land that is not participating. I felt I owed it to the stockholders to represent them in some way, since Boomtown isn't going to do it. So I applied for, and received, a special VIP variance. So here I am. I don't get to vote, but I can speak if I feel the need. Thanks for asking. Its good to see you guys again, but I need to run."

Ms. Black turned away to walk on, but as she did so she noticed Izzy had his notebook open. He had been sketching the crowd. She turned back to warn Izzy, "Be careful flashing your original work around here. You don't want to be gulled. I'm sure the sea gulls are lurking nearby."

The four friends wished Chairwoman Black good luck, and approached the VIP section, where they spotted Yucca and Elder 2. The cactuses were also just arriving, and the lone two comprised the whole cactus delegation. Yucca came over and gave JJ and friends a warm greeting. "It's great to see you guys here, JJ! I wasn't sure if you'd make it, but just in case, I registered your name, along with Frank, Izzy, and Statistic, into the VIP seating section. You guys have been so instrumental in helping us cactuses and the critters with our summit plans, that you have earned that honor. I know you'll want to see this historic event from good seats."

The Critterland contingent walked up as Yucca was finishing speaking. The critters seconded Yucca's sentiments. "We're glad to see you're here too. And we also put your names on the VIP list," said Critter 1. "We're hoping you can advise us in case we get flummoxed or befuddled."

"Or if things get perplexing and muddled," added Critter 2. "In fact, we're hoping you'll sit next to us. By the way, I've been thinking it over, and I thought you should know that my real name is Jeb. I really like the name you gave me, Critter 2, so I hadn't said anything yet. It's hard to get to be number 2 at anything. Usually someone can only get longer numbers, like 9345, for example. I don't think being 'Critter 9345' would be as good as just being plain old 'Jeb'. I sure am glad I approached you second when you walked into the picture."

"Yeah, me too," agreed Critter 1. "My name is really Bub, but I *love* being Critter 1. Critter 3 is pretty depressed about it, though. He wishes he had approached you first. He keeps asking us to play "pen, sword, dollar" over the rights to be 1 or 2. So now he's back to being just plain old 'Hal' again."

JJ smiled and explained, "The first ones to assert themselves or try something new, usually do get the most credit. It took leadership instincts to be the first few Critters to walk up and greet a group of strangers like us when we walked out of the cave, especially strangers as imposing as Frank and Yucca must have looked to you. Not to mention Statistic and I. So I'm glad to see you were chosen to be delegates. Thanks for the invitations to join you in the delegate section. I'm sure we'd all be glad to be of any help we can."

Yucca and Elder 2 were listening in. Elder 2 noted, "*We* don't use names at all in our society, which is perhaps why we respect others as if they were ourselves. But at my age, I'm fine with being called Elder 2. I only have a few things left to prove." Yucca was still digesting all the information about names and what they mean to different people.

JJ, Izzy, Statistic, and Frank all thanked the Critters, and Yucca too, and then proceeded to enter the VIP section. The Cactus delegation sat themselves at the far left end of the second row from the back and the Critters filed in next to them. Then Frank, Izzy, Statistic, and JJ, all of whom had always felt most comfortable sitting in the back anyway, sat next to the Critters. There were close to a hundred delegations from other lands in the VIP seating that JJ and friends hadn't met. The guy who seated himself next to JJ was a new face. JJ introduced himself, and the new guy responded, "Nice to meet you. I'm not really sure why I was invited. I'm just a barista, and I don't know much about this EcoSummit."

Surveying the crowd, JJ noticed that the Joneses from Southright-most County had seated themselves up in the front row. A few minutes later, Yucan the Toucan led the Jungle Birds delegation into the stands, and they sat right in front of JJ and his friends. They shook hands and the four friends told Yucan the Toucan how great it was to see him there. The Critters were also particularly thankful for all the help he had provided them. JJ leaned forward to be sure Yucan the Toucan could hear him over the crowd noise, and said, "Yucan, when this is over, let's talk about everything. We are heading home in the morning. I want to figure out a way to take your positive message back home with us."

The Seaside delegation filed in and seated themselves next to the Jungle Birds. Captain Gruzzly and The Witch Doctor were both within whispering distance of JJ and Izzy. There was a narrow aisle between the fifth row and the last row of seats where a few ushers and police were standing post. That final row of the VIP Section was already full of cooks, all wearing their aprons.

Frank was thinking, "This will be great. The governor has a whole team of caterers for the event. I can't wait to eat!" He leaned back and asked one of the cooks what was on the banquet menu.

"We're not cooks, you idiot. This is the journalists' section. We're covering the event."

Seated next to that journalist, was the cook from the diner in Hills-ville, who overheard Frank's question. He grinned facetiously at Frank, and asked, "Hey, what do you *think* you're doing here?" Before Frank could answer, the cook added, "My name is Clyde. You two almost blew my cover back in Hillsville. I've been writing a grass-roots perspective piece on the summit. I'm glad to see you and your friends are taking an interest in the green movement. Maybe those thought meters were working after all!"

18

A Twist and a Turn

It was time for the EcoSummit to commence. A spokesman walked out of a door from the conference center, across the veranda, and up to the lectern. The crowd, which had been very loud, hushed down in anticipation of the summit's opening. The spokesman tapped on the microphone to make sure it was working, and announced, "Ladies and gentlemen, thank you for coming to the EcoSummit. We weren't expecting such a spirited turnout, or we would have held this event in a larger venue. Please try to consolidate as closely as possible to make room for the crowd that is still coming in."

The spokesman paused for a second, and then began his build-up. "I will be today's Master of Ceremonies. As you all know, there is nothing more important to all of us than the protection of our environment. This is why *your* Right Governor took the initiative to examine and rethink all of our eco laws and to ask for real feedback and suggestions from each of you, the citizens of these Federated Lands. The Right Governor took all of the opinions you shared to heart, and proclaimed that this EcoSummit be convened. In conjunction with the EcoBureau, the Right Governor framed a list of the eco issues that are the most important to *you*, and asked that each and every land in these great Federated Lands form a delegation."

"Each of these delegations, seated before you today, are representative of the most concerned and knowledgeable citizens of every unique and diverse land. Every delegation in attendance has come prepared to debate all of the issues on the EcoList. They have journeyed from all across these Federated Lands to this EcoSummit, full of ideas and sug-

gestions, and carry with them the seeds for real solutions to our mutual
eco needs. Together, these delegations will work with The Right Governor's team of experts to hammer out a framework for the new EcoLaws
that you, the citizens, have demanded and deserve. I'd now like to ask
all of the delegations to stand up and face the crowd."

The delegations all rose and turned around to the gallery, and the
Master of Ceremonies continued his speech, "Ladies, Gentlemen, Citizens. These are the folks who have toiled thanklessly and sacrificed
years from their lives for *you*. Please recognize and welcome all of *your*
EcoSummit delegates."

A mighty cheer erupted from the crowd that took two full minutes
to subside. The Master of Ceremonies waited for the applause to wane,
and continued, "The delegates may now be seated. And without any
further ado, I would now like to announce the entrance of the leader
of the Green Movement, the protector of our environment, the leader
of these free Federated Lands, The Right Governor!"

A rousing cascade of applause serenaded the Right Governor as he
made his entrance from the same door the Master of Ceremonies came
from, and strode across the veranda, waving to the spectators in the
gallery the whole way. The Master of Ceremonies shook the Governor's
hand at the podium, and then he left center stage and sat in the first
row of the bleachers.

The Right Governor stepped to the lectern, and addressed the
crowd. "I would like to welcome all of the denizen of these Federated
Lands who have traveled from so far to be here this evening. I would
also like to thank those of you who have taken the time to correspond
with my administration regarding your individual concerns. I am always interested in hearing about all of my subjects' situations, habitats,
and living conditions. As you know, I have taken all of the information
you have submitted and will address these issues at this forum, The
EcoSummit."

There was a massive roar of approval from the crowd!

"I would like to start by personally thanking our VIP section for being here. Citizens, I know they've already been recognized, but I just want to emphasize that all of these special guests have been singled out for their extraordinary courage and outspokenness. These are the heroes that have helped make this EcoSummit happen."

Another massive roar erupted from the crowd.

"Now I would like you to welcome the EcoSummit panel of experts. These are the men who have taken all of your suggestions and presented me with *The List*. They will moderate this historic discussion. I hand–picked this panel of patriots myself. These are the foremost experts in the land, and are my most trusted confidants."

Twenty men walked onto the stage one-by-one from the same side door as the Master of Ceremonies, and filed onto the bleachers. Mr. Big was the first one in line! The next eighteen of them all looked *exactly* like Mr. Big. The crowd gave them a loud ovation as they each walked slowly out onto the veranda.

"I've never seen so many lifetime achievement awards in my whole life!" observed Yucca.

"Uh oh. Look at all those liberals," grumbled Critter 1.

The Witch Doctor suddenly became very fidgety. He began running his fingers up and down his rows of bones and softly chanting to himself. A serious look fired through the eyes of Elder 2. He said resolutely, just loud enough that the parties seated around him could hear, "This summit isn't what any of us thought it was."

The last expert in line looked a lot different. It was the Economist! The other 19 experts looked quite smug and cocksure, but the Economist seemed edgy, obviously uncomfortable. The barista nudged JJ, pointed at the Economist, and said, "*That's* the guy that invited me here! The Economist. He came to the restaurant and asked me a lot of hard questions. I quit the next morning. I don't need that kind of pressure. I mean, *that's* not why I went to college."

"That's not why I went to college either," agreed Frank. "When they ask hard questions, just remember the answer is always D, all of the above."

"I don't mean that kind of hard questions," responded the Barista. "I knew the answers. I'm the one that discovered them. They were easy to write, but they were hard for me to *say*. I kind of got a lump in my throat in the process. They involved theoretical economic scenarios in the impending technological age. I wrote my thesis based on these theories, and then they wouldn't let me graduate because my theories were 'heretical.' But the head of my economics department didn't understand technology to begin with. He was a member of the thesaurasaurus family, a nearly extinct reptilian species from an earlier age. He knew the meaning of every word of every theory ever advanced. Advanced up until about forty years ago, that is. Once he realized he knew it all, he started teaching and preaching and stopped learning and yearning. He still lives in the same world where his dusty old textbooks were printed. But he needs to start paying attention. We don't have much technology here yet, but it's coming. So is increased interfederated trade. Advances from Boomtown are paving the way. The Economist took an interest and told me that if my theories were true, they'd have to rewrite the textbooks. Some of my theories involve green energy technologies, which I guess is why I was invited here."

The Economist looked down over the crowd, and was visibly shaken when he noticed Statistic, JJ, Frank, and Izzy in the audience. He became very uncomfortable and started fidgeting as the Right Governor continued his speech, "And again, I'd like to thank everyone in attendance today for being here and showing your support. This is indeed an historic event, one that should bring all of you great pride and joy."

By that time the Critters were starting to get antsy. They had been seated for several minutes and hadn't had a chance to speak their mind yet. Critter 1 nudged the policeman posted near him in the aisle to his rear, and asked, "Hey when do I get my turn to let'er rip?"

He replied, "I don't think you get to talk. We're supposed to usher you out soon."

Critter 2 snapped back, "*You* are under-informed. Can you find out when we get to talk?"

"He's definitely supposed to get his chance to speak," JJ reaffirmed.

The policeman sneered at JJ, leaned over and replied, "You're not going to *think* your way out of this one, this time, buddy." The policeman walked up to Mr. Big on the pavilion. They exchanged whispers. The policeman walked back down to the aisle, next to the critter, and said, "You'll get your moment of glory soon."

The Right Governor glanced over at Mr. Big, and continued, "At this point I'd like to announce a last-minute change to our format, due to the overwhelming size of the crowd here in attendance. We had originally planned on having the entire debate right here on this stage for all to hear. But in order to maintain an orderly dialogue, we are now going to ask all of our delegates to exit to the right, down through the tunnel on the lower level of the Conference Center." The Right Governor motioned down to the tunnel entrance. "This tunnel leads to our state-of-the-art conference complex, which we have set up for this event. When we have reached the conclusion of this historic discussion, I will return to the stage and announce the results."

The crowd let out another roar, but JJ could hear a few boos scattered in.

The Right Governor continued, "And now our panel of experts will go to the chamber with our VIP guests and debate the specifics of the new Eco Laws. For the entertainment of everyone in the crowd, we have set up a jumbo screen and will show movies until I come back to announce the results of the debate. These films were produced by EcoCo and show all of the great things they are doing with green technologies in our Federated Lands."

As the moderating panel began exiting, a massive, one hundred foot wide movie screen was unfurled directly behind the VIP section, blocking the crowd's view of the stage and the delegations. The crowd let out another approving and deafening roar. *Finally! Eco progress was going to be made!* The movie started as soon as the giant screen was completely rolled down from the guy wires suspended above the VIP section. The crowd became immediately engrossed in the riveting Eco-Co documentary on clean energy.

The panel of experts exited the veranda through the door to the Conference Center, all except for Mr. Big, who walked down to the VIP section. He began assisting the police, who had quickly multiplied into a large force, to usher the delegates down into the Conference Center tunnel. They started in the front row, and when the front row had all filed out into the tunnel, the second row began doing the same. As JJ and Izzy watched the delegates being herded along, it dawned on both of them that something just wasn't right. Elder 2 gave an alarmed glance, and expressed in a loud enough voice for the others around to hear, "Why the change in format? Why are the government guys going upstairs, and yet we're going downstairs? I sense something is going terribly wrong here."

JJ noticed the Economist about to exit through the door on the veranda. He was looking back at the VIP section with a very unsettled look on his face. Elder 2 repeated his earlier observation, this time just a little more loudly and poignantly than before, "This summit isn't what any of us thought it was."

Some of the others seated around JJ and Izzy suddenly became very nervous also, and began asking each other questions in quick succession. Yucan the Toucan and the Seaside Mayor were hurriedly talking back and forth about the new format. Captain Gruzzly was trying to calm the Witch Doctor down. JJ, Izzy, Frank, and Statistic formed a huddle to discuss what might be happening. Elder 2 calmly, but urgently, explained things to Yucca in a hushed voice. And the Critters were angrily demanding, at the top of their lungs, that Mr. Big come over and explain why they hadn't had a chance to speak yet.

The police had now emptied two of the six rows of delegates, and were only two rows from where Yucan the Toucan's Jungle delegation, and the Seaside delegation were both sitting. Mr. Big heard the Critters hollering at him, and strode over to their seats with an angry look on his face and an evil look in his eyes. He leaned over to the Critters, who could barely hear him over the raucous crowd and the loud EcoCo movie, and said, "So you want to let'er rip, huh? Ok. *Now* we'll letter rip." With that he reached over to the VIP Delegates sign and ripped the V off of VIP. He turned it over and on the other side was an R!

There was a collective gasp in what was left of the RIP Delegates section. It instantly dawned on all of them that they were goners. The government wanted them to disappear so it could just keep up *business* as usual. But the crowd was oblivious. They were still cheering so boisterously they couldn't hear anything over themselves. They couldn't even see what was going on up front through the movie screen and the EcoCo documentary, which was making enough noise of it's own by that time. The Barista, thinking to himself, realized, "The Economist *doesn't want* to rewrite the textbooks." And the cooks realized that the government had finally figured out how to kill off investigative journalism once and for all.

When reality jolted Critter 1, he screamed, "We've been double-crossed!"

"Yeah, we've been E-Conned!" hollered Critter 2. "Mr. Big, How could you do this to us?"

"I said I was going to take care of you, didn't I?" replied Mr. Big. The police force suddenly divided into three columns and began ushering the RIP guests in the final three rows away simultaneously, urging them out of their seats, "Get up! Get up! Get up *now*!"

Then in an instant he couldn't afford, it dawned on JJ: It was all about the economy, stupid. This wasn't an Ecology Summit. It was an Economy Summit in disguise. All of the decisions had already been made. And the government was going to dispose of the dissidents and all of the evidence: *them*! But the masses in the gallery didn't know what was really happening. They were now cheering the EcoCo documentary, which had started with an exciting chase scene involving the EcoCo hero and the villainous bad carbons. JJ could hear the police through the din of the crowd and through the clouds in his own head. They were getting closer and were urging all of the delegates out of their chairs. "Get up! You need to get up *now*!"

JJ, Izzy, Statistic, and Frank huddled back together. They knew they had to do something. And do something quick. JJ especially felt the burden. He knew it was mostly his fault they were there to begin with. The lives of all of his friends, new and old, hung in the balance. *This time it wasn't somebody else's turn!* If he didn't think of something right now, and *act on it*, this would surely be their last night!

JJ's entire life flashed before his eyes. In about two long seconds he thought of everyone he loved. He thought about everyone he loved who had already passed, but who had always believed in him. He thought about all of his friends and loved ones who counted on him. He thought about his children and about his children's future children. And he thought about his devoted wife, whose settling voice had always reminded him that, in the end, she *knew* he'd make the right decisions...

19

Last Night's Turn

"Get up. It's time to get up now. It's time for breakfast."

As JJ was waking up, he recognized that familiar voice urging him on. His wife was standing over the bed, with a concerned look on her face. "I can't believe you had *another* bad, restless sleep last night. You tossed and turned all night. Your sleeping problem is really getting out of control. I mean JJ, you have *got* to figure out what is making you lose sleep at nights and do something about it."

"I know. I know. I was having a really crazy dream. My friends and I were in big trouble. I'm glad you woke me up. I don't know how we would have worked our way out of *that* jam," JJ replied, shaking his head.

"Well, I'm going downstairs to cook breakfast. You'd better get moving. Frank and Izzy will be here soon. Hopefully you won't have trouble sleeping while you're away. Did you finally decide where you're going?"

"Myrtle Beach, I guess. I was out-voted on the camping idea, but maybe they changed their minds. I packed my hiking boots just in case. Don't worry. I'm sure I'll sleep okay while I'm gone. We'll be staying up late watching games, so I'll be tired enough. They're starting the rookie on Sunday."

JJ began rising out of bed and added, "I'll take a quick shower and head downstairs."

As he walked towards the bathroom, his wife said, "I'd love to get a postcard or two from you this trip. You know, writing is very relaxing.

It might be therapeutic for you. You should consider doing more of it."

"I'll write, I promise. And doing it more often sounds like a good idea," replied JJ, as he approached the bathroom mirror.

His wife followed him to the bathroom door, and urged, "Well when you get back you need to get to the root of what is keeping you up at nights. I mean, *wake up,* JJ. Its time to *do something*! Problems don't go away by themselves. They just start running more and more amok until someone tackles them head on."

"I know, dear. I *know*," replied JJ as he looked into the mirror and took the time to shake the cobwebs out of his head.

20

A Toss and a Turn

Frank slapped JJ in the back. "Snap out of it! We need to do something quick!"

JJ's life instantly *stopped* flashing before his eyes. He had woken up from the daydream he had been shocked into, and knew it was time to act. And "it" meant *now*! There was nothing mystical about it. He leaned back into the huddle. He looked across at Statistic, and at Izzy and Frank to either side. JJ knew that each of his friends, and everyone else in the RIP section, had been experiencing the same emotions that had just flown through his own mind. The cobwebs were completely gone now. JJ lifted his head from the huddle and looked over at the delegations being escorted out, and at the three columns of police. He leaned back down, put his arms around Izzy's and Frank's shoulders, and urged, "We need to tackle this head on. We need to get to the podium. Remember trick play #73 from High School?"

Izzy and Frank both nodded their heads. Statistic said, "We practiced that play too. But we never got to try it in a real game!"

JJ looked at Statistic, and said, "Neither did we." And then he stepped back from the huddle and called over to Yucca, "Just Follow Me!" Next he leaned back into the huddle and barked, "Play 73. Break!" Frank and Izzy immediately ran towards the second row of police. Statistic fell in behind Frank and Izzy, rushing full throttle right behind them.

A big smile spread across the face of Elder 2 as he analyzed play #73 unfolding. He jumped up, just as spry as if *he* was still a teenager, all eleven feet of him! He tossed, okay he lateraled, his backpack to Yucca, whispered, "You know what to do," then went charging off towards the third row of police. JJ followed his blockers, with Yucca following closely behind.

Meanwhile, Clyde the cook, who was still seated in the last row with the rest of the journalists, realized what was going on. He knew it was *his job* to expose government corruption, so he immediately utilized an old trick he had learned in school. He reached back to the giant, one hundred foot movie screen, and yanked the cord that was hanging down so hard that it furled back up with a giant, resounding crash. Thwack, Thwack, Thwack, Thwack! The thunderclap was so forceful that it shook the trees lining the meadow and blew the hats off of most of the spectators! Clyde turned to one of his colleagues, and exclaimed, "Man, I've been wanting to do *that* again since I was in grade school!"

The EcoCo documentary movie had just reached the celebrity endorsement song-and-dance part, so the crashing screen startled the masses, whose eyes had been glued squarely upon it. The entire spectator gallery collectively gasped and watched play #73 unfold. They looked on in disbelief.

Frank and Izzy plowed right into the second row of policemen with a devastating one-two punch and knocked most of them down. Statistic ducked out from behind Frank and Izzy and hit the first row of them at full speed, taking as many of them out as he could. The trick play caught the police napping! Elder 2 knocked over all the cops still standing in rows one and two on his way to obliterating most of row three. The police went down like bowling pins. The whole row of journalists then formed a blocking wall and ran over and shielded JJ and Yucca from the police, who were trying to get back on their feet. Mr. Big was standing there, bewildered. He had never seen such a stunt in all of his lifetimes. He didn't hang around to see it to its conclusion either, because the whole Critter contingent was charging towards *him*!

The play worked! JJ and Yucca had a clear path and rushed onto the stage. The Right Governor panicked and ran away from the podium, across the veranda, and into the door to the Conference Center. He tried to gather the other 18 experts and the Economist, from inside the building. But they were all being pinned back in the hallway by, among other people, none other than Mr. and Mrs. Jones! The Joneses had rushed back out of the RIP chamber, not at all amused at being sent by the government to their imminent demises. All of the other delegates who had been ushered into the chamber also began rushing back out to help. Luckily none of them had been harmed yet. JJ ran up to the podium and grabbed the microphone, with Yucca right next to him.

A hush fell over the crowd as they wondered what was going on. Then a murmur began spreading and grew louder and louder as the crowd began noticing the RIP sign. The first ones to see it pointed it out to their neighbors, and so forth, and a collective realization of what was happening started growing quickly through the crowd. The spectators were in a total state of shock as they realized the conspiracy the government had tried to perpetrate upon them. The shock slowly turned to agitation, which quickly began turning into anger, and the crowd grew louder.

The rest of the delegations who had already exited into the RIP chamber, were just finishing making their way back out. They joined forces with the delegations that had never left, and the journalists, to line the edges of the stage. By that time, the cops were back on their feet and were also surrounding the stage. The delegations, journalists, and cops were jostling for position as if a rock concert was about to start, and they were all staring at the podium. The Right Governor urged the police to stand back, though. The last thing he needed was for the masses to turn on *him*. And he *knew* they were hungry. The Governor was sweating bullets, but they were blanks, wondering what JJ would say.

JJ looked around and realized the police and the Right Governor were going to let him speak. He tapped the microphone. The whole crowd quieted to hear. Without any further hesitation, he announced, "Citizens of these Federated Lands, I'd like to thank you for coming out today. Now we will hold a public forum on the ecological *and* economic problems you are all facing. I'd like to introduce the new moderator of the EcoSummit, Yucca the Cactus."

JJ stepped back, knowing that even after all those years, when the right time had come, he had executed his role in trick play #73 to perfection. And it had actually worked!

Yucca advanced to the podium and set his backpack on top of it. He began to speak. "I brought with me today a portion of the legendary Omnipotence, which I am now renaming 'The Whole Tamale.' It is the most powerful force in our world." He looked over towards the Right Governor, who looked panic stricken. The Economist, who had made it back to the edge of the stage, looked like he had seen a ghost!

Yucca continued, "My land's Council of Elders is the custodian of this power. And from this day forward they will wield this power, if and *only* if, the government takes any more unfair liberties against any of us with *their* power." Yucca glowered over at the Right Governor again, before he went on, "I would now like to nominate myself to be the Chairman of the new 'Citizens Eco Oversight Committee,' the creation of which I am hereby proposing. This committee will question every maneuver and every law the Federated Lands makes in regard to ecology *and* the economy. We will protect each and every one of the citizens of these Federated Lands with deep, probing questions. Our motto will be 'Do Ask, Do Tell.' We will have full veto power over all Federated laws and policy. I also hereby nominate my friend, the Witch Doctor, to be the Vice Chairman, and the Barista to head the Economic Department. All in favor of these proposals say I."

The masses erupted with one staggeringly loud "I."

Yucca glared at the Right Governor, and then glared at Mr. Big, who no longer looked like he wanted to boast about his lifetimes of achievement, and again he continued. "All those not in favor, don't say

I." There was a deafening silence. Not even the Right Governor dared to not not say I.

Yucca finished his speech by saying, "And now it is time for our public forum to begin. This is the event we are all here for. It is now my honor to introduce you to the new Master of Ceremonies who will be moderating the rest of this event. Citizens, please welcome the new Chairman of this EcoSummit, Yucan the Toucan!"

The crowd erupted with a welcoming round of applause as Yucan the Toucan flapped over to the podium and began to *lead*. "Ladies and Gentlemen, topic #1 affects our very survival. Yes, it shakes us to our primeval core....."

JJ knew it was time to leave the stage and let all his new friends do what they had to do. He grabbed Yucca's VIP diplomatic pass as he exited the stage. That souvenir was better than any tee shirt. Besides, you never know, it might help him get back through Hillsville on the way home. JJ glanced over towards the exit tunnel at the side of the stage, and it was a sight he would never forget. The Right Governor, Mr. Big, the Economist, and the rest of the Right Governor's crew of cronies, were all huddled together, powerless to stop the sweeping momentum of the movement that was unfolding before them. To a man, they all looked shocked, but JJ could also sense a feeling of simmering anger and steely resolve radiating from within them. To be sure, these men of power would do *what* they could, *as soon* as they could, to quell this insurrection, or at least minimize its damage to their status quo. But for now the Right Governor and his cabinet had no choice but to accept the conditions Yucca had set forth. The Federated Lands would now have to recognize the power of the new Eco Oversight Committee, and adhere to its rulings. Down the line, a lot would depend on the extent to which the citizens of the Federated Lands were willing to become involved in their own government, and to the true nature of 'The Whole Tamale'. Just what, JJ wondered, could Yucca let out of that bag? The Right Governor, the Economist, and Mr. Big were horrified at the mere mention of its name, that's for sure.

Frank, Izzy, and Statistic pushed through the crowd to join JJ, as he reached the bottom of the stage. The thick crowd at the foot of the stage respectfully parted to make room for JJ and his friends to leave. Even the police stepped aside. JJ passed one cop in particular that he recognized, the one that arrested him and Izzy in the District of Concrete. But then he did a double take when he remembered that he thought that trip was a dream. He nudged Izzy, who looked back at JJ with a mischievous smile and a twinkle in his eye.

Izzy confided to JJ, "Not all conspiracy theories are dreamt up, JJ. Some are true. But either way, an honest man can't just lay awake at night worrying about one. That's when the conspirators win the game."

JJ smiled and nodded his head understandingly. It was getting late and he and his friends knew they had to leave to head home. It would have been great to hang around and watch the surreal scene at The Meadows unfold to it's conclusion, and to have been able to say goodbye to Yucca, Yucan the Toucan, the Witch Doctor, and all of their other new friends. But their new friends would be busy gaining their eco-independence for some time to come. JJ, Frank, Izzy, and Statistic, on the other hand, were done with their work, and needed to make their way home from their vacations. They began hiking slowly up the hill.

As they were walking, Frank asked, "Can we make it all the way back to Seaside tonight? I'd love to have one more seafood plate at Bad Captain Billy's Mutiny before we head home in the morning. But tonight I need to play a dollar if we fight over the tab again. Somebody else needs to be the pen. I'm running low on doubloons!"

They all laughed, and Izzy replied, "Seaside sounds good to me. We can make it, as long as we take the back caves this time. The government employees have taken as much toll as they can squeeze out of us this trip. I have my map, so I know the back route."

JJ replied, "Seaside sounds great. Bad Captain Billy's Mutiny is the perfect place to discuss our exit strategy. Don't forget we still need to come up with a plan to make it past the thought police in Hillsville."

"Yeah, and the policeman and the Park Ranger at the campground," reminded Frank.

"Not to mention Mr. Big and the police in Critterland and the District of Concrete," added Izzy. "There's a chance that Mr. Big isn't done with us yet. He may be plotting his immediate revenge as we speak. We're probably public enemies numbers one through four right now."

Then Statistic said, "I doubt the Economist is very happy with me either. We have a lot to discuss tonight. I'm up for one more night in Seaside too, but I need to head off in my own direction in the morning, unless you can give me a lift to where I'm parked. The Economist brought me into the Federated Lands through a different entrance than you guys came through."

Frank was quick to say, "I'm sure we can give you a ride. Where are you parked?"

"Myrtle Beach," replied Statistic.

Frank, JJ, and Izzy all stopped in their tracks, their jaws dropped. They were in a collective state of shock. "*You have got to be kidding me!*" exclaimed Frank, who went on to stammer, "You *are* joking, right? I mean, are you saying that we could have gone to Myrtle Beach the whole time we were down here?"

Statistic smiled, winked at JJ and Izzy, and replied, "Possibly. But you know I'm not the type that would *ever* say anything to create any kind of rift or controversy. I just like to go with the flow and treasure what I *do have*. I don't spend much time dwelling on the thoughts of greener pastures somewhere else. Myrtle Beach is a long hike anyway."

The four kept walking slowly up the hill, and after a brief contemplative moment, Statistic continued, "You know, it's beginning to dawn on me why the Economist chose to bring *me* here, of all people, to assess during his travels. He's probably a part of this world, not our world, which is what I was led to believe. He obviously had ulterior motives that run much deeper than just looking for economic data. It looks like the depth of his designs could turn out to be quite frightening."

Statistic paused for a second. He noticed the pained looks on each of the other's faces as they suddenly began to contemplate what the Economist may have *really* been up to. They were all thinking, "Why had the Economist reached out to our world for his studies? Or if he really was from our world, why was he studying *the Federated Lands* for clues? And *why* did he hire Statistic, of all people, to help?" JJ and Izzy even got carried away with their thoughts: "Is Statistic even *a real person*, or just a figment of our runaway imaginations? Could it be that we were so caught up in our *own* worlds and chasing our *own* dreams, that everyone else and everything going on around us has just been one big metaphoric blur?"

Then Statistic said, "On the brighter side, it *will* be an easier decision for you to go to Myrtle Beach on your next vacation, won't it? I hope I'm still invited."

Izzy and JJ remained deep in troubled thought, but Frank's mind had moved on, so he replied, "I'll bet we end up playing 'pen, sword, dollar' to decide where we go. We'll just have to see which way the wind is blowing. But you'll be invited, wherever the wind takes us."

JJ and Izzy snapped out of their contemplative dazes, both realizing that, after all, not *all* outlandish theories are true, so they were quick to tell Statistic that they also certainly hoped he would join them next trip.

They walked up the slope, crossing the meadow, with Izzy the navigator leading the way, of course. When they reached the crest of the hill, they couldn't help but stop and stand on the toppled gate and look back down at the spectacle below. The eyes and ears of the throngs of spectators were fixed directly on Yucan the Toucan, standing at the podium. And Yucca, the Witch Doctor, Captain Gruzzly, the Critters, and the members of the rest of the delegations were all standing on the veranda directly behind Yucan the Toucan, who was now pacing back and forth, orating. The crowd was growing larger at the base of the stage, as the meadow full of spectators swarmed closer to the podium. The entire crowd of tens of thousands were cheering and repeating every word Yucan spoke.

Frank had to admit, "You know it took my eyes a while to adjust, but I *can* see the bright side now."

Elder 2 walked up to JJ and his friends, carrying his backpack, which he had retrieved from Yucca, and remarked, "That was a great game plan you came up with back there, given the situation. I'm glad you took the initiative to lead the way, and didn't leave it up to an old guy like me to come up with a plan. I'm journeying home now too. May I accompany you on your way back?"

"Sure," JJ replied. "But wouldn't you want to stay here with Yucca? Don't you think he may need your help?"

"No," responded Elder 2. "I would just be in the way at this point. Yucca has received all the guidance and wisdom that we Elders know to give him. Some lessons are best learned by the youth when they are left to work their way through situations on their own. Yucca will know what to do."

When Elder 2 finished his explanation, Frank asked, "*What* exactly is in that backpack, anyway?"

Elder 2 winked at JJ, Izzy, and Statistic, and told Frank, "The game is over now. Your team won. No more questions."

"But Elder 2," Izzy implored. "We weren't playing *against* each other. We were on the same side. Doesn't that mean you could share with us?"

Elder 2 mulled Izzy's logic and allowed, "I can't see how any harm could come from showing you our power. The government obviously knows the legends are true." He looked down at the four humans and explained, "The Omnipotence, which Yucca decreed will henceforth be known as 'The Whole Tamale', is hard to explain in words. It's a sort of universal reality authenticator. It reads all fields and all sequences encrypted by energy. The owners of The Whole Tamale can unlock the brain waves of anyone and everyone. It can read the trace signatures left behind by all beings anywhere they've been and whatever they thought while they were there."

JJ, Izzy, Frank, and Statistic were mesmerized and stunned as they tried to grasp what Elder 2 was saying. Izzy asked, "Do you mean it can read people's minds? And it can decipher the strata of xyzactas?"

"Yes, in a way," answered Elder 2. "I'm surprised you know about xyzactas, but it reads all of these energies. It does much more than that, too. But it's hard to explain."

"It's kind of like an algorithm, then?" asked Statistic.

"It's not an algorithm, but it's a little like the *ultimate* algorithm, except more powerful than any algorithm could ever be. It's a confidence unto itself. A being who is in possession of the power of The Whole Tamale doesn't necessarily need others to communicate with him or her, because they can see the truth on their own. They don't need to listen to the empty words of others. Reality is already obvious to them. They simply *know*."

Elder 2 paused again, as everyone struggled to grasp the concept, and then he went on, "So you can see why the government is scared of The Whole Tamale, and why they also covet it. It's an asset that can never be taken away from its possessor. If the government were to try to wrest it away, the truth would only become clearer. What is *unclear* though, is whether or not the government or any individual could ever find and understand The Whole Tamale on their own. And if so, could they gain anything from usurping a portion of it away from someone else for their own use? I don't think so."

"I'm not sure I understand any of this," admitted JJ hesitantly. "Can we look at it?"

"I suppose so," answered Elder 2. He slowly opened the flap on his backpack and JJ, Izzy, Frank, and Statistic all nervously gazed inside. It appeared to be *empty*!

"It's invisible!" exclaimed Statistic.

"That's because there's nothing in it!" barked Frank. "It's a scam. There's nothing there."

"You can't see energy, Frank," explained Izzy. "And you can't see the truth. They're both totally transparent. They're both something you feel, something you believe, something you *know*."

Elder 2 closed the flap on the backpack and tightened the clasp. He looked back down at the four humans, his eyes gleaming with fiery power and radiant knowledge, and averred, "It's no farce. The joke will be on he who dismisses this power. You need to look deep inside to understand. The Whole Tamale is the most powerful force in the world. It's all there for you to see. I'm not going to explain any further."

Elder 2's piercing eyes and statement froze JJ, Izzy, Frank, and Statistic for a moment as they thought. They contemplated not just the nature of The Whole Tamale, but the new light that it shed on the Economist's pursuit of it. They all stood still with dumbstruck looks on their faces for several long seconds before they collectively snapped out of it.

Then Izzy reflected, "It's ironic, isn't it? What if we all redirected our energies away from ourselves and instead focused them on what is happening around us. The clues *are* all there. The power surge created could effect governments to become totally transparent, couldn't it?"

Elder 2 replied, "You're close to seeing the truth, Izzy. I think you're on the cusp of grasping the power of The Whole Tamale." But Elder 2 wasn't *quite* ready to leave the four humans alone so they could leave. He looked back down into their eyes and mused, "Actually, I do have one last question for each of *you*. When you get home to your wives and families tomorrow, do you think any of them will believe a word of your stories about what happened on your vacation's last night?"

Worried expressions spread across the faces of Izzy, Statistic, Frank, and JJ, and they looked at each other and gulped. Then Elder 2 added, "You know we're not too far from the District of Concrete. I have half a mind to go back and visit. I wonder how many layers of stone walling have accumulated there since I visited in my youth?"

Frank and Statistic looked at each other, then grabbed JJ and Izzy in bear hugs, and Frank said, "Don't get any ideas. We need to get home."

They all started laughing and turned around to walk through the mouth of the cave, which now definitely looked more like an exit than an entrance. As they were passing into the cave they could just make out the end of Yucan the Toucan's speech. "Citizens of these Federated Lands, tonight we have witnessed the beginning of the end of tyranny!"

And as JJ, Frank, Izzy, Statistic, Elder 2, (and Benny Jr.) faded off into the distance, they could hear the crowd's cascading chant, "The End of Tyranny, The End, The End!"

A Toss and a Turn